THE ARMOR C

The House
— Of —
The Forest

Thomas
Summerlin

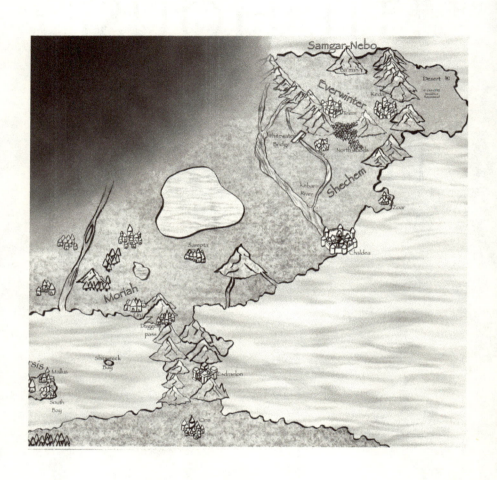

Trilogy Christian Publishers

A Wholly Owned Subsidiary of Trinity Broadcasting Network

2442 Michelle Drive

Tustin, CA 92780

Copyright © 2024 by Thomas Summerlin

All rights reserved, including the right to reproduce this book or portions thereof in any form whatsoever.

For information, address Trilogy Christian Publishing

Rights Department, 2442 Michelle Drive, Tustin, Ca 92780.

Trilogy Christian Publishing/ TBN and colophon are trademarks of Trinity Broadcasting Network.

For information about special discounts for bulk purchases, please contact Trilogy Christian Publishing.

Trilogy Disclaimer: The views and content expressed in this book are those of the author and may not necessarily reflect the views and doctrine of Trilogy Christian Publishing or the Trinity Broadcasting Network.

10 9 8 7 6 5 4 3 2 1

Library of Congress Cataloging-in-Publication Data is available.

ISBN 979-8-89333-295-7

ISBN 979-8-89333-296-4 (ebook)

Dedication

To my companion, Sarah. Thank you for showing me what it truly means to put on the Armor of Light. The world would surely be dimmer without you in it. You inspire me to be a better man and are an endless well of encouragement. You are my best friend, and I am beyond blessed to go through this life with you. I would also like to thank my friends and family for their support. Without you, I would have no reason to write.

Table of Contents

Chapter 1 1
Chapter 2 11
Chapter 3 23
Chapter 4 38
Chapter 5 54
Chapter 6 66
Chapter 7 72
Chapter 8 78
Chapter 9 89
Chapter 10 98
Chapter 11 105
Chapter 12 113
Chapter 13 120
Chapter 14 127
Chapter 15 133
Chapter 16 144
Chapter 17 154
Chapter 18 163
Chapter 19 170
Chapter 20 180
Chapter 21 185
Chapter 22 194
Chapter 23 201

Chapter 1

Putting on her glasses, Neviah pushed the heavy covers off, swung her feet to the wooden floor, and stood. The room was dark, with slatted shutters blocking out most of the morning light. The narrow rays leaking through revealed walls and ceiling made from the same wood slats as the floor. Simple furniture was scattered around the place. Everything smelled like herbs.

The home, which also served as an apothecary and recovery ward, belonged to a widow named Elna. The woman had taken care of Neviah from the day she arrived in Uru, the capital city of Moriah, the largest of the northern kingdoms. Neviah and Adhira had spent several weeks in Sarepta before joining a caravan traveling to the capital.

She was told they were hundreds of miles from Chaldea, where they'd battled with an army of corpses indwelt by Lesser Shayatin and controlled by Ba'altose, the King of the Undead. Months in the past, it all seemed like a distant nightmare.

Walking over to the heavy front door, she grabbed the handle and took a deep breath. The breath wasn't to test her ribs, which had been cracked in their final skirmish with the undead king, but to steady her for what she knew was on the other side. She opened the door and couldn't keep her eyes from drifting up. A mile above the city floated Alya. It was an enormous spherical landmass, like a small moon that had gotten way too close to its planet. Alya's surface was covered in thick forests and rivers. Though everything seemed upside down from her perspective, Neviah suspected the water was held in place by the land's own gravity. It was its own world, held in place by an enormous chain connecting Alya to somewhere at the center of Uru. The entire scene was dizzying yet breathtakingly beautiful. She couldn't help the death grip she had on the door frame.

Alya was home to the Chayyoth, the flying creatures who'd saved them from Chaldea. She remembered nothing from the flight but was told the Chayyoth had somehow known they were in trouble. She could see a few of the lion-like Chayyoth flying around, though they rarely came down to Uru. The humans did not interact much with their flying neighbors, though they were said to be allies. Turning back to the room, she grabbed her coat, shoes, and a simple-looking book titled *Prophecies* before stepping out into the cool morning air. She closed the door behind her and took a seat on the steps.

The city was mostly quiet. She halfway expected to hear car horns blaring in the distance but knew that sound was likely gone forever. Earth itself felt like a distant memory, a dream even, since appearing in that strange new world. The sun was up and hung between the horizon and the landmass above. The blue planet, Colossus, wasn't viewable from her position, but its golden rings extended far to the east. She wondered at it all, unable to keep herself from marveling at its beauty.

Opening her book of prophecies, a gift from Re'u, a man she'd never met who'd somehow saved their lives before bringing them to that world, she read through a few of the prophecies. More and more, the strange words made sense to her. Out of the four of them who'd come from Earth, she seemed to have the greatest understanding of the book. Along with *Prophecies*, Re'u had given each of the four of them a gift, which was a unique and extraordinary ability. Her gift gave her the ability to see the future, part of which allowed her to decipher the meanings within the book of prophecies.

A smile came to her face when she read, "They shall mount up onto wings to soar as the birds do." The words were often beautifully written, almost poetic at times.

The smile faded as the interpretation came to her. There was flying in their future. The day before, she'd climbed a stepping stool to grab a jar from the top shelf in the apothecary's house and became frozen with fear after looking down. How could she possibly fly with such a crippling fear of heights? She took a steadying breath.

"It's okay," she told herself. The prophecy could have been fulfilled when she was flown unconscious from Chaldea to Moriah.

The House of the Forest

Or maybe the prophecy wouldn't be fulfilled for years.

At that exact moment, she spotted a lone Chayya walking down the cobblestone street toward her. The creature was male, evidenced by the thick mane, like a lion's, around his neck and flowing around his shoulders. His mane was entirely white, shining like silver in the morning light. It was strange enough seeing a Chayya in that part of the city but even more so to see one strolling about instead of flying.

As he drew closer, she saw why he didn't fly. One of his wings was gone completely, replaced by an ugly white scar, and the other was half missing. His face showed many more old wounds, with a long scar passing across his snout. He strode forward with heavily muscled legs and shoulders, more so than the other Chayyoth she'd seen. There was a sinking feeling in her gut he was coming to talk to her. She was right.

The Chayya walked up the hill to stand before the stairs where she sat. "I was told you were the leader of the Sword Wielders," he said in a powerfully deep voice. It was the first time she'd been called a Sword Wielder.

"We have no leader. Not really."

"Very well," he said without any change to his expression. "I am Corban, professor and schoolmaster at the School of Flight." Neviah thought it ironic that a flightless Chayya taught flying, though she would never say so in front of the large creature.

"Hello, Corban. I'm Neviah. What can I do for you?"

"I have come to invite the four of you to the opening ceremonies tomorrow."

"Ceremonies?"

He showed a little emotion then: surprise. "Once a year, we accept new students to the School of Flight and the School of Soldiering. Each candidate will be tested and evaluated before admittance is granted."

Variations of the word "fly" had become far too common for her liking. "We don't have any training in such things," she said, trying to find a way out.

"That is preferred. It is always more difficult to re-train a recruit. We will be evaluating candidates based on potential, not experience."

"Oh."

"Will you be attending?"

"I don't know. I have to talk to the others."

"Understood. I should tell you that I am also a prophet of Re'u, just as I've been told you are. I have seen you in a dream, riding on the back of a Chayya. If you apply to the academy, I am positive you will be accepted."

She immediately knew his words to be true, with the kind of certainty that only came when her gift revealed something to her. She would be riding a Chayya by the end of the next day. It was an unavoidable event.

"Thank you," she managed with her suddenly dry mouth. "I'll let the others know."

"Tomorrow then," he said with a respectful nod and left, walking with his head high. She noticed another scar down the side of his front left shoulder. It must have been some battle.

Swallowing the panic welling up inside of her, she closed her book of prophecies and went back inside to put it into her backpack before finishing her morning routine. With shaky hands, she squeezed the smallest drop of toothpaste onto her aging toothbrush before putting the tube away. It had lasted her nearly a year, but it was almost out. When she was done prepping, she wrote a quick note to Elna, explaining where she was going, grabbed her backpack, and left. Elna, the herbalist/apothecary/doctor, was still asleep in the other room. The woman kept late hours with house calls.

First, Neviah stopped by the house where her friend Victoria was staying, a tall stucco building like many of the city's structures. Elna's wooden house was one of the few exceptions. Neviah opened the door and peeked in. It still felt strange opening people's doors without knocking but the culture of these people held that it was rude to knock.

The third time she'd come over, the woman of the house had said to Neviah, "Why do you keep knocking? You don't know if there is a baby sleeping or not. Besides, if we didn't want anyone coming in, the door would be latched." With so little crime in the city, people only locked their doors when they weren't home or when they didn't want company.

Victoria was sitting at the table with the home's two parents and three pre-teen daughters. Her fair skin made her stand out from the dark-skinned family. Victoria's hair was put up in a perfect golden bun. The girls loved playing with her hair. Their own was black, like Neviah's, so the novelty of blond hair intrigued them.

"Can I borrow Victoria from you?" Neviah asked politely.

"Certainly," the mother said, shooing off one of the daughters who was incessantly stroking the blond hair. Victoria grabbed her backpack and was out the door in seconds.

"What are you in a hurry for?" Neviah laughed when they were away from the house. "Don't you want to see what your next hairdo will be?"

Victoria widened her eyes in horror and slowly shook her head.

"Have you read anything interesting in your book of prophecies lately?" Neviah asked as they turned down the street where Adhira was staying. The homes looked the same, but the street transitioned from rough cobblestones to smooth bricks, showing a slight rise in wealth for the area's occupants, though the citizens as a whole were quite wealthy. Victoria shrugged and nodded but didn't say anything. Neviah was determined to get the girl to open up more.

When they came to Adhira's door, he was just walking out. "Good morning, ladies," he said with a cocky grin, attempting to smolder his eyes. They ignored him and kept walking. "Do we get to take Asa with us today?" he asked, obviously annoyed at having to ask his question. His gift from Re'u was the ability to always see the immediate future.

Neviah had decided she would wait to answer any questions he asked so he would be forced to hold any conversation in real time. His continually seeing fifteen seconds into the future was super annoying.

"Maybe," she said, stringing him along.

"Well, what's up? Where are we off to?" he finally asked.

She counted down to zero before saying, "To see Asa, of course. I have news that affects all four of us, so I'll tell you when we're all together. Victoria, can you lead the way?"

He harrumphed but didn't say anything. He was so used to seeing into the immediate future that it annoyed him not to know her responses ahead of time. She would have to use the waiting strategy

The Armor of Light

more often.

When they arrived at Asa's door, as per custom, they opened it and walked in. The owner was a baker, and he and his family had likely already been at the shop for hours. Asa was sitting on the floor stretching.

"Oh, hi, guys," he said after a quick glance. Neviah made it a point not to look at his limp when he stood and walked over to them. His knee had been badly dislocated in the fight with Ba'altose, some ligaments partially severed, whatever that meant. He also couldn't lift his right arm above his shoulder without pain. Neither she nor Asa had been in good shape after their fight with Ba'altose, the King of the Undead. Adhira and Victoria were the only ones who escaped unscathed.

Her injuries had been serious but not as bad as his, keeping her bedridden for nearly a week because of swelling around her spine. It had been frustrating. Asa could have healed her with a touch, his gift from Re'u, but the doctors in Sarepta refused to allow her to travel to Uru until she felt better. Oddly enough, her injuries should have kept her bedridden longer, but the Moriahns had access to the waters of Alya, which had amazing regenerative properties. Adhira had stayed with her in Sarepta until they traveled to join Asa and Victoria in the capital.

"What are you up to?" Asa asked.

"I've got a few things to run by you three and thought we could go up to the wall," she said.

"The wall?" Asa asked. "Are you sure?"

"I'll make it up this time," she assured him.

"Sounds great," he said but looked at her sideways before limping over to a coat rack to grab his coat. "Did you overcome your fear of heights?"

"Not even close," she said. "But I'm tired of being afraid." Thoughts of her riding on the back of a Chayya crept in, but she pushed them away.

After moving a few books off a chair, he found his backpack and stuffed his book of prophecies inside. The room was filled with so many borrowed books there was no way Asa would remember who they all belonged to. After locking the door behind them, they were off.

"What's the news?" Asa asked from beside her.

"Have you guys heard of the School of Flight or the School of Soldiering?"

Asa nodded. "I've heard of them. Tomorrow, they'll be accepting new admissions." He'd been spending a good bit of time with Rafal, the Chayya he'd saved and who subsequently helped save them. It was likely Asa knew more than Neviah did about the event.

"Well, we'll be part of the new admissions," she said.

"According to the rules of recruitment, they accept very few outsiders," Asa said. "You might blend in with your dark skin, Neviah, but the three of us will stand out."

Ever since they arrived in that world, Neviah had felt like an outsider. Everyone they'd met, aside from the scaley Shedim, was fair-skinned. The roles had reversed, and now she fit in, and her friends stood out. Race wasn't a big deal to her, but she still found herself comforted to feel like she blended in somewhere.

"The Chayyoth don't view us as outsiders," Adhira added to the conversation. "They think there's something special about us. And besides, we defeated the Army of the Undead. That has to count for something."

"Most people don't know that," Neviah pointed out. Asa had been the one to kill Ba'altose, but Tanas was the one many believed killed him.

The city wall came into view, rising above the three-story buildings around them. The wall was older than the gray stone buildings next to it, having been made from some type of sandstone.

"I'm guessing you're going for the School of Soldiering," Asa said to Neviah. "You know, with the whole dislike of heights and all." Saying "dislike" was the understatement of the year.

"Unfortunately, no," she said, shaking her head. "There is flying in my future." Actually, there was a Chayya in her future, but that likely meant flight. Unless she found a way to ride a Chayya without actually flying. She let the thought linger.

"That's something I would pay to see," Adhira said with a smirk. "Neviah, flying, the girl who would rather face death than heights, actually flying."

"What do we have to do?" Victoria squeaked from the back.

"I don't know," Neviah admitted. "Have you learned anything, Asa?"

"The School of Soldiering simply has some of their top graduates fight the new recruits with practice swords. They won't really be trying to hit us or anything. It's just to test reflexes, agility, listening skills, and stuff. The School of Flight has a different test every year and only the schoolmaster knows what the criteria are. If the blade master is there, he may be looking for a new pupil."

"What's a blade master?" Neviah asked.

"He's the best swordsman in the country. Blade masters only train one recruit at a time, who sometimes end up becoming the next blade master." Asa did know a lot.

"Is it possible to be a member of both schools?" she asked.

He shook his head. "Just one. If we get accepted to both, we get to pick which one we want. The School of Flight is on Alya." He pointed to the floating country above. "The School of Soldiering is here in the city."

"What if we get accepted to different schools?" Victoria asked, the question undoubtedly aimed at Asa. Asa looked at her for a moment.

Neviah glanced at Adhira, who clasped his hands by his cheeks and fluttered his eyes. Asa and Victoria were cute and completely clueless.

"That won't happen," Asa said confidently.

"And even if it did happen," Adhira added. "Whoever is in the School of Flight can fly to visit whoever is in the School of Soldiering."

That seemed to comfort Victoria since she slowed her pace to take up the rear again. They came to a tower built into the fifty-foot walls, which circled around the large city, even on the side that bordered the ocean. They ascended the spiraled staircase that wound around the interior of the tower. Even though they were protected by walls on all sides and the stone provided no view of the outside world, Neviah felt the blood quicken in her veins the higher they went. She counted it as a small victory every time she took a step. When they came to the top, she made it a point not to look over the four-foot barrier that traveled along the top of the wall.

The wall was wide enough for five men to walk abreast, and the walkway gave them plenty of room to spread out. Asa and Adhira sat in a couple of the rectangular groves built into the parapet. Neviah and Victoria sat on the stone walkway, far from either edge.

"Now that Ba'altose is dead, and I'm mobile again," Asa said, "have you had any prophecies or heard anything from Re'u about our purpose here?"

"Do you remember when we first came to this world and I said there was a danger looming to the east?" They nodded. "Well, the danger feeling went away when we defeated Ba'altose. It's back. I feel a darkness to the east. It's growing stronger every day."

"I'm guessing the schools aren't for recreational purposes," Asa stated.

"Re'u is definitely preparing us for something."

Asa sighed and looked over the wall at the view Neviah couldn't see from her seat. "I guess nothing could be as bad as fighting an army of undead soldiers." He paused and quickly turned his head back toward Neviah. "Unless Tanas comes here. And if Tanas comes, he will likely bring dragons with him." Asa had just voiced one of her greatest fears.

"That would make for an interesting day," Adhira said.

"Have you flown with Rafal yet?" Neviah asked to change the subject somewhat.

Asa shook his head. "It is forbidden for a Chayya to carry a human before they are bonded and trained. Emergencies, like ours in Chaldea, are the exception."

"Bonded?" Neviah asked.

"When a human is accepted to the School of Flight, they must choose a Chayya, and they are bound to each other for life."

"If I'd known I was getting married tomorrow, I'd have rented a tux," Adhira said with a laugh.

"You joke, but the edict makes it sound very similar to a marriage," Asa said. "Just not romantic in any way."

"Have you read all the rules?" Neviah asked Asa.

"Pretty much. Rafal let me see the scroll they are written on."

A soldier in hardened leather armor walked behind them on his patrol. He smiled and nodded his head in greeting before continuing on.

"How much time is there between choosing a Chayya and the first flying lesson?" she asked. Neviah wanted to smack Adhira's smirk off his face.

"Putting it off as long as possible, are we?" he said. "If there's a loophole, Neviah will find it."

Asa did a decent job not smiling at Adhira's jibe. "I don't know when the first lesson is, but the school is on Alya. We have to get there somehow."

As if she was expecting it to fall on her, Neviah ducked her head and looked up at the massive landmass above her. It was more than intimidating to think about. The sun had risen higher and was behind Alya. The city of Uru dwelt in the shade for the greater part of every day. It was a great city to live in during the summertime, which it was.

She was thinking about how she would get the nerve to fly when she felt a hand on hers. Victoria smiled at her reassuringly. Neviah squeezed the other girl's hand to say thank you.

She still felt a pang of guilt when she remembered their escape from Nebo's prison. Even though her friends were depending on her in a life-or-death situation, she couldn't make herself face her fear of heights. Next time, she would have to face her fears. She told herself the following day was still a long time away. But it wasn't.

Chapter 2

The next morning, it was Neviah's friends who came to get her. With everything she owned packed into her backpack, she gave her hostess a hug.

"Thanks again for all your help," Neviah said.

"You are welcome to come back any time," Elna said with a motherly smile. "I just hope you don't need to."

When the door was closed behind her, she turned to her friends and took a steadying breath. "I'm ready."

"We'll see," Adhira said with a smile.

They made their way deeper into the city, Neviah taking up the rear this time. The stout homes were traded for shops with open shutters. Many people were out buying, more than usual, to be so early in the morning. The recruitment day was kind of an unofficial holiday for the city, bringing in many people from the countryside.

The press of people became more and more stifling. There were vendors selling everything from food to weaponry to jewelry. Neviah forced herself not to linger at the shops they passed as they made their way toward the coliseum as best as they could. The teens came to the corner of an intersection with a sign with an arrow and the words "New Recruits" painted on it.

There was still a crowd as they pushed toward the large entrance, but most of the faces were young like them. Their progress slowed considerably when a tunnel bottle-necked the flow of recruits. The tunnel spilled out into an enormous arena larger than a football field. The seats were only about a quarter full but filling fast. Human soldiers stood guard around the field and stands.

An older soldier with ornate armor walked along the recruits with two young soldiers who were forming the newcomers into

The Armor of Light

ranks. When they came to Neviah and Victoria, they paused and looked back at the older man who furrowed his thick gray eyebrows, looking thoughtful.

"We'll deal with it later," he said, and the soldiers continued down the line.

The encounter prompted Neviah to look around. As far as she could see in either direction, including the ranks behind her, every recruit aside from her and Victoria was male. Her friends were obvious outsiders, which she thought would be a problem, but it was the girls' gender that gave the men pause.

They stood there while a few hundred more teenagers filed onto the hard-packed dirt of the arena. There was a long wall that cut the field in half. It was only four feet high, allowing her to see an obstacle course on the other side. Since the course was made for younger soldiers, it was short enough that it didn't make her nervous, not at the moment anyway. Atop the wall were several humans, some in armor, some in flowing robes, and there was Hayrik, father of Rafal and king of the Chayyoth. When the last of the recruits were in formation, the older soldier wasted no time assuming a position that was centered and facing them.

"I am Dimtri, overseer of recruitment. Today's testing will commence now," he said, loud enough for all the recruits to hear. "The first set of tests will evaluate you for the School of Soldiering. The following tests will evaluate you for the School of Flight. You will face the first tests alone and must have your partner for the next set."

Neviah hadn't known they needed a buddy. She looked over at Victoria, who smiled and nodded. That was easy. She had her buddy.

The soldier was still speaking. "Blade Master Mordeth will be sitting in on the ceremonies today," Dimtri said, waving his hand behind him to indicate a handsome man dressed in black. The crowd cheered and whistled at the mention of his name. He occupied one of the chairs on the short wall. "He is ever looking for an apprentice who can learn the sword as he has. If you do well today, perhaps you will impress him." Excitement spread among the recruits as hundreds of hushed conversations started up.

The soldier held up his hand, palm out. Then he quickly closed it into a fist, silencing everyone. "Two more things before we begin.

One, you may quit at any time. No one is forcing you to be here. Two, I have the final say for the School of Soldiering. Show me your best," he finished as he turned to take his place among those on top of the wall.

A handful of soldiers in hardened leather armor with wooden shields and wooden swords walked into the arena to stand before the recruits. The recruits were split into several different lines. One at a time, the front row of recruits began to file onto the field. A man gave the first person in Neviah's line brief instructions while he handed him a wooden sword and shield before sending him onward.

Neviah watched as the boy approached the first soldier. The recruit swung with his sword, but the skilled soldier easily sidestepped the blow. He blocked the next swing with his shield. This went on for a minute before a little gong was sounded. The first recruit moved on while another took his place. At the next station, the same recruit did all the blocking as the soldier struck out at him. The next station was archery, with the last being some type of strength test. Simple enough.

The atmosphere was rather festive. The people in the stands provided a constant background of conversations. Every now and then, there would be catcalls and cheering for a particular recruit as he walked out onto the field.

With a couple hundred recruits in front of them, Neviah and her friends waited a long time before it was their turn. Asa was up first. She noticed he held the shield in his right hand and the sword in his left. He would have to learn how to fight left-handed, she realized. The injuries to his shoulder greatly limited his range of motion, and as long as he couldn't lift his right arm above the shoulder, it was useless in a fight. Asa stepped out onto the field, and suddenly, not a voice could be heard in the entire stadium. It was like someone had cut off the conversation switch. Was it because Asa was an obvious outsider? Had everyone heard of them? She heard the words "hero" and "Ba'altose" passed around by the recruits behind her.

Asa paused only a moment before continuing to the first soldier. The soldier actually looked a little nervous as the teen approached. Asa attacked, but his swing was slow and awkward-looking. The man easily dodged it. Asa made several swings that hit nothing but air.

Conversations sprang to life again. This time, it was a den of whispers. The soldier only had to block one of Asa's swings, which was a stab. Then, the soldier set the shield on the ground and just continued to dodge Asa's strikes. There was laughter from the crowd. Neviah couldn't see Asa's face but could tell by the set of his shoulders he was embarrassed.

Egged on by the crowd, the soldier danced around, and when Asa tried another stab, he moved and smacked Asa on the butt with his sword. The crowd roared with laughter.

"Stop it!" Neviah yelled but her voice was drowned out by the crowd. In front of Victoria, Adhira was already outfitted with shield and sword. His knuckles were white from his grip on the pommel. He looked back at Neviah.

She gave him a nod. "Go be you."

The gong sounded, and like a horse loosed from the stocks, Adhira ran across the short distance to the soldier. Seeing Adhira coming, he quickly picked up his shield, but it didn't do him any good.

Adhira used his own shield to knock the soldier's shield out of the way. He then punched the man square in the face, causing him to stumble back a step. While he was off balance, Adhira tangled his shield in the man's legs, which made him fall over. When he tried to stand, Adhira sat on his back and smacked him repeatedly on the butt with his sword. The crowd went wild with cheering, but Neviah didn't care about their applause. She was already mad at them for laughing at Asa, who she couldn't see anymore because he was further down the line of soldiers. It was impossible to pick him out of the crowd of recruits who were training everywhere.

The gong sounded, and Victoria walked out. Adhira moved on without looking back. Humiliated, the soldier quickly made his way off the field. Neviah was handed a sword and shield.

"The first bout is to test your strength, speed, and dexterity," Neviah was told. "You will be on the offense. The next bout will test your ability to follow instructions as well as your fortitude. Any questions?" She shook her head. She'd watched enough recruits to where she knew what they were expecting.

Victoria was doing okay. She made a few strikes, but she was obviously aiming at the shield and not the soldier. Neviah smiled. Victoria had a gentle heart.

The gong sounded again. "Try not to go crazy like your friend did," the instructor said as she walked away. The soldier was waiting with his shield raised. Unlike Victoria, Neviah was trying to hit the soldier.

She swung at his helmet, but the shield was quickly raised, and the blow was deflected. When he brought it low so he could see, she struck again, but again, her sword was deflected. When he lowered it, she did the same thing again but jumped to the side and tried to get her sword around the edge of the shield. He turned, and suddenly, the shield was in front of her again.

She knelt and tried hitting his legs, but he danced back out of reach. Very few recruits had scored a hit, but if she managed to, it would make her stand out. An idea popped into her head, and she smiled. It was just the sort of trick Asa would use.

She swung at the soldier's head, and when he lifted his shield, she tossed hers to his right. He turned to face her shield, but she was no longer with it. She had moved around his other side and struck him in the back with her sword.

The soldier was stunned at first but smiled and nodded his head at her slightly. There was a modest amount of applause from the audience, but she didn't know if it was for her or not. When she picked up her shield, the gong sounded.

She made her way to the next soldier, who was accompanied by another instructor. "Try not to get hit," was his first command.

The soldier came at her, swinging his sword slowly to her right. She easily blocked it. He did the same to her left, and that was blocked, too.

"Put your shoulder into the shield so it can absorb more of the blow." The soldier swung harder, and she put her shoulder into the shield. It stung her arm on impact. "Don't take your eyes off your opponent." He swung again, and she forced herself not to turn her head away. "When you block a strike to your face, regain sight as quickly as possible."

The swing at her face was slow, and she held up her shield. Right after she felt the impact, she lowered her shield. There was suddenly a fist hovering an inch from her nose.

"When you lose sight of your opponent, even for a second, you want to put distance between yourself and him." The soldier swung at her head again, and she took a quick step back while blocking her face. When she lowered the shield, the man was further from her. The gong sounded. "Nicely done," the man said before turning to the next recruit.

A soldier took her sword and shield, and she was handed a bow and quiver of ten arrows.

"Hit the target," the next instructor said.

Not really knowing what to do, she put an arrow in the string, pulled back, and let it go. The arrow came nowhere near the target, which was only thirty feet away.

"This time, pull the string back to your cheek."

Neviah did so and the arrow still missed the target by a wide margin.

"Aim the tip of the arrow at the center of the target."

She did so, and the arrow buried itself in the dirt in front of the target.

"What should you do differently?"

"I need to aim above the target to hit it," Neviah guessed.

"Do so and spend the remaining arrows."

The next shot hit low on the target, making her smile. Archery didn't seem so tough. The rest of her arrows hit somewhere on the target, though none hit the bull's-eye. The gong sounded.

When she moved to the next test, there was a series of stones.

"Start with the smallest and lift each one above your head."

The first one was easy, as was the next one. The third one was a stone about the size of a soccer ball. She was able to lift it onto her shoulder but couldn't get it any higher. She tossed it onto the ground.

"Now, toss this javelin as far that way as you can. Like this." He held the javelin like he was about to throw it and went through the motion.

When he handed it to her, she stood where he pointed. There were markers every ten feet or so. She pulled it back and threw it as hard as she could. It wobbled awkwardly through the air before burying itself in the dirt. She was feeling good about the throw until she saw the other javelins sticking in the dirt, nearly all much further away than hers.

That was all he had her do. She stood there a moment, waiting for the gong. When it sounded, a man who'd apparently been rating her approached and gave her a red ribbon before walking away. She studied the ribbon, wondering if red was a good thing or a bad thing. Then, she noticed a soldier waving her over to the other side of the wall. There, she met up with her friends. Asa and Victoria also had red ribbons, and Adhira had a green one.

"I know what red means now," she said to them.

"They can keep their stupid ribbon," Adhira said, throwing his on the ground. "We're here to fly anyway." The Indian looked like he was still ready for a fight. Asa remained as quiet as Victoria.

"What's next?" Neviah asked to get Asa talking.

She didn't think he'd heard her and was about to repeat the question when he said, "The Chayyoth have two tests. The first one takes a while."

He was right. There were three lines formed in front of a small building erected at the northern end of the colosseum, and they were hardly moving.

"What happens in there?" she asked. The others shrugged.

"You will see," came a deep voice from behind her. It was Corban, the Chayya who'd invited her to the tryouts.

Neviah introduced everyone. Corban nodded to each in greeting. After seeing Adhira's green ribbon on the ground, he picked it up with one of his large paws and handed it back to him.

"I don't want to be a soldier," he said as he took the ribbon.

"The School of Flight also uses these ribbons to keep track of a recruit's progress. They are the only way to keep up with so many. This ribbon will let us know you passed the first portion of the assessment."

"Does this mean we fail?" Neviah asked, showing him her red ribbon.

"Negative. Green means the recruit's physical capabilities are acceptable to both the Moriahns and the Chayyoth. Red only means the School of Soldiering does not accept your application to their school."

The Armor of Light

"Why wouldn't the School of Flight disqualify us too?"

"We have different ideas about what makes a good warrior. Asa was given red because of his injuries. I, however, know how he received those injuries and therefore know a warrior's heart beats in his chest."

Asa stood a little straighter under the praise.

"Victoria wasn't accepted by the soldiers because she is meek and lacks aggression. I see these qualities as akin to patience and mercy, both of which every warrior needs a good portion of. Anyone can swing a sword, but knowing when to sheath it is the very essence of wisdom.

"And you, Neviah, did better than many of the male candidates but received a red ribbon solely because you are not as strong as the males. I value speed and cunning as much as strength. The four of you still have an equal chance to be riders."

"Oh," she said, trying to look relieved.

"I will be monitoring your progress," Corban said before walking away.

"What do you think happened to his wings?" Asa asked. "I haven't seen a Chayya so scarred."

"That must have been one nasty fight," Adhira said.

After a while, Adhira and Asa entered the small building, making Neviah and Victoria next. The door eventually opened, and a Chayya waved the girls in. Neviah grabbed the other girl's hand as they stepped inside. Another Chayya, one without the large mane of hair like the others, stepped up to them. The voice was distinctly feminine.

"Go ahead and put these on." She held out two pairs of bracelets. "I must separate you now," she said, looking down at their clasped hands.

Neviah gave Victoria's hand a squeeze before letting go. They were then led to separate rooms. There was a black button on a waist-high stand. Otherwise, the room was bare.

The female Chayya followed her in. "The rules for this test are simple. Each of you has been given pain bracelets." Neviah already didn't like the test. "Pain sensations will be sent directly to your nerves, beginning with a mild discomfort but growing more intense as time goes on. You and your partner will share the pain for as long as you can. When you cannot take the pain anymore, push the button, and the pain will switch to your friend. In this way, last as long as you can. When you want to end the test, call out 'done.'" She hesitated a moment before saying, "There has never been a female rider before. I hope you do well."

The door shut, and Neviah braced herself for the pain. What if the pain started with Victoria? She stilled herself just in case the pain came all at once. Her wrists began to itch with the anticipation. Then she realized the itch wasn't psychological. She rubbed them and walked around the room. It felt like she had a small burn under the bracelets. She looked at the button.

As the fire began to spread up her arm, she considered taking a break from the pain. But it would give the pain to Victoria. She turned her back on the button and began pacing again. She shook her arms and pulled at the bracelets, but it brought no relief. Only the button would take away the pain, and she refused to go near it.

"I can't do that to her," she said quietly as tears leaked from the corner of her eyes. It became excruciating. She couldn't pace around anymore. Her arms started to spasm uncontrollably, and she wrapped them around herself. They were on fire. She sat on the floor, rocking back and forth, trying to think of the words to any song that would comfort her, but she couldn't focus on anything but the pain.

She didn't let herself look at the button for fear that she would push it. How could anyone pass this on to a friend? She couldn't take it anymore. "Please, stop it!" she yelled at the door. Suddenly, the pain was gone. It was as if it had never happened, and the door opened immediately.

The female Chayya strode in and took the bracelets off. Her face was unreadable. Neviah stood and wiped her eyes on her sleeves before following the Chayya out of the room.

"Where is Victoria?" she asked, gathering herself.

"She is not done with the test yet," the Chayya said.

"Shouldn't we have finished at the same time?"

She didn't answer but instead asked, "Why didn't you press the button?"

"I didn't want to pass that kind of pain to my friend."

After several minutes, the female Chayya went in. Victoria was led out with fresh tears on her cheeks and wrapped her in a hug. There was no time for comforting each other, though.

"You must move on to the next trial," a male Chayya said from behind them.

They exited into the arena.

There was no time to speak before another Chayya approached them.

"You have until the sandglass is empty," he said as he led them around a wall where they could see a sprawling obstacle course. A human soldier walked up and flipped over a large sandglass. The sand started to trickle down. It looked like they only had a few minutes' worth of sand.

Neviah and Victoria turned to the first obstacle. It was a pair of balance beams. Neviah climbed on one while Victoria tried to stand on the other. It was impossibly thin, making the girls wobble on the first step. They took a second step. Neviah lost her balance and fell.

"Back to the beginning of the obstacle," the man with the hourglass said. "Both of you."

Victoria hopped down, and they started over. They stood on the narrow beam again, and this time, Victoria immediately lost her balance. Neviah reached out her hand and steadied the other girl. Then, it hit her. This was a team obstacle course. Holding firmly to the other girl's hand, they took another step, much more stable. They easily finished the first obstacle and came to the next.

It was a rope swing across water, but the rope was hanging in the center of the pool. Victoria wordlessly held out her hand, and Neviah grabbed it. Leaning back to counter her friend's weight, Neviah eased her out over the water. When she was almost parallel, Victoria grabbed the rope.

She easily swung over before throwing the rope back to Neviah. When they were both over, Neviah looked back at the hourglass. They were half out of time. The next obstacle before them was a platform with a zip line over water. It ended at the ground but started about six feet off the ground, high enough to trigger Neviah's fear of heights but not enough to cripple her. There was only one set of handles, not unlike the handlebars on a bicycle. If one of them slid down, she would be too far away to slide the handle back to the other person.

Victoria grabbed one-half of the handlebars. Neviah smiled and grabbed the other side. They stepped off, the wind whipping ponytails as they descended, stopping in front of a ten-foot wall. Neviah immediately cupped her hands, and Victoria stepped into them, reaching high until she was lifted to the top of the wall. She swung her leg over and climbed up into a seated position. She held her hand out to Neviah, but it was just out of reach.

Neviah jumped and grasped the other girl's hand, nearly pulling her from the wall. Victoria held on to the wall with a hooked elbow and was pulling hard, but she was unable to pull Neviah up. Neviah let go and thought for a second. Maybe they should switch.

"Time," she heard the man behind her call out. The hourglass was empty on top; all the sand had settled into the bottom.

Neviah looked up at Victoria. They hadn't finished. What did that mean? Her dream told her she would be on the back of a Chayya. She'd assumed that meant she would be in the flying school.

After Victoria dropped back to the ground, they were led to the rest of the waiting recruits. She couldn't shake the feeling that she'd failed everything. The School of Soldiering had already refused her. She had only lasted in the pain test for a few minutes or so and they hadn't completed the obstacle course. She decided it was out of her hands and didn't let herself worry about it. The bright side would be she wouldn't have to fly. She soon found herself hoping she'd failed.

A Chayya walked around with ribbons, taking their old ribbons and giving them new ones. Adhira received a silver one, but the other three received purple ones. They looked at all the other recruits around them. Most had yellow ribbons, though some had silver. Neviah couldn't reason them out. An hour later, the venerable soldier who'd started off the tests stood before the recruits.

"Now for the results," he said. "Yellow means you have been accepted into the School of Soldiering." He had to pause as a wave of cheering passed through most of the recruits. "Silver means you have been accepted to both schools and must choose."

Neviah patted Adhira on the shoulder to say, "Good job." She didn't see many other silvers.

"If you have received purple." Neviah tensed, waiting for the declaration they had failed. "Purple means you are not accepted to the School of Soldiering but have been accepted to the School of Flight. If you still have a red ribbon, you are invited to try again next year."

Victoria and Asa looked at each other, excitement and surprise plastered on their faces. Neviah forced herself to share their smiles, but she had to fight the sudden urge to flee. She, Neviah, the girl who was terrified of heights, was about to fly.

Chapter 3

"We can all go to the same school!" Asa said excitedly. There were similar statements from hundreds of different groups of teenagers. Suddenly, everyone grew quiet. The blade master, Mordeth, had approached the soldier spokesman. After a quick deliberation, the old soldier addressed the gathered recruits again.

"It appears that Blade Master Mordeth has chosen a new pupil from among you."

Neviah knew who it would be, even before a young soldier was sent their way.

He stopped in front of Adhira. "Do you accept the blade master's offer?"

Adhira looked back at Neviah. Every boy wanted to be a swordfighter. She knew this was the opportunity of a lifetime for anyone in the city, but she also knew Adhira didn't want to be separated from his friends.

"Just because we are in different schools doesn't mean we won't still be hanging out all the time," she said. He looked genuinely happy over her consent. He nodded at the young soldier and followed him to where Mordeth stood.

"The blade master has an apprentice!" the soldier declared.

Cheering followed, none more fervent than Adhira's friends. Neviah hoped she was right about being able to see him often. He was a constant annoyance but had grown on them all. Like a cyst that made her laugh every now and then.

"Now, report to your schools!" the soldier finished. There was still cheering from the audience as the recruits were led to separate ends of the coliseum.

When the three of them reached the end with the scarred,

flightless Chayya, there were only thirty other recruits.

"You have been accepted into the school of flight," Corban said to the small group.

Behind him, several younger Chayyoth began landing with heavy steps, folding their wings and waiting.

"The next step is to find a companion. Just because you have been chosen by the school doesn't mean you will be chosen by a Chayya. If you do not find a Chayya who will bear you, you cannot join the School of Flight. The rules state that only Chayyoth on the choosing field are eligible as choices. If you offer yourself as a companion and are rejected, you will receive a black ribbon. Two such ribbons will disqualify you from the school. If you only receive one black ribbon or none but still have not found a companion, you may try again next year."

More Chayyoth had arrived, their youth obvious in the way they moved around, trying to look around Corban to see the new human recruits. The Chayyoth were all male. The female Chayya had said there'd never been a female rider before. Apparently, that was true for the mounts as well. Neviah was by no means a feminist, but the obvious exclusion of females by both species was annoying.

"You will have as much time as needed to speak with the Chayyoth. I have seen conversations go on for days before a choice was made. When you make your choice, you will have your first flight together." Corban said a few more things, but Neviah forgot about the rest of the world. First flight. Why so soon? Shouldn't there be months of training first? Neviah wiped her suddenly sweaty palms on her pants.

Corban must have given permission to start because the other humans moved toward the Chayyoth, though hesitant at first. Only Asa was confident. He strode up to Rafal, his limp more pronounced when he hurried, and the Chayya dipped his shoulder so the teen could climb up. After Asa's feet were tied together around the Chayya's neck, they took off into the air.

She swooned slightly at the sight, desperately trying to think of a way out. After picking Asa's brain concerning the rules, she still hadn't come up with a plan. Looking around at the gathered Chayyoth, most were already in conversations with the humans, she didn't see any looking her way. The larger riders were talking to the larger mounts. The strong favored the strong. It was only natural. The female Chayya from the pain test was on the field, too, helping to tie the feet of the riders. She held several pieces of rope with slip knots on each end for easy tying. A second and a third pair flew into the air. Neviah still hadn't moved.

"They don't bite," said a friendly voice from beside her. She looked to see Corban towering to her right. "There is nothing to be shy about. I've seen you riding a Chayya in a vision. You will find a companion today."

Neviah nodded and slowly walked toward the Chayyoth. She kept her face calm, but her mind was screaming for a way out. She couldn't do it, couldn't fly. But it was prophesied. What was she going to do? Then, something Corban had said popped into her mind. Looking back at the gnarled Chayya, she knew what she would do.

No longer afraid, she walked up to the largest Chayya recruit on the field, though he was not nearly as large as Corban. "I wish to be your companion," Neviah said without even introducing herself. The Chayya shared a sideways look with the human he was talking to.

Looking back at Neviah, he said, "I decline your offer." The female Chayya walked up to her and gave her a black ribbon. One more, and she would be dismissed from the School of Flight forever. The female Chayya looked at Neviah with a raised brow, but the girl didn't explain herself.

Neviah turned and walked back to where Corban stood, frowning. His eyes were stuck fast to the ribbon she held. "You said I could choose any Chayya on the field?" He hesitated before nodding. "Then I choose you. Will you be my companion, Corban?"

The Chayya looked angry. "I cannot fly. This you can see. I cannot accept your request."

The female Chayya walked up, carrying another black ribbon.

"What are you doing?" Corban demanded.

"You have declined her offer," the female said without making eye contact. "The rules state that she must be presented with a ribbon."

"Hold on," Corban said, running a large paw through his thick mane. "It only counts as a declined offer if I am eligible, which I'm not. Have one of the Moriahns fetch the rulebook so we can get this matter settled quickly."

They had drawn the attention of many of the people left in the stadium. It was impossible for them to hear what was going on, but it was obvious there was some rule dispute when an elderly gentleman whose hair had gone completely white walked up carrying a book that looked older than he was. He wore white robes with a blue fringe at the bottom.

"What is the nature of the question?" he asked in a slow draw as if the act of speaking were a great effort.

"I am head instructor at the School of Flight," Corban said, "and I do not wish to have a new companion. Is this girl allowed to solicit me for companionship?"

When Corban had said "new companion," she realized he may have had one before. She hadn't considered he may have lost one. Was she opening up old wounds? If so, the Chayya didn't show any signs of emotion on his hardened features.

Without opening the rule book, the man said, "Any Chayya without a companion on the field may be asked for companionship, and any may refuse. If you do not wish to be companion to this girl, you must refuse her offer and give her a black ribbon."

The Chayya turned his attention wholly on Neviah. She did her best not to shrink back from his scowl. He'd said Chayyoth didn't bite but she was starting to have her doubts.

"You must reconsider your choice for mount," he said, almost pleadingly. Though Neviah knew he would hate her for it, she shook her head. Her offer would stand.

His white brows flexed down in thought, but Neviah knew he had no way out. They both had visions of her on the back of a Chayya, and if he refused her, she wouldn't be allowed to have a companion. Ever.

Without making eye contact with her or raising his head from a study of the ground, Corban nodded. "I accept," he breathed. The humans and Chayyoth recruits stared at the disabled Chayya in disbelief. "Shouldn't you be mingling?" he growled, rising up to his full height, his moment of weakness gone. The recruits were suddenly eager to talk among themselves again, not even daring a glance at Corban.

The House of the Forest

The remaining humans and Chayyoth continued to speak with each other for several hours. One at a time, they took off into the sky in pairs until only Victoria remained. In her left hand, she carried a single black ribbon.

Her eyes were rimmed with red as she looked desperately at Neviah. Victoria had not been chosen, and no recruit Chayyoth remained. She looked up at the sky and back to Neviah. Asa had a mount, and she didn't. Without one, they would be separated. The remaining humans and Chayyoth started to disperse, the formalities and ceremonies over.

Corban approached Victoria. "I am sorry, young one. Since you only received one black ribbon, you may try again next year." The wind began to blow in gusts, and the sky rumbled with the sound of thunder.

Victoria looked at Neviah again, not knowing what to do. The female Chayya came and took the black ribbons from her and Neviah to put them into a box. Looking at the Chayya, Neviah had an idea. Catching Victoria's eye, Neviah nodded sideways toward the female.

The other girl looked back and forth between Neviah and the Chayya a few times. Then, in wide-eyed realization, she moved to stand in front of the female Chayya.

"What is your name?" Victoria asked quickly.

"I'm Enya," the Chayya said, a little startled.

"Hello Enya, I am Victoria. Would you be my companion?"

Enya shook her head. "Only males are allowed to be mounts."

"Where does it say that?" Neviah asked. She had squeezed through the wording of the rules once. Maybe Victoria could, too.

Corban scowled down at Neviah before turning to the man with the rulebook. The man shook his head. "Female Chayyoth are not allowed to be a companion," he said flatly.

"Where does it say that?" Neviah dared, though she could tell she was wearing on everyone's nerves. Victoria was worth it.

With a sigh, the man opened the book in his hand and flipped through the pages until he found the words he was looking for. "Here," he said. Then read, "'The firstborn *male* Chayya of each house must offer *himself* as a possible companion in their first year of ascension into adulthood.'" He looked at Neviah as if to say, "Satisfied?" She wasn't.

"It says the male must. It doesn't say a female can't." The man opened his mouth to speak but paused. Shutting his mouth and turning back to the book, he read it again.

"What is it?" Corban asked, looking over the man's shoulder to read what he was reading.

"She," he paused, flipped to another page, and read a moment before shaking his head. "She's right, Professor Corban. There is nothing in here that says a female Chayya cannot offer herself as a companion." Looking at Enya, he said, "But she still has the same rights as all the others and may refuse. Since she shook her head, she must offer this young girl a black ribbon."

Enya shook her head again. "I only shook my head because I thought it wasn't allowed." Turning to Victoria, she smiled and said, "Yes, I would love to be your companion."

"Young woman," the man in the white robes said to Neviah. "One day, when you retire from guarding the skies, you will have a promising career in law." He walked away with his book tucked under one arm.

Victoria hugged the Chayya tight before mounting up. Corban hesitated but slowly tied Victoria's feet for her and watched as the pair took off into the air. The large Chayya had a rueful smile as Victoria and Enya flew away. He saw Neviah watching him, and his face became stone.

"Are there any more centuries-old traditions you'd like to challenge, Neviah?" he asked.

Feeling more than a little sheepish, she shook her head. He lowered his shoulder for her to get on. She hesitated.

"I thought you couldn't fly," she said.

"I can't," he confirmed. "But the rules state that the new companions must ride together to the School of Flight."

Neviah climbed on. She thought the School of Flight was on Alya and didn't know how they were supposed to make it to the floating country. Corban would have the answer, but she was done being a nuisance. His fur was soft, but corded muscles were taut beneath. He straightened once she was seated, and a young male Chayya came over with a rope to tie Neviah's feet.

"I do not think that will be necessary," Corban growled. The young Chayya backed away quickly.

All eyes were on the new companions as Corban moved toward one of the large, gated entrances to the stadium. Neviah shifted uncomfortably under their scrutiny and kept her eyes on the ground in front of them. It wasn't until they were passing between the stands that a few peals of laughter came from the people gathered along the railing.

Neviah felt Corban's muscles tense momentarily at the first jeer. He kept his head high and his eyes straight ahead as he walked. Pride may have shown outwardly, but Neviah knew he was wracked by the humiliation she had caused him. She never in her life hated herself as much as she did at that moment. Instead of facing her fear of heights, she had chosen to disgrace the Chayya, who had been nothing but friendly to her.

Even once free of the onlookers in the coliseum, the pair became an outlet for the city's curiosity. Eyes followed them through the streets. Neviah alternated between looking at Alya above, the people, and the Chayya's white mane. It was as if everyone looking their way was condemning her for being so selfish. Corban stuck to the main roads, taking them through what seemed an infinite number of city blocks. He didn't once pause until they came to a squat stone building.

There were several thick ropes stretching from the building all the way to Alya. The enormous chain that connected the Chayyoth home world to Uru was so close its sheer size was dizzying. Craning her neck, Neviah saw large square lifts going up and down the ropes. That was how they were getting to Alya. She forced herself to loosen the sudden death grip she had on Corban's mane, telling herself she could do it.

"What's the deal with the chain?" she asked, attempting to stall their ascent as long as possible. Corban looked up at the chain for a moment.

"Alya is said to have been created thousands of years ago as a prison, and the Chayyoth were charged with its keeping. The chain keeps Alya from falling and destroying Uru." How could the chain possibly hold up the enormous landmass above them? What kept it from crashing down on the city? Was it filled with helium like a moon-sized balloon?

"A prison for who?"

"The most merciless abomination to ever walk the world of man."

"Corban!" said a short man with light brown skin, abruptly ending the Chayya's story. The guy carried a ledger and stood beneath an awning that circled the building. "I see you brought company this time."

"Two to go up," the Chayya said curtly.

Seeing Corban was not in a conversational mood, the man consulted his paperwork. "Lift four is ready to go. The lady must dismount and occupy her own harness. Will she be paying, or will her ride be credited to the school as well?"

"The school," Corban said, walking into the building. He stopped in front of a large box that had the number four written above it. After kneeling to let Neviah off, he walked into the elevator. Neviah halted at the door and looked in. There were other humans sitting in chairs that appeared to be fastened to the floor.

A man motioned to the seat next to him when Neviah slowly stepped into the elevator. It felt sturdy enough. There were windows to the side, but nothing could be seen out of them except for the wall of the building. The man with the clipboard looked into the box, checked something off on his sheet, and closed the door. Sweat immediately broke out on Neviah's face. She looked over to Corban. He was strapped into a large harness that allowed him to remain standing. He looked at her curiously.

The elevator rumbled and jerked as it came free of the landing. Light poured in from the windows as it was lifted into the sky. Neviah rushed to her seat and quickly strapped herself in, closed her eyes, and put her head between her knees. She knew the lift was taking her hundreds of feet above the city, but if she didn't look, maybe she could stave off the panic threatening to consume her. Closing her eyes didn't keep her from feeling the sway of the lift, however.

She told herself over and over she was perfectly safe. Each lift probably made hundreds of trips a day. The longer the ride lasted, the more relaxed she became. It was going to be okay. Suddenly, she felt herself rising above her seat, her shoulders pressing against the restraints. She let out a scream when she realized she had become weightless.

"It's okay," the man next to her said. "We are switching between gravities." Without opening her eyes, she was still able to tell everything was shifting. She felt disoriented, like they were hanging upside down. Then, it passed and it felt like the elevator wasn't rising anymore but going down. After a few more minutes, she braved a peek. They were about twenty feet above the ground, then ten.

She breathed a sigh of relief when the elevator came to a rough stop on the ground. They'd made it. Everyone unbuckled and filed through the door that was opened from the other side. She eagerly unstrapped herself and rushed through the door into the structure the elevator occupied. When Corban emerged, he wordlessly knelt so she could climb on his back again. Once mounted, they left the building.

Another more terrified scream escaped Neviah's lungs when they came out into the daylight. She wrapped her arms around Corban so tight, it was a wonder she didn't pull out any of his mane. Above them, sprawling for miles in each direction, was the kingdom of Moriah. They could see the curve of the planet from the surface of Alya. It looked so close she was afraid its gravity would pluck them right from where they stood. At the same time, it appeared so far away that she felt bile rising in her throat as the dizziness assaulted her. They were standing upside down on a planet above the world.

She felt a slight rumble coming from the Chayya's back. Was he laughing? "You will get used to it," he said, continuing to walk. "It helps if you think of Alya as down."

They traveled for quite some time before she was able to loosen her grip on his mane. She kept her eyes below the new horizon, which allowed her to feel mostly normal again. Alya was down. They weren't hanging upside down. She was relieved when they came under the cover of large trees. The leaves were green with purple veins running down their length and connecting them to the white branches.

"You are afraid of heights," Corban stated without looking back at her.

"Yes," she admitted.

"And that is why you chose me; because I can't fly." She was afraid to answer, but she didn't need to. His comment was more of a statement than a question, anyway. He turned to look at her with his right eye. She pretended like she was looking at the trees, unable to meet his steel gaze.

He looked back at the path in front of them and froze, his muscles rigid. She followed his line of sight and saw an animal caught in a thicket ahead. Its fur was a magnificent white, almost iridescent, color. It had horns like a deer, a great large rack, which was caught in a tangle of vines. It pulled against the restraints, but its horns wouldn't budge. Neviah put her arms around Corban and swung her feet to the ground. She slowly approached the animal, though the Chayya remained glued to the path.

The animal saw her coming and pulled more frantically against the vines. Suddenly, a blinding light flooded the woods around her. It was so bright that closing her eyes wasn't enough to keep out the stinging rays. She had to cover her eyes with her hands as well. Turning her back to the brilliance, she took off her backpack and pulled out her clip-on sunglasses. Once the shades were over her glasses, she turned back to the trapped animal. It was still painful to look at, but she could see by squinting her eyes nearly to the point of being closed. The source of light was the animal itself. Its fur shone like the sun.

She continued her approach. Slowly. The animal was panicked, seeing its light defense had failed. It jerked so hard that Neviah was afraid it would hurt itself. When she reached the creature, she lightly placed a hand on its shoulder, which was as tall as Corban's, though not nearly as muscled. It tensed, expecting some harm to follow, but instead, it received a gentle stroke from Neviah's fingers. The fur felt like silk to the touch.

"It's okay," she cooed. "I just want to help." She placed her other hand on its neck, slowly winning its trust with continued stroking. The creature relaxed after a minute or so of this treatment. Then, as if a switch had been turned off, the light was gone.

She could see into the creature's eyes better. Its terror had been replaced by curiosity. A fierce intelligence burned behind those purple and gold eyes. Her stroking brought her hand across something wrapped around the creature's neck. She followed the golden chain to a silver key that hung on it. She stared at the key, trying to discern its purpose, but it looked like an ordinary key to her. The creature gave the thicket another pull as if to say, "Can you hurry up?"

Neviah pulled out *Prophecies*. It was an amazing source of guidance for her and her friends as they navigated that strange new world. It was also a weapon. With a thought, the book turned into the Sword of Re'u. The two-edged blade reflected beautifully in the sun's rays penetrating the canopy. It had the word "spirit" etched into each side of the blade.

The sudden appearance of the silver sword gave the animal a start, but it quickly relaxed. She had gained its trust. Careful not to sever one of its white horns, she cut through the vines holding them. Once free, the creature gave its head a quick shake, showering Neviah with leaves and vines. They stared at each other for a second before the animal turned and bounded through the forest.

When it was gone from sight, she became aware of Corban standing behind her. She turned to see him staring at her with his head slightly cocked.

"What?" she asked.

"You have no clue what manner of creature that is, do you?" She shook her head. "That is a Neri; actually, the last of the Neris. When Re'u hid his armor throughout the world, he hung that key around the Neri's neck."

"What does the key go to?" she asked.

"The House of the Forest. Inside lay the Forest Shield." He looked where the Neri had been trapped. "Many have sought the beast, but it is difficult to catch something you can't look at. You are the first person to touch it since Re'u."

She didn't know what to say. It felt good that she had done something no one else had done, but she felt dumb for not grabbing the key. When he knelt, she remounted.

"Where is the House of the Forest?" she asked once they were back on the path.

"It lies on Alya's uppermost region. The air is too thin to breathe, and even if someone did make it there, they couldn't enter without the key."

"Even with the key, how could anyone get the shield if they can't breathe?"

"A human can hold their breath long enough to reach the door if they are flown there."

"But once the door is open, will they be able to breathe inside?"

She was lifted slightly as the Chayya shrugged. "That journey would require the utmost faith," he said. "No one knows exactly where it is, anyway."

The sun sank low on the horizon belonging to the planet below just before the forest opened up into a clearing with short-cropped grass. The other recruits were there with their Chayyoth. Asa and Rafal were the only ones standing near Victoria and Enya. The others were several yards away in their own group.

Everyone straightened when they entered the field. Corban stood facing them. Shocked expressions were prevalent at the sight of the odd pair. Even Asa stared at Neviah with his mouth open. Victoria hadn't told him about Neviah's choice of companion. At a command from Corban, the humans and Chayyoth attempted a semblance of a formation.

There were human and Chayyoth instructors around the glade. They also gawked at the pair. Corban looked over the recruits as he walked down the line. Neviah avoided eye contact with everyone, shifting awkwardly as they passed before each recruit. When he had completed his inspection, Corban stood before them again. Neviah didn't know what she was supposed to do, so she sat and tried not to attract any undue attention to herself while her new companion spoke.

"You are among the very few to be chosen for the School of Flight. That does not mean you will pass." Neviah could see awe mixed with fear as the recruits suffered under the head instructor's glower. "Whether you finish or not, the companion you have chosen will be bonded to you for life. Mount up, humans," he ordered. The other recruits quickly scurried onto their Chayya's back. "Everyone, repeat after me. 'I swear to put the needs of my companion above my own.'"

Neviah repeated the vow with everyone else.

"'I will be a lamp in the darkest times and a help when times are good. I will treat them how I would like to be treated. There is no enemy my companion will face alone and no friendships we will not share in. Only in death will this vow be lifted.' You are now bonded to your companion for life," Corban finished flatly.

There was no pomp about the ceremony, but there it was. Official companions.

"Tomorrow, you begin the hardest year of your life. You must be broken before you can be made whole into the wind warriors you are meant to be. Tonight is your last night as civilians. Get to know one another. I will see you in the morning."

With that, he walked away from the recruits and approached one of the instructors. "Have two cots and two mats taken to the old armory. It will serve as a barracks for the three females."

"But two mats, sir?" the Chayya asked.

"I will be joining my companion in the makeshift barracks," he said.

"Yes, sir," the Chayya said.

When he hesitated, Corban asked, "What is it?"

"I was only wondering how training was going to work."

"Are you referring to my training status or me being head instructor?"

"I guess both, sir."

"We will coast that current when we come to it. For now, treat me as a recruit as it pertains to training." The other Chayya nodded and walked off.

"We will be in a separate barracks?" Neviah asked. "I don't want special treatment."

"Both for safety and human standards of propriety," Corban stated. "Don't worry. You will be just as miserable as the other recruits."

Asa and Victoria approached. Their Chayyoth companions stood away, not wanting to approach the venerable Chayya. When Neviah's friends had come as close as they dared, Corban let her down so she could walk over to them.

Victoria wrapped her in a hug. "Thank you," she whispered in Neviah's ear.

"So, what happened after I left?" Asa asked, staring between her and Corban.

Neviah quickly filled him in.

"Thank you for helping Victoria," he responded. "But why did you choose the head instructor?" Neviah shrugged, though she knew why. Asa likely knew as well. He had a strange look in his eye as he continued to look between her and Corban.

"How are the other companions reacting to having a female Chayya and female riders?" Neviah asked to get the topic off herself somewhat.

"Not too good," Asa said. "The other riders won't talk to Victoria at all and treat me indifferently. The Chayyoth haven't said a word to Enya. They talk to Rafal, but he *is* the son of their king."

"They'll come around," Neviah said, watching the other companions mingling. "No one likes change." After thinking for a moment, she said, "Come with me, and bring your Chayyoth."

Without looking to see if she was being followed, she made a straight line for the group of companions. She might be terrified of heights, but she wasn't afraid to socialize. The others saw her coming and conversations ceased as she stopped in front of the group.

"Hello, everyone. I'm Neviah."

They stared at her. She waited patiently. One of them had to be brave enough to overcome the wall being wedged between their group and hers. She wanted there to be one group.

At last, the largest of the recruits stepped forward and introduced himself. "I am Ebbe. This is my companion, Biyn." Following his lead, a few of the others introduced themselves.

"Have you met my friends?" Neviah asked as Asa and Victoria approached, Chayyoth in tow. She introduced them all, not forgetting a single new name.

She saved Asa for last, adding "Slayer of Ba'altose, Lord of the Undead" to his name. This piqued their interest.

"He's that Asa?" a Chayya asked.

"He's still healing from the fight, but yeah, that's him."

Asa flushed red but managed to say, "It wasn't just me. I may have struck the killing blow, but without my friends, I would have died."

The large boy, Ebbe, puffed out his chest as he looked Asa up

The House of the Forest

and down. "I heard that a king named Tanas was the one who killed Ba'altose."

Ebbe was supposed to be her bridge to the other recruits. She couldn't lose him. "I assure you it was Asa."

He shook his head, unconvinced. She thought about showing him the Sword of Re'u but even that wouldn't be proof Asa had slain the undead king. Ebbe walked off, and the others followed. Neviah kicked the grass at her feet. She had been so close!

Asa put a hand on her shoulder. "We'll win them over eventually."

Corban approached. "Neviah, Victoria, and Enya come with me." Waving goodbye to Asa and Rafal, the females followed the large Chayya.

They were led to a small wooden building. It was dusty and dark, even with the oil lamps hanging from the ceiling in the center of the single room. Two beds were against one wall, and two very large mattresses were on the floor on the other wall. All four were complete with blankets and pillows, made up perfectly with the sheets and blankets tucked in tightly. There were clothes folded at the end of the beds for the two girls.

"Each night, I will give you three privacy while you prepare for bed. Let me know when you are ready. Only then will I come in. I must remain near my companion."

He walked out of the building and stood under a nearby tree. Neviah looked through her new clothes. They were blue and white colored shirts and pants mostly. She did find a nice set of cotton pajamas, also blue. When they were dressed for bed, she walked to the door and called to Corban. She saw him standing in the same place, but he wasn't alone.

Asa and Rafal were speaking to him as Corban shook his head. The Chayya said something back, which made Asa shrug his shoulders and walk away. What was all that about? Wordlessly, Corban walked in, turned the lamps down low, and sat by his sleeping mat. His face was unreadable.

Still feeling horrible for what she was putting the Chayya through, Neviah fell asleep.

Chapter 4

She wasn't sure if it was the yelling that first woke her or the banging of the door against the wall. Either way, all remnants of sleep evaporated as Chayyoth barged into the barracks, yelling for them to wake up. She sprang up in bed, disoriented for a moment, not knowing exactly where she was. The oil lamps were turned up to full brightness.

"I'm sorry princess, did I disturb your beauty sleep!" a Chayya yelled, his face inches from her own and the smell of a fish breakfast fresh on his breath.

Suddenly, there was another Chayya beside the first. "You will answer 'Yes, sir' or 'No, sir' when a flight instructor addresses you! Is that clear, recruit?"

"Yes, sir," she said.

"I can't hear you!"

"Yes sir!" she yelled, letting her anger at being woken up in such a way show.

"Well, recruit? Are you going to stay in bed all day?"

"No, sir!" She jumped out of bed.

"Did I tell you to move, recruit?" the first Chayya asked, trading his yelling tone for one of incredulity.

"No, sir!" she yelled, not knowing if she should get back in bed or not since she had already moved.

"Get back in bed!"

"Yes, sir!"

She climbed back in. The Chayya moved, and Neviah could see Victoria, Enya, and Corban standing at the foot of their beds, straight and at attention. Another flight instructor was walking back and forth, yelling at them, too.

The Chayya who'd been addressing Neviah turned to the room. "It appears as if this recruit hasn't gotten enough rest! Get in the pushup position!" Victoria got down on her hands after squeaking a "yes, sir." The Chayya beside her yelled at her to speak up several times before Victoria managed a response loud enough to satisfy him.

"Now, the three of you will do pushups until her highness has had enough sleep."

"I'm fine," Neviah said. As if by magic, three Chayyoth faces were yelling at her, spittle flying all over her face as they shouted. She didn't catch everything they said, but the gist of it was not to speak unless spoken to. When they were done yelling, Neviah had to lay in bed and watch for several minutes while the others did pushups. Victoria was the first to tire, unable to push herself up anymore. This attracted the instructors. Next, Enya couldn't do anymore. Corban, however, was a pushup machine. He cranked them out as if he started every morning with a hundred pushups. None of the instructors approached or addressed him directly.

"Are you finished sleeping in, recruit?"

"Yes, sir!" Neviah yelled as loud as she could.

"Stand in front of your rack, you lazy excuse for a recruit!"

"Yes, sir!" In seconds, they were all standing in front of their beds again.

"I don't know what kind of latrine hole you crawled from," the Chayya yelled, addressing all of them, "but at the School of Flight, we make our racks in the morning!"

Neviah wanted to say that they hadn't told them to make their beds yet but knew there was no winning the argument. She had been yelled at before in her life, but she never thought she would have someone yell the words, "And make sure that pillow is fluffed!" while she smoothed the wrinkles out of a pillow. Corban remained at attention the entire time. His bed was already perfectly made, just the way it had been the night before. He must have woken early to make it, knowing what was coming.

Even after Victoria's and Neviah's beds were perfectly made, Enya was still struggling to make hers. She lacked the dexterity of the humans.

Victoria was the next target of their attention. "Are you going to stand there while your companion struggles? You make me sick! Are you just going to leave her to die in combat? You would, wouldn't you? You would tuck tail and run and leave her to die!"

"No, sir!" Victoria yelled louder than Neviah thought possible for the other girl.

"Then, help your companion!" After quickly following orders, she and Enya were soon back at attention.

"I want you all dressed and outside in five minutes!" One instructor yelled as they left the barracks. When the door banged closed behind them, Neviah just glared. It was going to be a long year.

"That was fun," Enya said with a laugh. The Chayya was actually bubbly!

"You'd best get dressed," Corban said as he left.

The clothes fit snuggly. The girls decided it was best to leave their backpacks in the chest at the end of their bed, along with their weapons. Neviah hesitated at the door, looking back to where she left the book of prophecies. After carrying it around for the better part of a year, it felt odd leaving it behind.

The other recruits were coming outside into the darkness just as the girls and their companions were. The Chayyoth eyes reflected the blue light of Colossus, almost as if they were glowing. Three human instructors, who were likely the companions of the three Chayyoth, were yelling at the males. The instructors formed them all into two lines. One with the human recruits. The other with the Chayyoth recruits.

"Double time, march!" one Chayya instructor yelled. Neviah soon found out what that meant. They broke into a steady run as the sun's rays just began to peak over the horizon of the world below. A wave of dizziness came upon Neviah for a moment, but she reminded herself she was not hanging upside down over the world. She was right side up.

The run took them through a wide path snaking through the woods. After the first mile of the run, they were still headed away from camp. The instructors stopped them several times to do calisthenics. Several miles later, they found themselves standing in the courtyard in front of the barracks. A few recruits, man and Chayyoth, retched to the side of the formation. Most were doubled over and gulping air.

Victoria and Neviah were the only humans largely unaffected by the run. Aside from the way Asa stood to keep weight off his injured knee, he seemed otherwise unbothered by the run as well. Running wasn't so hard when nothing was chasing them. It seemed like there was always something chasing them.

Corban and Enya stood at attention behind them. Corban breathed normally as if he had just taken a stroll through the forest. Enya was breathing hard but stood at attention, doing her best not to show weakness. Like a pack of wolves, the instructors descended upon the other recruits until they were all standing at attention.

With big toothy grins, the flight instructors promised to see them again soon. As they walked away, a tall, lean man with short-cropped hair approached. He had the darkest skin Neviah had ever seen, and she was pretty dark herself.

"To your rear are the showers. To your right is the chow hall." The man paused, looking at the females, then at Corban. Corban made a scissors motion with his right paw. The man nodded. "The females will shower first. When they are done, the males will shower. Food will be served in fifteen minutes. Understood?"

Everyone yelled, "Yes, sir!"

"Good. Dismissed."

The water was cold, which encouraged everyone to be quick. Corban waited for the boys' turn, which was the only time she was separated from him. Fifteen minutes later found all the recruits seated, the Chayyoth on the floor in front of the massive table, and the humans seated across from their companions. The meal was fish, bread, and something that looked like potatoes but tasted like carrots. It wouldn't have been Neviah's first choice for breakfast.

She was the first to break the silence that blanketed their meal. "This water is delicious! I've never had anything like it."

"That is water from the Life Spring here on Alya," Corban responded from across the table.

"I drank some while I was back on Moriah," she said. "It was good, but it didn't taste this good."

"It wasn't fresh," Corban said. "This was drawn from the spring this morning."

"It is the only water the Chayyoth can drink," Rafal said.

"How do you venture away from home then? I've seen Chayyoth far to the north of here." She was referring to the battle at Samgar-Nebo.

"A Chayya can go nearly a week without a drink," Rafal said. "We also carry canteens. Beyond that, we can dehydrate just as humans can without normal water."

"You guys are like camels," Neviah said.

"What's a camel?" another recruit asked from across the table.

She shoved a piece of fish in her mouth to give her time to think.

"Are all the flight instructors so mean?" Asa asked Corban to save her from having to answer the question. Everyone perked up, eager to hear this answer instead.

Corban smiled at their eager faces. "You will see."

A Chayya came in and stood at the edge of the tables. "Form up outside," he said simply.

Everyone rushed outside, the humans lining up beside their companions.

"Follow me," he said once they were assembled.

They were led to a small building, barely large enough to hold them all. Inside were chairs and mats for everyone to take a seat.

"Before we begin your first lesson, I would like to go over your training schedule." This Chayya was far more laid back than the others. "Every other day, starting today, you will begin the day with physical training. This will be followed by the communication class, flight training, and tactics. The days between will be combat training. Are there any questions?"

No one said anything.

"Then, I will turn over your first communication course to my companion, Har."

A middle-aged man wearing solid-colored light blue pants and a tunic walked to the front of the class. As he spoke, he made motions with his hands. "Hello. My name is Har. This is the hand motions that correspond with saying 'my name is.'" He made the hand motion again. "Now, I want everyone to introduce themselves."

Why were they having a class on sign language? Everyone took turns saying their names, making awkward hand motions. The Chayyoth had a very difficult time making any semblance of the motion.

"What did you notice during your introductions?" Har asked, continually talking with his hands.

"We have a hard time doing the motions," one of the Chayyoth said.

"That is correct," the man said. "A Chayya can, at best, do a select few of the signs. Only humans have the dexterity to master all of them." He sat on the edge of the desk at the front of the class. "I bet you are wondering why I'm teaching sign language to all of you when only the humans can perform it."

Neviah was wondering about the purpose of learning sign language, period.

"When you are flying with the wind rushing in your ears, it is difficult to hear speech. Companions can speak with one another, but if you want to communicate with someone further away, you must use sign."

Neviah had never thought about not being able to hear when flying. She remembered how hard it was to hear when she was riding in a car with her head out the window. Sign language actually did make sense.

They spent the rest of the class going over basic signs. When the class was over, her hands and eyes were tired, and she had a slight headache. Another Chayya instructor and his companion led them from that class at a jog to a green field a mile or so away. This was where their flight training would take place. The first thing the instructor did was have the humans mount up.

More than a few glances were spared for Neviah, mounted upon her flightless Chayya. She pretended not to notice.

"I know you are excited about flying," the Chayya instructor said, "but aside from your first flight yesterday, you will remain grounded for the first month of instruction." A wave of complaints moved through the recruits. The expression on the flight instructor's face soured, quieting everyone. His anger disappeared, and he smiled. "Soon enough, younglings."

The instructor's companion mounted up. "Note how my companion sits," the Chayya said, turning sideways so they could all see. "His feet fit perfectly in the crevice above my shoulders."

Neviah pulled her feet up above Corban's shoulders. This brought her knees up to rest on the back of his neck. "That doesn't hurt, does it?" she asked. He looked back at her and shook his head.

"Now, grab a handful of your Chayya's mane," the instructor continued.

Neviah grabbed her companion's mane lightly.

"You cannot hurt me, Neviah," Corban said over his shoulder. "If you pulled with all your might, I would barely feel it," he assured her. She held more firmly. Looking over at Victoria. The other girl didn't know what to do. Her Chayya didn't have a mane. The other recruits snickered.

The instructor approached Victoria and Enya. After experimenting, they determined that Enya's fur was long enough and Victoria's hands small enough that the girl could hold onto the fur instead.

"Now, we are going to play a game," the instructor said. "Without leaving the ground, I want you, Chayyoth, to try and make your companions fall off. I also want the humans to try to stay on as long as possible. If there is one human that has not been dismounted by the end of the exercise, the Chayyoth will run an extra mile tomorrow. If all the humans have been knocked off, they will run the extra mile instead."

The faces of humans and Chayyoth alike were quickly set in grim determination.

"Go!" the instructor called out.

Suddenly, Corban reared up onto his hind legs. Neviah barely tightened her grip in time to keep from falling backward. He put his front legs down and simultaneously bucked his back legs. Neviah found herself unseated and flipping over her Chayya's head. She held on tight, twisting the mane of hair in her hands. Corban grimaced in pain, so she let go and fell to the ground. Then, he smiled.

"Wait. You weren't really in pain!" she said, shaking her fist at him.

"I told you I wouldn't feel any pain, no matter how hard you pulled," he said with a grin.

Neviah looked around. She was the first human unseated, though a boy was tossed to the ground shortly after. Soon, another followed.

Then, there were six still mounted. In a few seconds more, all the humans were thrown to the ground except for Victoria. She had put her head next to Enya's and had her arms wrapped halfway around her neck. The humans were all cheering for Victoria, the Chayyoth for Enya. It was a beautiful sight.

Enya opened her wings and shrugged with them, knocking Victoria sideways. "Hold on!" Neviah yelled with a laugh.

Victoria's legs swung around, almost striking the ground, but she managed to pull them up and wrap them around Enya's neck. Firmly attached, there wasn't much the exhausted Enya could do to dislodge her.

"Time!" the instructor said.

Cheers went up for Victoria as she dropped to the ground. Some of the companions rough-housed over the results until the instructor called them to attention. They were put through a few more basic riding techniques before being taken to lunch and then to their last class of the day. It was in the same room as before but a different Chayya and human taught.

"This will be your favorite class until you are allowed to fly," the human assured them. "Here, we will teach you how to think and give you the skills necessary to be the wind warriors you are meant to be."

He walked over to a stack of scrolls and picked one off the top. After walking back to the front of the class, he hung it on a nail, allowing the scroll to unroll to the floor. There was a life-sized painting of a Shedim.

"This is the enemy you are most likely to face in the sky. It is a Shedim, the enemy of all that is good. They are dragon servants, carrying out their will. Who has a guess as to the easiest way to kill a Shedim in aerial combat?"

One of the humans said, "A sword through the heart."

The instructor shook his head. "Shedim have naturally scaly skin that they cover with hardened leather armor. Piercing their heart is possible but far from the simplest way."

"By biting their head off," said the largest Chayya recruit, Biyn, grinning with his razor-sharp teeth. Everyone laughed.

"While that is an effective method, it requires that the Shedim be first disarmed or distracted. Otherwise, young one, you will receive a blade to your throat for the effort."

The thought made Neviah shudder. She looked over at Corban and his battle scars. She instantly knew the answer. "By disabling their wings," she said.

The instructor gave her a slight nod. "Precisely. No matter how armed or armored a Shedim is, their wings are their most vulnerable assets. It is also the most vulnerable part of a Chayya," he said, making it a point not to look at Corban. "In the weeks to come, we will show the riders how to protect this vulnerability."

After that, the man went through the basic strengths and weaknesses of many other creatures. According to the instructor, one of the greatest weaknesses of humans was that they couldn't see in the dark. Chayyoth, on the other hand, could see quite well in the dark when they chose to. He showed the class a painting of an all too familiar rock monster, stocky hairy creatures, giant spiders, and a few other creatures that looked like monsters out of nightmares. He showed one picture of what appeared to be a man but seven feet tall with lightning covering his skin and fire in his eyes. The face was elongated like a dog's.

"This was a Gibborim, the most dangerous land enemy the Chayyoth or man ever faced. It would usually cost the lives of hundreds of men to kill one, so fierce were they in combat. Some people think the reason the bow was invented was to deal with these formidable warriors. Be thankful you will not have to face one of them."

"What happened to them?" one of the humans asked.

"Thankfully, they dueled themselves into non-existence," the instructor said. "The Gibborim believed they gained the strength and speed of their opponent when they defeated them in honorable combat. They also believed the only way they could be at peace in the afterlife was to be defeated by a superior warrior.

"Legend has it there is only one left alive, the greatest warrior the Gibborim ever produced. Siarl, known as the Imprisoned One, is bound by the very chain which holds Alya at its place in the heavens."

The human recruits were leaning forward in their seats upon hearing the tale. Corban had mentioned something to Neviah about the chained creature the day before. She wondered if it was true but figured it was only a tale meant to excite them.

The instructors spent the remainder of the class touching on a few more enemy types. "And that is the basics concerning each of the more common races," the Chayya instructor said. "More detailed classes will be taught on each creature, their combat strategies, beliefs, and more. Are there any questions?"

Neviah knew that people always hated it when someone asked a question when it was time to leave but she had one that was burning in her. She raised her hand.

"Yes, Recruit…"

"Neviah," she said.

"Ask away, Recruit Neviah."

"Umm, I was wondering what the best way to fight a dragon was?"

The instructor smiled. "It is impossible to kill a dragon. The best way to fight one is to run."

"It is possible to kill a dragon," Neviah countered. "Asa killed the dragon Nebo."

Everyone was looking at her and Asa in disbelief. A few openly rolled their eyes. They wanted to be done for the day.

"Then, you should ask him," the instructor said, amused.

Asa spoke up. "When we were fleeing the fortress of Ba'mah, we were able to trap Nebo in the tunnels and kill him."

"It is true," Corban said, wiping away the skeptical looks on the faces of those gathered. "When King Hayrik's son, Rafal, was returned, I had a vision that convinced the king to lead a small party north. The dragon never showed."

"I knew of the expedition," the instructor responded. "But the slaying of a dragon? Why hasn't this been sung in the streets?"

"The king saw it fit not to compromise the search for the Sword of Re'u. Their fame would have made them targets, and there is still much they have left to do."

Neviah realized she may have overstepped by revealing the death of the dragon. But secret mission or not, she'd definitely heard people whispering "Dragon Slayer" in the streets.

"If it is the will of the king, then this knowledge will not leave this room," the instructor assured Corban. He looked around the room at each recruit until they all nodded in agreement. To Asa, the instructor said, "Next class, however, I would like you to give a detailed account of how you accomplished such a feat. If there is a way to defeat them, I would like to know it."

"Yes, sir," Asa said, giving Neviah a playful scowl that said she'd embarrassed him.

They were given the rest of the evening to do what they wanted.

"We should go find Adhira," Asa suggested.

To Corban, Neviah said, "We were thinking about going to see our friend. Would you like to come?"

"Wherever we go, it must be together," Corban said.

"Would you accompany me to go see Adhira?" Neviah asked a little more formally.

"Yes, we can visit your friend, but I have business on Alya later this evening."

Victoria and Asa asked Rafal and Enya if they wanted to go, and they both agreed. The ride down the lift wasn't as bad for Neviah. She still didn't open her eyes but was able to suppress the urge to scream when it turned upside down. Victoria and Enya actually giggled when they flipped between gravities. With their feet firmly on the ground again, Neviah was able to slow her pulse.

"Do you know where Adhira is being trained?" Neviah asked when they were at the bottom, or was it top, since coming from Alya.

For some reason, Corban smiled. "Yes, I do." He walked off toward the western side of the city.

There were many people out. Conversations were abuzz concerning a strange messenger who'd ridden into the city.

Corban was troubled. "When we have seen your friend, Neviah, it is necessary that I speak with the king. Is that acceptable?"

"Of course," Neviah said, embarrassed that the venerable Chayya needed her permission. The whole companion thing was going to take some getting used to.

They continued on. Enya and Rafal hung back, still intimidated by Corban. There was still a good bit of light in the sky when they came to an extremely congested intersection. Neviah immediately saw why.

Standing on a pole on one foot, high above the crowd, was

Adhira. He was balanced on the ball of his right foot with a wooden sword held out straight in each hand. Sweat glistened on his tanned chest and back.

A group of giggling girls sat watching the Indian, the muscles on his arms flexed with the strain of holding up the practice weapons. Neviah wondered at the sudden feeling of anger she felt toward the girls. They had just as much right to watch her friend as anyone else did.

Asa opened his mouth to yell something, but Adhira's head spun toward them first. With the help of their three Chayyoth, they were able to push to the front of the crowd.

"What are you doing up there?" Asa asked.

"Mordeth said I lacked grace," Adhira called down. "This is supposed to teach me balance." His leg was shaking uncontrollably. It was a wonder he hadn't fallen yet. "Is it too late to fly instead?"

"What did you expect becoming the best swordsman in the world to be like?" Asa taunted.

"Honestly, I thought I would be waxing cars or painting fences."

"This isn't a movie," Neviah laughed. Corban looked at her sideways. Oh, yeah, no one in this world would know what a movie or a car was. They had to be more careful. "What happens if you fall?" she asked.

"Then, I have to do the next exercise."

"What's the next one?"

"I don't know, but they've gotten progressively worse, so I don't want to fall."

"Don't you do it!" Adhira called down. Neviah had been thinking about shaking the pole.

"You would shake it if I was the one trying to balance," she said with a wide grin.

"But you're nicer than me," he pleaded.

"Whatever made you think that?" she asked as she pushed on the pole. It was firmly attached to a large platform, but it did sway slightly. He waved his arms and kept his balance, pleading with her to stop. The more she pushed, the more the pole swayed until it was wobbling back and forth. His leg buckled, and he fell, landing in a seated position atop the pole.

A shadow unfolded and rose from where it had been leaning against a wall. The crowd gasped in surprise. It was Sword Master Mordeth.

"Adhira, drink water and speak with your friends. I will be waiting for you in the training yard. You don't want me to have to wait long." He moved through the crowd, which parted for his passage.

Adhira climbed down and took a long draw from a water skin. When he'd put it down, he gave Neviah an evil smile. "I've missed you so much!" he said as he picked her up and crushed her in a very sweaty hug. His sweat slicked the side of her face and dampened her clothes.

"Gross!" she yelled, though the feel of his arms around her sent her heart racing. "Corban, help me!" The Chayya just laughed. When Adhira was satisfied his vengeance was done, he let her go.

"What are you guys up to?" he asked, stepping out of Neviah's immediate reach.

"We wanted to see if you were free to hang," Asa said.

"I will be free in the evenings in a week or two. Mordeth feels the need to break me in this week."

"That bites," Asa said. "Will you teach us what you learn when you're free?"

"Do you mean, do I want to use my time away from sword training to do more sword training?" he asked with a raised brow. "Maybe. But you have to convince Rafal to let me fly a few times."

"We aren't allowed to fly for the first month."

"That's great," Adhira said with a laugh. "I'm learning how to swordfight even though we haven't done any swordfighting, and you guys are in a flight school that doesn't allow you to fly. This all makes perfect sense."

"Shouldn't you get to your training session?" Neviah asked.

"Can I have another hug before I go?"

"I'll have my companion bite your arms off," she said.

"Maybe later then. Bye, guys." He moved off the way Mordeth had gone.

"We must be off to see the king," Corban said.

"Can we come?" Asa asked.

Corban looked at the teens, then the two Chayyoth. Rafal was

King Hayrik's son, so he had a right to be practically anywhere. As his companion, Asa would be allowed, too, but Victoria and Enya were not royalty.

Corban nodded. "I see no harm in it."

Enya and Victoria lit up with excitement. Rafal seemed indifferent. He had seen the king many times in his life. A short walk brought them to the lifts that connected to Alya. Even in the fading sunlight, the enormous silver chain connecting to the strange planet shined brilliantly.

Corban asked the man with the clipboard if King Hayrik was on Moriah or Alya. Though the king flew, and so didn't need the lift, his human servants and advisors did. The man quickly confirmed that the king was on Moriah. Corban was sure where the king would be and led them through the city again.

They eventually came to stand before an enormous building with pillars several feet in diameter and rising several stories to support the outer entrance. Large, darkly stained wooden doors stood open wide enough that a dragon could pass through. There was a crowd of people in the courtyard outside, eagerly awaiting news. After pushing through the crowd, which wasn't so hard with Corban leading, they made it to large side doors.

Guards nodded at Corban as he passed through the line with the five youths in tow. No one bothered to ask him any questions. They found their way to a side staircase with wide stairs. Each step was a little high for the humans but perfect for a Chayya.

The polished gray stone floor at the top was free of anyone else aside from the occasional human guard as the party moved down the wide hallway. They eventually arrived at a pair of large wooden doors.

"You two must wait here," Corban said to Victoria and Enya. "You come with me," he directed at Neviah and the male companions." Her companion paused and looked back at her. "I apologize. I am accustomed to giving orders. Will you accompany me?"

"Yes," she said.

They walked through the door and into an auditorium large enough to hold several hundred people. Neviah stood with Corban and two other Chayyoth on a balcony. She recognized one of them as King Hayrik.

"Good evening, young ones," the king said with a smile.

Neviah offered him a deep curtsy. "It is good to see you again, King Hayrik," Neviah said. He looked the same as he did that day she met him at the base of Nebo's mountain.

"Who are they?" Asa asked, looking over the rail at a large group of Moriahns gathered below.

"Those are the Patriarchate," Corban said. "The rulers of Moriah, chosen by the people."

Neviah counted seventy men, mostly elderly, seated like a choir in a choir box, so those further back were higher than those in the front. All seventy of them, as well as everyone else gathered, were staring down at a large figure that stood at the center of the great hall. It was a Shedim.

The creature wore shining armor with the emblem of a red horseman painted on the front and back, the seal of Tanas. Its gray wings were folded across its back. The Shedim was addressing the gathered.

"It is a most gracious offer," he said.

"You dare to threaten us with war?" one of the seventy said, rising briefly to speak before sitting again.

"If war was desired, I would not be here. High King Tanas wishes you as allies, not enemies. When the nations of man were assembled to face Ba'altose and his army of the dead, we received not one soldier from Moriah. I mention this only to say that had you been there, you would have seen the wisdom of following the king. There are many forces in the world that would see an end to the kingdoms of man and Shedim. Only united can we endure."

Another of the Patriarchate stood. "And what will your king do if we refuse this alliance?"

The Shedim froze for a moment and snapped his head high to his right, where Neviah stood. She thought he was looking at her until she realized Asa was by her side. The Shedim was looking directly at him. How had the creature known he was there?

The Shedim smiled and turned back to the seventy elders. "Tanas will not allow any to remain neutral in these dark times."

"You claim this alliance is for the safety of mankind, yet your king thinks killing men will save them?" This brought about a stream of agreement from many of the gathered and more than a few curses against the Shedim.

"A horse," the Shedim said, unaffected by the mood of the room, "must be broken before it can be made strong. Since you obviously prefer bluntness, I will be blunt. There will be an alliance between all the kingdoms of man, whether willingly or not. I will return in one month for your decision. If your answer is no, then the next time you see me will be at the head of an army."

The crowd erupted in angry shouts and yelling. The Shedim remained where he stood, seeming to revel in everyone's hate. Raising his hand, he waited several minutes before it quieted enough for him to be heard.

"One last thing," he said with a triumphant smile. "Not only do men and Shedim serve High King Tanas," he paused to make sure everyone heard his next words. "He also has command over the dragons." The Shedim spun on his heel and marched from the room amidst utter pandemonium.

Asa looked at Neviah. "I saw that Shedim before, in Samgar Nebo, when we were prisoners," he said. "And again, when we defeated Ba'altose. I have no doubt his threats are true."

King Hayrik and Corban were in deep conversation while the rest of the room was full of heated discussions, some fearful, some angry. Not everyone, Neviah noticed. Many of the Patriarchate sat in silence, apparently weighing the Shedim's words.

"What happens now?" Neviah asked Corban as he turned away from his conversation.

"The rulers must return to their provinces and speak with their towns and cities. After that, they will vote to decide whether to fight or submit."

"What will the Chayyoth do?"

Corban looked at her as if the question were absurd. "We will fight."

"What if the Moriahns don't?"

"Then, we still fight. There can be no peace with the likes of Tanas. This, you know."

Neviah nodded as any sense of security faded away. In a month, they would be at war.

Chapter 5

The tone of their training changed. When the Chayyoth yelled them awake in the morning, their manner was different. While the previous morning was difficult and all the yelling annoying, there had been a somewhat comical edge to everything the flight instructors did. That was gone. They still yelled, but there was a grim determination behind each word. The run was different; quiet. If someone couldn't keep up, an instructor fell back and ran with them.

They were all walking off the field at the end of the run when one of the instructors said, "Where do you think you're going? All Chayyoth are to run an extra mile. Form back up!"

The human companions laughed and taunted the Chayyoth as they fell back into formation. Neviah had a thought. Companions were supposed to do everything together. She jogged forward to stand by her companion in formation. Victoria and Asa fell in beside their companions, followed shortly after by the other recruits.

Out of the corner of her eye, she saw Corban looking at her before giving a single respectful nod of his head. She acted like she didn't notice but couldn't keep from smiling.

"There may be hope for this group yet," the flight instructor said, starting their extra mile.

After breakfast, they were all ushered down to Uru. The flight students soon found themselves in the large courtyard within the School of Soldiering. If Neviah thought she was shunned by the other companions, it was nothing compared to standing in the training yard amidst hundreds of human soldier recruits. The only comfort was the other flight students were equally as excluded as she was. The soldier recruits stared at them as if they were from another planet, which Neviah thought was ironic because she and her friends actually were. Come to think of it, the Chayyoth sort of were, too.

The yard was quite large, easily spanning the length of a football field back on Earth, but any grass had long ago been trampled until only dry, cracked clay remained. The army recruits looked equally drab, with plain brown tunics and matching pants. The flight humans stood out in their blue and white uniforms.

A crusty old man walked into the courtyard, and everyone snapped to attention. "The flight students will be with us every other day so we can teach them to be warriors!" he yelled so everyone could hear him.

The soldier recruits gave a loud "Hurrah" in unison.

"I am Weapons Master Instructor Nadab. Today, you will all learn the basics of the sword. To your stations!"

All the recruits grabbed wooden swords and stood in lines, the companions doing their best to mirror the young soldiers.

The instructor walked over to the flight students. "You will be at a disadvantage in every class," he said, speaking normally. "Only half your training will be spent on the art of combat. You will, however, only be learning the sword, spear, shield, and bow, so the days you miss will usually be spent going over the many other weapons, husbandry, and land tactics. Now, ready your practice sword and learn fast."

The next hour was spent going through sword drill after sword drill. Then, they went through shield technique. Close to noon, they were all moved to the archery arena, where everyone was issued a bow.

"There is no such thing as a practice bow," the archery instructor said as soldiers passed out bows to the newcomers. "The bow you are issued will be your bow. You will be shown how to care for it."

When they came near, Asa pulled out the Sword of Re'u and let it turn into a beautiful silver bow.

"I already have one," he said, drawing everyone's bewildered stares.

Neviah and Victoria pulled out their swords and willed them to become bows as well.

None of the students were allowed to shoot a single arrow in that class but instead learned how to set a bowstring, how to keep it dry and strong, and how to prevent fraying. It was a boring class, especially since Neviah didn't need any of the information, knowing her bow was indestructible. She managed to pay attention anyway, telling herself that anything she learned could be useful one day.

The pace changed for the evening classes, which were held back on Alya. It was the Chayyoth's turn to learn how to fight. After sitting around most of the day watching their human companions, they were excited to try their paws at fighting.

Classes for the Chayyoth recruits were much fiercer, involving wrestling matches with each other and mutilating dummies with their claws and teeth. Instead of wrestling one of the recruits, Corban wrestled one of the instructors to be fair. It still wasn't fair. Neviah could tell her companion was going easy on the instructor so he wouldn't lose any credibility in front of the recruits. Corban would have ripped the instructor apart in a real fight. When class ended, Neviah looked at the setting sun with dread. They were one day closer to war.

The sign language class the next day hadn't changed much, though the instructor didn't allow anyone to speak. Everyone had to flip through a large picture book with the many different hand gestures painstakingly painted on the pages. It was fun in a way, almost like charades. It was fortunate that many of the hand gestures resembled what they meant.

The instructor had to get on them for monkeying around after one of the boys found the sign for "I have to poop," which consisted of putting the back of his hand on his butt and wiggling his fingers. All the males were running around signing it over and over. Even Asa was doing it. Though Victoria didn't join in, her laughter certainly didn't discourage him.

The tactics class had Asa recount how he killed Nebo. The students and instructors hung on his every word as he recounted the tale: their imprisonment, his plan to slay the dragon, the failure of the original plan, and the slaying of the beast by trapping him in the tunnels while he was transforming from his human form. Asa used the word "we" a lot, stressing that it was teamwork, but Neviah knew they would still be trapped or worse if it hadn't been for his plan to break out.

The events sounded impossible, hearing them put together like a story. Asa did leave out the reason for his sudden urge to kill the dragon. How he thought Nebo killed Victoria. Neviah looked at the shy friend sitting beside her. Asa killed a dragon for the girl.

He continued the story beyond the death of Nebo so he could incorporate Rafal into the tale. The Chayya stood proudly while his name was put with the battle. It didn't matter that he didn't do any actual fighting. Having been there was enough.

When the story was over, the instructor asked, "Do you think it was the fiery explosion that killed the dragon or the crushing tunnels?"

Asa shrugged. "I think either could have done it. If I had to choose, the tunnels did the trick, though the explosion stopped him from escaping."

The rest of the class was spent going over human and Shedim anatomy, both being the most likely enemies in the coming war. The biggest shock of the day came from the flight class.

"You will be flying next week," one of the flight instructors informed them. At first, Neviah wondered why their training was being accelerated. Surely, they wouldn't have the inexperienced companions ready to fight in time for the coming battles. Would they really want inexperienced fighters in the air?

Then, it hit her. The Sword of Re'u was the only way they could defeat a dragon. It could cut through anything. The training was being accelerated because the sword was the only hope of winning. She looked over at her flightless companion. She would be desperately needed in the sky, yet she'd chosen a flightless Chayya.

They were rushed through flight techniques, teaching the humans how to hold on and the Chayyoth how to move without losing their rider. The class went long, keeping them an extra hour to teach the humans how to fall.

"When you fall from your Chayya," the human instructor was saying, "face your shield and weapon down, but spread your arms and legs wide to give your companion something to grab onto." He laid face down on the grass and demonstrated.

"Sir, will we have parachutes?" Asa asked.

The instructor stood and frowned. "What's a parachute?"

"That answers my question," Asa said under his breath to Neviah.

"Did he just say *when* we fall?" Neviah asked.

"Anyway," the man continued. "Chayyoth, you must be quick. Your wings can only counter so much force. If your companion is falling too fast, you will not be able to bank out of the fall, and you will both die."

"So, you can see it is best to stay on your Chayya," his companion said.

When the class was over, as Neviah walked across the clearing, she could not help but think about how horrifying it would be to fall off a Chayya miles above the world. The thought made her shudder. She paused when she realized Corban hadn't followed.

He and Asa were standing off to the side of the clearing, talking. Asa was nodding, and as if they sensed her eyes, they looked toward Neviah at the same time. What could they be talking about? With one last word for Asa, Corban walked her way.

When he had caught up to her, Neviah asked, "What were you guys talking about?"

"He has an idea of a way to make fighting dragons more effective," he said without stopping.

She followed him to a meeting of flight instructors. It was mostly administration stuff, and Neviah was more than happy to be done with it when they left. Victoria and Enya were already asleep when they made it back to the barracks.

After the morning exercise session, this one giving them a break from running to do some boulder climbing, they found themselves in the sword training yard again.

"The best way to drive home your lessons is practical application," Master Instructor Nadab said, looking around to take in everyone. "Meaning, the best way to learn is by fighting each other. The instructors will walk around and give you directions."

Neviah felt the edge of her wooden practice sword. It was made out of a soft wood with a rubber-like quality. The edge was blunt instead of sharp, though it would still hurt very much to be hit with one. After everyone was issued a battered wooden shield and hardened leather helmet, they were paired off. Neviah got a tall boy who looked annoyed at being paired up with a girl.

"Fight!" the instructor said, and the courtyard erupted into an amateur battle scene. The boy came at Neviah with an overhead strike, which she managed to block with her shield, though the weight of it made her movements slower than she liked.

Before she could counter, he'd already stepped to the side and hit her in the arm with his sword. It stung horribly, and she dropped her shield to rub the bruise she knew was forming.

An instructor came over to her. "When you block with your shield in a way that makes you lose sight of your enemy, you should expect an attack from one side or the other. Therefore, you need to block the strike you know will be coming. Like this." He pretended like he was holding a shield and blocking up. As he brought down his shield to cover his left shoulder, he brought up his sword to cover his right. "It is also wise to gain distance by backing away from your opponent."

Neviah nodded. It was good advice, similar to what she was taught during tryouts. She decided to take the offensive and sliced at the boy, who blocked with his sword and ran into her with his shield, bowling her over and knocking her to the ground. That really annoyed her. The soldier recruit let her stand, and the fight continued. Even when she blocked with the shield, the strikes jarred her all the way down to her feet.

She spared a glance at Victoria. She wasn't doing any better, with several large bruises on her forearms. Neviah exchanged another round with the tall boy, earning a welt on her shoulder. She found Asa in the crowd. He seemed to be doing okay. He sported a nasty bruise on his cheek, but his opponent was gingerly holding his sword. Asa must have gotten him in the hand.

Another round and Neviah received the first strike to her head. Despite the helmet, her vision swam for a moment. When her sight normalized, she yelled in anger and let loose all her strength on her opponent. He blocked and parried every blow until she had spent all her energy, then struck her in the stomach. Either the boy was extremely good, or she was extremely bad. When the sword training was over, she hurt everywhere. Asa healed Victoria of her bruises, but Neviah wouldn't let him heal her.

"Why not?" he asked.

"I just don't want you to," she said more angrily than she meant. She knew she should apologize but was too frustrated to talk. Corban wasn't.

"Why do you keep your bruises?" he asked.

"Because I earned them. They're mine." She'd meant the statement to be sarcastic, but he nodded.

"I understand," he said, with something very close to approval in his voice.

The archery training was much better. Far away, there were fifty targets, which everyone lined up across from. The instructors walked down the lines, giving instructions where they were needed. By the time the first group had spent ten arrows, most were at least getting near the target. Very soon, it was Neviah's turn. Victoria gave her a pat on the back before she stepped up to shoot.

Using the Sword of Re'u, she let it become a bow and drew back her arrow, holding her fingers against the side of her cheek so she could look down the shaft of the arrow. When she let loose the string, the arrow shot forward like a bullet. There was a loud crack as the arrow hit the bottom right edge of the target and traveled through it and through the stone wall behind it. The instructor beside her looked between the hole in the wall and her. Neviah and her friends were immediately issued regular bows.

"You can practice with your magic bows outside the city walls," the instructor told them. With the wooden bow, Neviah was able to hit the target nine times out of ten, with one hitting the yellow center. She received one of the better scores.

Then, Victoria took her place. She looked around shyly, waiting for Neviah to clear her arrows. When she was far to the side and out of the way, the instructor signaled for the next wave of recruits to begin shooting. All let their arrows fly, Victoria in time with everyone else. Less than ten shots hit targets. Not only did Victoria hit the target, but the arrow also struck dead center.

"Great shot," the instructor near her said. "But can you do it again?"

The recruits took aim and let loose another volley. There was a shower of splinters against Victoria's target as the arrow she shot struck the nock at the rear of her first arrow. The second arrow had destroyed itself on the first. The instructors exchanged looks of wide-eyed shock before one of them walked over and removed the first arrow.

"Again," the instructor told the girl. No one else shot as Victoria notched an arrow and drew down on the target. The arrow flew and thudded home, key-holing the last shot perfectly. "Impossible," the instructor beside her said.

Moving the other recruits out of the way, the instructor drew Victoria to the opposite side of the courtyard, effectively doubling the distance between her and the target. She looked at Neviah worriedly, not liking all the attention. Neviah pumped her fist and nodded, letting the other girl know she was doing great.

"Show her some support," Neviah said to Ebbe, who was standing beside her. He stared at her for a moment before turning his attention back to Victoria.

"You can do it!" he yelled to the blond-haired recruit. "Show these soldiers what the School of Flight is all about!" This got the other companions cheering for her until the instructor raised a hand for silence.

Victoria's last arrow was removed, but she soon put the fourth one in the exact same spot. The recruits were abuzz with excited wonder. Neviah looked between the girl and the target. Normal skill with the bow couldn't duplicate what her friend had done. There had to be something else at work. Borrowing a bandana from the recruit next to her, she approached her friend, who had five very stumped instructors around her.

"May I try something?" Neviah asked as she stepped up to their circle. She stepped up behind Victoria and placed the bandana over her eyes as a blindfold. The instructors quietly stepped back as Neviah helped Victoria ready an arrow.

"What are you doing?" her friend whispered.

"Just try to hit the bull's-eye like you've been doing." Neviah stepped back and waited. From her position she could tell Victoria was aiming a little too low but didn't say anything. The arrow flew and actually split the one that preceded it.

A round of applause came from the recruits, who were getting quite a show. At last, Neviah understood. Somehow, Victoria was using her gift to guide the arrow. Though she was convinced, she had to do one more thing, this mostly for the others' sake.

"Did I hit it?" Victoria asked as Neviah helped her ready another arrow.

"Yes."

"How?"

"Just shoot one more," Neviah said and faced Victoria the completely wrong way. The recruits moved out of what they assumed would be the path of the arrow. She had to quietly wave them out of the way of the targets, too. "Now," Neviah said when the path was clear.

The arrow sped from the bow and, as if it had a mind of its own, it turned, flew the opposite way, and drove home into the dead center of the target, dislodging the previous arrow.

Everyone was silent, not knowing what to think of this obvious show of power they didn't understand. Victoria took off her blindfold and realized what Neviah had done. She looked at her friend, the obvious question left unspoken. How?

"It's your gift," Neviah said. "You are controlling the arrow somehow."

It was several minutes before the instructors were able to restore order and get the recruits lined up for the next round. In the next group was Asa, who Neviah knew had to be a good shot because he killed Ba'altose with an arrow through the heart. When the instructor gave the order to fire, every eye was on Asa, even those belonging to the shooting recruits. His arrow soared through the air and didn't even strike the target. The next missed, too, sailing far over it. In fact, only one of his arrows even hit the target.

Had Victoria guided Asa's arrow that day? Had she unknowingly helped slay Ba'altose? It was time to find out more about her friend's strange gift.

The combat training for the Chayyoth that day was actually fun. Each Chayya was decked out in hardened leather armor and the humans had to throw rocks at them to teach them how to move so their armor took the impact.

"Stop dodging Rafal!" an instructor yelled when the Chayya ducked under a rock. "Are you trying to get Asa killed?"

The recruits' instinct was to shy away from projectiles or to dodge them altogether. If a Chayya's instinct was to duck in combat, the move could leave their companion vulnerable. Corban excelled at this, though Enya showed agility that surprised the other Chayyoth.

That night Neviah convinced Corban to keep the oil lanterns on after their normal bedtime. He and Enya watched as the girls sat on the floor with a glass jar in between them.

"I don't think I can do it," Victoria said at length.

"You've done it before," Neviah said. "I've seen you make lightning before."

"But I can't control my gift like the rest of you."

"You controlled it today. How did you make the arrows hit the target every time?"

Victoria shrugged.

"Were you thinking about Re'u?"

"No. Do you guys think about Re'u when you use your gifts?" Victoria asked.

"No," Neviah said. Their gifts came to each of them naturally.

"I wasn't thinking about anything. The instructors told us to clear our minds and focus down the arrow."

"Maybe that's it," Neviah said, happy to have a clue on how to begin. "I want you to do that now. Forget about me, Enya, and Corban. Don't think about anything except for making lightning. In the jar," she added quickly.

Victoria closed her eyes for a moment. Nothing happened. She tried staring at the jar but still nothing.

"Do you feel anything?" Neviah asked.

"Sort of," came the slow response.

"Can you describe it to me?"

"I see energy, I guess. Different energies. It's everywhere. There are three enormous tree trunk-like beams of energy connecting to everything. It's like I can almost touch things." She reached out a hand while looking at something Neviah couldn't see.

"Can you touch the energy tree things?" Neviah asked.

Victoria opened her eyes wide and shook her head. "No. I think it would be like touching a powerline."

"Okay, never touch those. What about other, smaller energies?"

"Living things have energy. Each of us has a little ball of energy in us."

"That's neat, but maybe we don't touch those either," Neviah said.

"I can feel the static in the air," Victoria said.

"Perfect," Neviah said, feeling like a blind person trying to teach another blind person how to drive a car. "Concentrate like before, but try to touch the static."

"I'll try," Victoria said and took a calming breath. She stared at the jar for a minute.

"You've got this," Neviah whispered encouragingly.

Victoria nodded and softened her stare. Slowly, she lifted her hand as if she were reaching for something. Suddenly, there was a spark in the jar. Then another. In seconds, there was a little lightning show. Enya quietly rose and cut the lanterns down low.

"Amazing," Corban said in awe. "Re'u has given you something wondrous." The lightning was beautiful, the way it danced around the jar.

Tears were flowing from Victoria's eyes.

"You did it!" Neviah whispered as tears welled up in her own eyes. She stared at the lightning for several minutes. Why was it so hard for Victoria to use her gift? Asa didn't have to concentrate when he healed. Adhira's gift was simple and constant. Even her own gift of prophecy only required her to wait sometimes. Something was consuming the other girl internally. Neviah could see it in the way she withdrew from people.

Grabbing Victoria's hand, Neviah lifted her to her feet. The lightning show continued as Neviah led them through a simple dance, which made the other girl laugh. The lightning reflected off the wall and their faces as they twirled around it. Neviah allowed her dance to become more complex until the lightning finally vanished, and they were standing in the dim light of the lanterns.

"You held your concentration for quite a while," Neviah said.

"I did!" the other girl said excitedly. "Can we do this again tomorrow?"

They got together every night for the next few days, practicing with fire, water, and anything else they thought she could do. Each time, they would dance until Victoria lost hold of her manifestations. It was so new and exciting. It wasn't until Neviah woke on the tenth day that she realized there were only three weeks left in the month.

Chapter 6

Immediately, she knew she was dreaming. Everything felt real enough, but sounds, colors, everything was almost muted, not quite the same as in the waking world. She was on top of a yellow-stone castle, though it was larger than any castle she'd ever seen. The walls stretched for miles. No, it wasn't a castle. She was standing atop a heavily fortified plateau. The distant sound of yelling brought her attention to something below.

Walking over to the edge of the wall she stood upon, she looked out over the plains below and froze. The entire landscape before her was covered in moving figures. Troops of varying armor were mixed with creatures of shadow, their inky black skin sending shivers through her spine. Millions. Never had she seen so many in one place before.

Below her, men yelled, and archers sent arrows flying out over the battlefield. Neviah almost laughed. Several thousand men were manning the walls below her, but what could they do against so many?

A shadow loomed above the walls. Neviah screamed and jumped out of the way as an enormous, three-headed dragon landed atop the wall near her, shaking its foundation and sending stones tumbling toward the ground. It breathed fire down at the men below, their screams rising, then stopping as they were killed. One of the heads turned toward Neviah and breathed fire at her!

She shot up in bed, heart racing as she felt her skin for burns.

Breathing a sigh of relief, she looked over at Corban. He was watching her, eyes alert. She climbed out of bed and went to sit on the floor beside his mat.

"Did you have a dream, too?" she asked.

He nodded.

"Mine had a three-headed dragon in it."

"I think Re'u showed us the same dream," he said.

"What does it mean?"

"That dragon needs to be stopped," he said, looking at something unseen. "No matter the cost."

"Do you ever wish Re'u was a little clearer?"

"Yes," Corban said with a smile.

"Why isn't he?"

Corban looked thoughtful. "Your friend Adhira, he can see into the immediate future. If he makes a different choice because of what he sees in that future, he can change the outcome. Likewise, if Re'u knows the end from the beginning, if he can see far enough into the future to write the book of prophecies you carry, then he should also see how your understanding will change the future."

"Wouldn't being clearer, therefore, be more effective?" she asked.

"If he showed you the exact time and day Victoria died, what would you do?" Corban asked slowly and quietly.

"I would stop it," she said.

"What if she needed to die? What if her death played a role in the future Re'u is trying to shape?"

She didn't know what to say. His words set off a flood of prophetic images she'd been repressing.

"Sometimes the prophecies are clear," he spoke into the silence. "Sometimes they're not. In the end, we have to have faith that he knows what he's doing. I think the strengthening of our faith is what the prophecies are really about. This strength leads us to the perseverance we will need in the coming years." They continued to talk until the flight instructors barged in.

After the morning physical training, it was sword training time again. Neviah was paired up with a stocky boy of average height. She already had several bruises from their exchanges, he having received not one. No one was ever struck by her.

Whack! She rubbed the stinging spot on her arm and grimaced at her opponent. Why was everyone so much better than she was? Though Asa was regaining mobility in his knee and shoulder, he was still injured, and he was doing better than her.

Corban approached and waved her away from the fight. She was more than happy to postpone her next bruise. When she stood next to him, he said, "How is the sword training coming?"

She scowled at him. He knew full well how it was going. "No matter what I do, I can't beat these guys."

"Why not?"

"I don't know. I practice just as hard as everyone else, but I'm just not as strong or fast as the boys."

Corban smiled. "Then why are you fighting like they do?"

She opened her mouth with a curt reply but closed it. As the question settled on her, she looked back over to where her opponent waited. How else was she supposed to fight?

"I've seen you dance with Victoria each night. You have the grace of a water treader." She didn't know what a water treader was but assumed it was meant to be a compliment. "Do not cater to the enemy's strengths."

She nodded, though she had no clue what he was talking about. Sword fighting was sword fighting. It was a man's invention, so it was natural that men were better at it than she was. Walking back over to the patiently waiting recruit, Neviah readied herself for the bout.

The boy attacked, a sideways slash meant for her midsection. She blocked it with her sword, the jolt hurting her arm.

"Graceful," Corban said from behind her.

The recruit rushed her, using his shield as a ram. She braced herself with her own, but the boy easily knocked her to the ground and tapped her on the shoulder with his sword. She wanted to knock that grin off his face, but he was too good at blocking with his shield.

"Stop catering to his strength," Corban said. Neviah gritted her teeth and tried to ignore her companion.

The recruit slashed down, and she blocked with her shield and managed to strike back. He easily knocked her blade wide and struck at her midsection, knocking the wind from her lungs.

Before she'd fully recovered, Corban repeated, "Graceful."

That was it! If he wanted graceful, she would give him graceful. Clearing her mind of her sword fighting lessons, she picked a tune and hummed it to herself. When her opponent struck with an overhead swing, she didn't bother blocking it but slid to the side and spun with her sword stretched out. She was doing her best imitation of a ballerina executing a pirouette. The recruit couldn't suppress a grunt as her sword struck him across his back. She stared at her sword in disbelief. She'd done it! She'd actually hit someone!

A couple of recruits who saw the hit laughed and jeered at the recruit for getting hit by a girl. He squared off with Neviah again, his brow set, determined not to let that happen again. He made a stab at her stomach. She took a quick step away from him, gliding out of reach.

Following, he put his shoulder into his shield to ram her again. Training told her to put her shoulder in her shield and lean into the charge, but she ignored it. Instead, she jumped up and back. This stole all the momentum from his charge and allowed her to rise above his defense and hit him in the face with a roundhouse from her shield. If the leather strap of his helm hadn't taken most of the blow, he might have lost some teeth. The blow still drove him to his knees.

An instructor told him to go shake it off in the recovery box, where a few other recruits were being tended to by medics. She was assigned a new partner, one of the bigger soldier recruits. Three of the trainees in the recovery box were his doing. Neviah had dreaded facing him. He was a brute.

"You won't find me as merciful as the others," he said.

Graceful, she told herself and took the offensive. She stabbed at his chest, which he immediately protected with his shield. She didn't follow through with the stab but, instead, let the blade turn low toward his knees. He was able to lower the shield in time and swung his own sword. She ducked, and he tried to smash her in the face with his shield. She used the opportunity to drop into a split and as the shield passed over her, her sword flew forward with all the force she could manage, and the point drove up into his groin.

A collective "ooh" came from those who had seen. His eyes closed, and he fell to the ground beside his dropped shield and weapon. She and another recruit helped him to the recovery box.

The rest of the training session was spent with another recruit. He got in some hits but so did she. When it was over, she gave Corban a kiss on his furry cheek and wrapped him in a hug.

"Thank you," she said into his fur.

He was taken aback by the sudden show of affection, but he did pat her on the back briefly.

In archery training, Asa and Neviah had gotten much better, but Victoria still stole the show. She never missed, not once, any of the days. That day was no exception until she got to her last arrow. The instructors were watching her, critiquing her form, though she hit the bull's eye no matter what.

She put the final arrow to the string and drew it back. One of the instructors was chatting casually with another. "You know, my father is the former bow master. I should bring him here to see this prodigy before she's gone."

Victoria let the arrow loose, and it flew past the target to bury itself in the ground at the feet of a very frightened recruit. They had become so sure of her ability that some of the recruits had gathered around her target to see the impact. Shock was on everyone's face, including Victoria's.

After a moment, Asa said, "Well, it's about time you missed one." Everyone laughed, and the training continued.

Her miss bothered Neviah, however. The instructors' conversation couldn't have distracted her. People talked around her all the time while she shot. If it wasn't the talking that distracted her, maybe it was something about what they were saying. It nagged at her until they were sitting on the floor of their barracks with Victoria practicing her gift. She was making a small ball of fire hover in the air above the floor. Corban and Enya had buckets of water standing by, just in case.

The girls were dancing for a while before they collapsed to the floor, giggling. The fire remained in the air. It seemed like nothing could break her concentration now. Well, maybe there was one thing.

"You've come so far, Victoria. Do you ever wish your parents could see you now?" The air immediately exploded in fiery heat, forcing Neviah's eyes closed with its intensity. Water soaked through her clothes as Corban and Enya poured their buckets out on the scorched floor.

"I don't know what happened!" Victoria exclaimed. "I suddenly lost control of it."

"There's no reason to apologize," Neviah said, knowing the fault lay with her, not Victoria. But she had to know, and the burst of fire confirmed it. There was something in Victoria's past that was haunting her and somehow interfering with her gift. It had something to do with her parents. "Is there anything you want to talk about?" Neviah pressed.

Victoria shook her head. "No, I must have lost my focus."

They spent the next half an hour cleaning up the water and scrubbing the blackened floorboards. She was returning the cleaning supplies to the closet when the world around her disappeared.

The room was replaced by a vision. She was surrounded by darkness; the only light was a flickering fire to her left. As she approached, the fire grew. She stood as close as she dared, holding up a hand to protect her face from the intense heat.

The sound of crying brought her attention to the center of the blaze. The intensity dimmed enough for her to see Victoria sitting among the flames. She was holding something unseen, rocking back and forth, sobbing.

"This is her past and her future," Re'u said from behind her. Neviah turned, but all she saw was the barracks. The vision was over.

Chapter 7

In the morning, the room still smelled of burnt wood. After their run, the sign language course was typical, which focused primarily on tactical signs ever since the ultimatum from Chaldea. Tactics went over a few different flying formations, though Neviah could tell the recruits didn't learn much. Everyone was waiting for the last class of the day. When they moved to the flight field, Neviah dragged her feet while everyone else practically ran there.

"What's the matter?" Corban asked.

The truth was she still felt awful for the embarrassment Corban had to go through, the snickers and wide-eyed stares people gave him for having a companion though he couldn't fly. While everyone flew around today, they would remain on the ground, reminding the Chayya of his disability.

"I'm fine," she said to her companion's concerned face. Once they were on the field, everyone was told to mount up. Corban lowered his shoulder for her to get on, and there they were: the eyes, everyone watching them while pretending not to. There was pity on some of their faces, and that cut deeper than any snicker would have. They pitied Corban while they resented her for bringing the humiliation down on him.

She sat atop Corban while everyone's feet were tied around their Chayya. The human instructor came up to them and raised an eyebrow to ask if Corban wanted Neviah's feet tied. He nodded. She looked forward with her back straight. She didn't know why he was making it worse by having her feet tied like the other recruits, but it added to the guilt.

"Today, we will practice taking off, gliding, and landing," one of the Chayyoth instructors said. "The training ropes do not come off until next week. Is that understood?"

"Yes, sir!"

"First, a few reminders. Now, during the first flight, I saw some of the humans snapped around like an egg in a jar." The recruits laughed. "This is because you Chayyoth are used to jumping straight into the air and pumping your wings." The instructor demonstrated by jumping into the air and flapping his wings until he was ten feet off the ground. Straightening his wings, he let himself glide to the ground in a tight circle. "When you have a man on your back…or woman," he added as an afterthought, "you need to run forward a few steps before going airborne. "This will prevent your companion from being jerked around as much. Understood?"

"Yes, sir!"

The Chayya instructor's companion hopped on his back. "Gliding and landing will be the same technique you have used since you were young, but keep in mind you are heavier with your rider. This means you need a longer landing path. Follow me!" the Chayya finished as he ran forward a few steps and sprang into the air.

The human recruits all hunched low as the Chayyoth joined the instructors in the air. Asa and Rafal remained, standing a few feet from Neviah and Corban. The last pair of instructors on the field hesitated but after a nod from Corban, they took off after the other recruits.

"What are you guys doing here?" Neviah asked as Rafal walked them closer. No one answered her. "Wait, what's going on?" She was missing something, she was sure.

When Rafal stopped, Asa said to Corban, "If this works, there is no going back."

"Going back to what?" Neviah demanded. Their plan flashed through Neviah's mind like a bolt of lightning. Was he trying to heal Corban? Could Asa heal old wounds?

"Do it," Corban said determinedly.

When Asa reached out his hand and placed it on Corban's neck, a wave of energy washed through Neviah's body as Asa healed Corban. It felt like a cold shiver but warm, making them both gasp. Her vision suddenly went blurry. She took off her glasses to rub her eyes, but she didn't need to. Her vision was perfect. She put them back on for a moment in disbelief. Blurry. When Asa healed Corban, he must have indirectly healed her by accident. Healed Corban. The Chayya was whole!

She looked on in astonishment as two brilliant white wings opened, one on each side of her, stretching for several feet in each direction. Without hesitation, Corban ran forward and pulled them into the air. Neviah dropped her glasses, closed her eyes, and grabbed ahold of as much mane as her hands could grasp.

Corban's body jerked as they moved higher and higher. They spun once, taking them out of the gravity of Alya and out over Uru. Though Neviah saw nothing through her tightly shut eyes, she could feel the transition. There was a loud screeching sound in her ears that she couldn't quite place. Then she realized it was coming from her. She was screaming uncontrollably at the top of her lungs. Her head swam, and she knew she was close to passing out. Her voice turned hoarse, and she sobbed into Corban's mane.

Her body suddenly jerked as Corban landed. "Let me down!" she demanded, screaming it over and over until he cut the rope on her feet with a claw. She didn't wait for him to lower his shoulder but jumped to the ground, where she stumbled and lay on her hands and knees, her body racked by uncontrollable sobs.

"What is wrong with you?" Corban demanded, the last word coming as a growl.

She ignored him, wondering if she should just go ahead and throw up or try to hold back the bile rising in her throat.

"Why are you so afraid!" he yelled, walking around to where he could see her face.

"I just am!" she yelled back, rising to her wobbly feet. They were standing face to face, though she had to crane her neck to look at him.

"You, the girl who marched into the desolate north, who faced a dragon, braved desert and sea, and fought through legions of undead to face the most feared abomination the world has yet to see, are afraid of something so trifling as heights?"

"I just told you I was! What can I say to drive this home for you, Corban? I-can't-fly!"

"Why?" he yelled, his hot breath blasting in her face.

"I just can't!" she repeated.

"Tell me!"

"Because that's how I die!" she shouted at the top of her lungs. Silence fell as they stood staring at one another. Tears flowed freely from Neviah's eyes. She rested her head against his cheek as she whispered, "That is how it ends. A fall kills me, Corban. I can't fly, or I'll die."

"I'm sorry," he said, wrapping a furry arm around her and pulling her close to his neck. "I didn't know. Forgive me."

"There is nothing to forgive. It is my fault, you see." She decided to be completely honest. "That's why I chose you as my companion. I knew Re'u wanted me to ride a Chayya, so I thought if I chose a flightless one, I wouldn't be going against his wishes, but at the same time, I wouldn't have to fly. I'm so sorry. I know it's been torture having me as a companion."

"Fifteen years ago," Corban began, his voice thick, "my companion Micah and I were sent with a host of one hundred companions to put an end to a group of Se'irim who were raiding a border village."

Se'irim were squat and hairy creatures with claws that could cleave stone and teeth able to bite a spear in half.

"The Se'irim are not who we should have been worried about. They are fierce in combat but lack the ability to fly, making them easy targets for our archers. The enemy was quickly broken but we pursued them beyond our border into the mountains. There was a horde of several hundred Shedim waiting for us. They flew down from the highest peak with the sun behind them and were on us before we'd taken our eyes off our quarry below. We fought back fiercely and managed to gain the upper hand. There were humans with the Shedim, and they'd set up siege weapons."

He paused to take a steadying breath. "Micah was fighting a particularly nasty Shedim above us when the bolt tore off my right wing." He unfurled the wing and looked at it, now whole. "I remember spiraling out of control and seeing Micah a great distance from me, falling too. He didn't scream or flap or anything that most falling riders do. He calmly looked over at me, smiled, and gave me a salute with his sword. Everything went black after that. Then the worst thing imaginable happened."

"What?" she asked as fresh tears ran down her cheeks.

"I woke up," he said, turning his head away.

"How did you survive the fall?" Neviah asked softly, stroking his mane.

"There was a forest below us. I broke several bones, and my remaining wing was a mess, all but ripped off, but the trees slowed my fall enough to spare my life." He was silent a moment before saying, "Micah was not so fortunate."

"I'm so sorry. I couldn't imagine."

"I was in a dark place for a long time," Corban said. "I went through the motions, but I wasn't really living. I was a cripple. Everyone pitied me. I couldn't escape their staring eyes because I couldn't fly. For so long, I wished I'd died at the foot of that mountain with Micah."

He looked at Neviah. It was her turn to look away. She added to the humiliation when she chose him as her companion.

"Then, one day, out from behind the clouds came a girl, a stubborn girl who chose me as her companion." Neviah smiled and turned to bury her face in his mane. She wasn't stubborn. Was she? "I knew she was destined to be a rider, and so I had no choice but to accept. I was angrier than I'd been in years. I was angry until I met her friend Asa, who could heal someone simply by touching them." She made a mental note to give Asa a good punch for leaving her out of their plans. Then again, she knew she would have fought the idea.

"And you realized you might be able to fly again."

"Yes, and it terrified me."

"No, it didn't," she insisted. The Chayya couldn't possibly be afraid of anything.

"Try falling a hundred stories and see how it makes you feel." He had a point. "But I wasn't just afraid of being in the air again. I was afraid that by flying with you as my rider, I was fully replacing Micah. I felt like I was betraying him in a way, so I turned down Asa's offer of healing." He looked at her, but she was at a loss for words.

He was baring his soul to her. "Then, I got to know you. You have his spirit, Neviah. You're a fighter, yet you are gentle. I've watched you with Victoria, and only one who truly loves her friends would be so patient. When Tanas sent his ultimatum through his Shedim messenger, I knew Re'u was telling me that it was time; I just didn't want to admit it until now."

Neviah nodded. "So, you overcame your fear and let Asa heal you."

"Not at all," he said. "I decided to let Asa heal me, yes. But if anything, I'm more afraid now than ever." He couldn't continue, but he didn't have to. At last, Neviah understood where he was going.

"You are afraid I will die the same way Micah did."

"And now you tell me you have prophesied your own death, a death brought about by a fall from a great height. I can't lose another companion."

She rubbed between his eyes as she put her forehead on his cheek. "Maybe we'll die together," she said.

Corban was quiet for a while. Then he suddenly laughed. "I believe that is the first time I've ever heard the words 'maybe you will die' in a way that was supposed to be comforting."

She laughed, too, which felt so good after such a good cry. "I guess I don't really know what I was trying to say."

"Come," he said as he started back toward the city. "Let's walk back to Uru before it gets late. If we get lucky, maybe we will die on the way, so we won't have to do the run in the morning."

"I am an idiot, though, aren't I?" Neviah said.

Corban raised a single white bushy eyebrow.

"I know Asa is a healer and yet I never made the connection."

"I admit," Corban said, "I was surprised you hadn't considered it."

"I guess it's just that he is always healing people who are bleeding, sick, or in some type of pain. It never occurred to me he could heal people of *past* injuries." She touched her face where her glasses should have been.

They continued to chat as they walked but didn't talk about the big question that needed answering. What were they going to do about Neviah's fear of heights?

Chapter 8

The next evening, they had a very special treat. Adhira had finally earned his evenings off. Neviah barely recognized him with his black leather armor over a black tunic and pants. His beautiful black hair was cut short and square-top. He was leaner and walked lighter, leading with the balls of his feet instead of his heels. Neviah didn't see his backpack, but he wore a satchel, which likely carried his book of prophecies. Neviah and Victoria gave him quick hugs, but Asa just smiled and nodded. Why were men always trying to be so macho?

"Why don't you show us some stuff?" Asa asked eagerly.

"Will you let me take a ride on Rafal?"

Rafal lifted an eyebrow. "And what's in it for me?" he mused.

"I can get you a big ball of yarn if you'd like."

"What?" Rafal asked, confused.

"Or I can try to find some catnip or a good scratching post."

Neviah rolled her eyes and said, "He's teasing you. Those are supposed to be things that will make a cat happy."

"What's a cat?" Enya asked.

"It's a little furry animal that people keep as a pet," Asa said.

Rafal smiled mischievously. "Sure, I'll give you a ride."

"No, you won't," Corban spoke up from beside him. "You can only fly humans outside of training when the instructors say you're ready, and then only when deemed necessary."

"Later, then," Rafal said, looking pointedly at Adhira.

"I want to practice with my bow, too," Neviah said, holding up her book of prophecies. "We'll have to do that outside the city."

The humans and Chayyoth agreed getting away from the barracks for a while would do them all some good. A little over an hour later, they found themselves on a field of grass that was hidden from the walls of Uru by a low hill. Using the Sword of Re'u, Adhira took them through a few drills he called sword art.

"How did you get so fluid?" he asked Neviah after watching her practice her sword art for a while.

"What do you mean?"

"You move like Mordeth." Was he actually giving her a compliment? "Only you're slower, sloppier, and stiffer."

"Corban has been helping me to be more graceful."

"Graceful is good, but you need to anticipate too. Here, you and Asa have a quick bout."

Neviah hadn't fought her friend before. She felt awkward as she squared off with him.

"I don't take anything personally," Asa assured her as he readied his wooden sword.

They knew the Sword of Re'u wouldn't hurt each other, but it would slice through their wooden shields.

"I want to get better," he said. "If you can hit me, hit me."

She nodded with relief, having been worried about embarrassing him since his injuries prevented him from performing certain movements effectively.

She took the offensive, slashing down at his head with the wooden sword. Asa stepped out of reach of the blade and brought his shield up to deflect it. She was thrown off a little with him being a leftie now.

"Good footwork, Neviah, but you're driving your heels. Keep your weight on the balls of your feet like when you dance."

"Graceful," Corban reiterated.

Asa made a stab at her, but she easily side-stepped it and swung at his head. He held up his shield just in time to block it.

"Asa, why did it take you so long to raise your shield?" Adhira asked. "Wasn't it obvious she was going to slash down at you?"

"I guess it was her best option," he said. They were both starting to understand what he meant by anticipate.

Asa stabbed at her again, but again, she sidestepped it, and as he raised his shield, anticipating the strike, she rolled to the side and slashed across the back of his leg. The sword slid along his leg but didn't hurt him due to its rubbery edge. Their small group of friends congratulated her on her hit.

"What should I have done there?" Asa asked, not the least bit angry at being hit by a girl.

"Remember to anticipate, but don't expect. When she sidestepped you, her weight wasn't on the leading foot but the back one. She wasn't planning a strike like last time because she wouldn't have been able to put any strength or speed behind it."

Asa nodded. "It's like chess," he said. "I only have to be able to plan one move ahead of my opponent."

Adhira nodded. "That is a big part of it. Your enemy has a fight plan, too, and you need to be ready for it. This time, while you fight, I want Victoria to call out what each of you is about to do."

Victoria didn't look too happy at sharing in their spotlight but she did call out moves when she saw them. Neviah stepped forward, and Victoria said, "She's going to slash down."

Asa apparently agreed because he raised his shield and blocked the blow.

"He's going to kick," Victoria said, and sure enough, Asa kicked Neviah in the leg. It didn't hurt but knocked her off balance. "Duck!" Victoria yelled, forgetting to be shy and getting lost in the fight.

Neviah ducked, and Asa's sword swished through the air above her. She rolled back out of his way, but he was on her again before she could stand to her feet.

"Back up, Asa," Victoria said, but it was too late; Neviah had grabbed his leg and tackled him to the ground. They rolled, losing their shields, but Asa managed to push her away, and they both stood.

Asa raised his sword first, letting it stop just under her chin, but she managed to mirror him with her own sword. That bout was a draw.

"Not bad, guys," Adhira said as they pulled grass and weeds from their hair and clothes, laughing. Asa's long hair was matted with debris. "And great job, Victoria. How did you know what they were going to do?"

"I didn't watch their weapons. I watched their feet and shoulders as you told me to."

"Exactly," Adhira said. "Your feet and shoulders will betray you every time. When you see their weapon moving, you are not anticipating but reacting. Only by watching how they move will you be able to see the strikes coming ahead of time."

Adhira would make a great teacher, Neviah decided.

"I bet you do even better with your gift," she said. "You'll always see the strikes coming."

"That's true, but even though I absolutely know what is coming, I have yet to land a single strike on Mordeth."

That surprised her. Surely, Adhira would be able to win against the blade master with such a large advantage coming from his gift.

"Mordeth is too fast for me," Adhira said in admiration. "It is almost as if he does see what I'm about to do. His stamina is amazing. When I am collapsing in a puddle of sweat with my heart pounding out of my chest, he is barely breathing hard. I still have so much to learn."

He spent the next hour taking them through exercises meant to make them faster on their feet. Some of the moves she remembered from dances. Sword fighting really was just dancing with swords.

It was getting toward evening when they were done practicing with their silver bows, having been shooting at an old rock formation a few hundred feet away. They left it looking like a large wheel of Swiss cheese. Adhira said goodbye to them at the lifts going up to Alya. Now that his evenings were free, they would be seeing a lot more of him, so the goodbyes were nothing fancy.

Walking through the forest on their way to the barracks, Rafal nodded toward another path leading off through the woods. "Did you want to go for a swim before we head back?"

Asa nodded. "Sure, Rusty, that would be fun."

Neviah and Victoria froze. Asa walked on a few steps, not realizing his slip.

"Who's Rusty?" Rafal asked.

Asa took a long time answering, but there was no way around saying what he had to say. "He was my pet."

"A pet?"

"He was my dog. I think you have those here, right?"

"Is that what I am to you, a pet dog?" Rafal said, the hurt obvious in his voice.

"No, it's not like that at all. Rusty wasn't just a pet. He was my friend."

"I thought I was more than that," Rafal said and flew off into the night.

"Go after him," Corban said to Victoria and Enya. "Don't let him do anything stupid, and be careful yourselves."

Victoria mounted up. Enya's eyes suddenly shone blue before they went airborne and flew out of sight.

Neviah put a hand on Asa's shoulder. "Are you okay?"

"Yeah, I'm fine. Just an idiot is all."

"I know you still miss your dog," she said.

"I do." He looked up at the gap in the trees where Rafal had disappeared. "Rafal is a close friend. He's my companion. I don't see him as a pet at all."

"I know," she assured him. "He knows, too. I think Adhira's joking about him looking like a cat made your slip sound worse than it was."

Asa nodded, but he hung back as Corban and Neviah walked out in front to give him his space.

Their only warning was the loud snap of a tree limb behind them. They turned just in time to see Asa snatched up by a Shedim. His yelling was muffled by the cover of the foliage overhead.

Without thinking, Neviah swung herself onto Corban's back. With only two powerful steps forward, he jumped into the air in pursuit of the Shedim. The trees flew by at impossible speed, Corban deftly dodging limbs until they broke free of the canopy. Neviah quickly spotted the assailant, who was attempting to rise higher into the sky.

"It means to drop Asa to his death!" Corban shouted.

Suddenly, the Shedim changed course, some force pulling it toward the ground. Asa had gotten his arm around its neck and was pulling its head down. The Shedim was fighting him, causing the pair to lose altitude. With the crunch of breaking limbs, the pair crashed back into the forest. They struck a glancing blow to the ground, hovered above it, and then tumbled until they were thrown from each other.

When Corban landed, Neviah jumped from his back, the Sword of Re'u in her hands. Asa was already standing, his sword ready as well. The Shedim stood, facing them with a snarl on his face in the dim light. One of its gray wings was hanging broken behind it. It showed no fear of being outnumbered, and they soon found out why.

An arrow sped from the woods and struck Asa in the back, its tip breaking through his chest. Asa stumbled forward, looking down at the arrow in disbelief.

"No!" Neviah screamed as darkness descended on them from above. There was a confusion of wings and scales as Neviah swung her sword at anything that came into view. A sword struck out at her, which she instinctively parried before severing the arm that swung it.

"To me!" She heard Corban yell over the battle cries being shrieked by the attacking Shedim. The heavy thump of boots landing on the ground dogged her steps as she ran for Corban's voice. "To me!" he yelled again.

Cutting through the mass of bodies and wings in front of her, she made it to him. His blue eyes glowed fiercely in the dim light.

To his left side stood Asa, leaning against a tree. He was still conscious and still holding his sword. Blood poured from the wound, soaking the front of his shirt. Two Shedim lay dead at his feet. Asa still had some fight left in him.

Turning her attention to the Shedim, she raised her sword just in time to parry a spear and slice through a Shedim from shoulder to thigh, armor and all. While Asa and Neviah protected his flanks, Corban did the real damage. He didn't bother blocking swords or spears, clawing and biting through the enemy as if they were parchment. Dark Shedim blood mingled with his own as the enemy kept coming.

A spear got past Asa's weakening defenses and pierced Corban's side. Neviah let her sword turn into a silver bow before putting an arrow through the Shedim's chest. It passed through him and dropped two more enemies before disappearing into the woods.

Her shot left an opening for the attackers, and she was only able to partially deflect a mace that was meant to split her skull. The strike nearly broke her shoulder, knocking her back against a tree. Though slightly disoriented, she was still able to cut the weapon in half.

The Shedim grabbed her with his other hand and pulled her into the mass of enemies. Cuts crisscrossed her back, where her practice wooden shield still hung, thankfully absorbing the damage. A shot of pain came from her leg as a sword slid across her hamstrings. She was on the ground then, her sword ripped from her hand. Three swords stood poised to strike her dead.

Suddenly, the midday sun shone through the forest, blinding friend and foe alike. Neviah quickly pulled her clip-on sunglasses from a pocket, and no longer having glasses to clip them to, she held them over her eyes. Through slitted lids, she could barely make out the dark figures of the Shedim as they recoiled from the light. A magnificent white stag, the last of the Neri, broke through a thicket and charged into the fray.

The first Shedim the creature came to was gored by the horns and fell limp to the ground. The other Shedim, sensing their doom, were swinging blindly with swords, axes, and maces, cutting down each other in their panic. Neviah found her sword with her right hand, and with the other holding the sunglasses to her eyes, she stood. Blood ran hot from the deep gash on the back of her left leg. It refused to support her, so she was forced to hobble to a Shedim whose wild swings were bringing it close to the Neri's flank.

Neviah sliced the blade in half before driving her sword through the creature's chest. She looked around for another enemy, but none stirred. Neviah was about to slump to the ground, but the Neri was by her side, the bright light immediately dimming until it was gone. With all her weight on the animal, she was able to move over to where Asa lay on his side.

His blood matted his shirt and covered the ground around him. Corban knelt by his side; the many wounds he'd sustained miraculously gone. Asa must have healed him. She took Asa's hand in hers as she fell to the ground beside him.

"I'm here, Asa."

Suddenly, a wave of power flowed through her body, healing her completely. Even in his current state and barely conscious, he thought only of his friends.

"Get him to a doctor," Neviah said to Corban.

The Chayya tenderly took Asa into his arms, a moan escaping the boy's bloody lips. "What about you?" Corban asked.

"I need to warn the others," she said. She used the Sword of Re'u to cut the tip off the arrow protruding from Asa's chest. She hoped it would be much easier to get it out of him that way. Still, he hesitated. "I'm fine," she insisted. "Go!"

They disappeared into the sky, Neviah watching long after they'd gone, not moving from the battlefield. She started when she realized the Neri was still there, watching over her silently.

"Thank you," she said, reaching out and gently stroking the Neri's glass-like fur. "You saved my life."

The animal gently nuzzled her cheek, careful not to touch her with its blood-covered horns. She cut a piece of cloth from one of the Shedim and used it to clean the animal's horns.

When she was done, the Neri stretched its neck upward and moved closer, putting the key that hung from its neck at her eye level. She slowly reached out and grasped the key. It was held on by a thin chain, which she cut through with her sword. With a low nod, which was almost a bow, the animal ran off into the forest.

Neviah ran her fingers over the smooth surface of the key, which looked silver in the dim blue light given off by Colossus above. She found Asa's book of prophecies where they'd made their stand against the ambush. She tried not to look at the many faces around her, all twisted in the pain of death. Without really trying, she counted twenty of them. How had they made it to Alya undetected, and why did they single out Asa? It was as if they were homed in on him.

Then, she ran, setting a blistering pace away from the battle, making her way to the barracks. It was several miles away, but adrenaline fueled her muscles. Asa's healing had also rejuvenated her. Panting as she made it to the school, she ran up to the first instructor she saw, Trym, one of the men. His companion was a little way off, talking with a pair of recruits.

"There has been an attack!" she blurted. "Twenty Shedim ambushed me and my party."

The instructor immediately became alert, yelling, "To Arms!"

Instructors seemed to materialize out of nowhere, weapons drawn, watching the sky and woods for danger.

"Corban, where is he?" Trym asked, looking around worried.

"He is fine, but Asa is severely wounded. Corban flew him to a doctor. Do you know where he'd have gone?"

"To the hospital near the palace. The best surgeons are there."

"What of the Shedim?" another instructor asked.

"Dead," she said and briefly explained what had happened.

"I will spread the word to the other companions," Trym said. "They can notify the garrisons to increase patrols." He mounted up and flew off. Other instructors moved to guard the perimeter as others took to the skies to patrol the immediate area.

"Is Rafal here?" Neviah asked anxiously.

"Yes," an instructor said, pointing to the flight field. Rafal could be seen sitting in the meadow, Enya and Victoria nearby. They were staring anxiously at all the commotion.

Neviah ran toward the lone Chayya.

"What's going on?" he called out to her anxiously. "Where's Asa?"

Enya and Victoria approached now that Neviah was there.

"Why are you covered in blood?" Enya asked.

For the first time, Neviah realized blood was splattered all over her clothes and face. That must have been why the instructors took so little convincing.

"We were ambushed," she began slowly.

"Asa," Victoria and Rafal breathed together.

Rafal spun Neviah to face him. "Where is Asa? Why isn't he with you?"

"Corban took him to the hospital, to the one near the city palace, I think." Victoria was on Enya, and they were gone into the sky before Neviah could utter another word. Neviah stopped Rafal with an upraised hand. "Take me with you," she said, then climbed on when he bent his shoulder. "And if I start screaming, just keep flying," she added.

The wind rushed against her face as they flew through the night. Fear assaulted her, but it wasn't overwhelming. Asa was more important than she was. She could risk her life to be there for her friend.

There was enough room for them to land on the roof of the hospital with lamps along the edge of the roof like a runway. It must have been common for Chayyoth to land there, likely acting as flying ambulances in some situations.

Rafal preceded her down the wide staircase and, after consulting with a few people, found where they'd taken Asa. He was in a large room with many curtains dividing the patients. Corban stopped them with an upraised paw.

"He is through there, but leave the surgeons to their work."

Victoria had her arms around Enya in near hysteria. As the doctors moved in and out of the curtained room, Neviah caught glances of Asa through the openings. The arrow had been removed, and two men hovered over him. One poured a liquid to clean the blood away while the other inspected the wound. The worst part was that Asa remained conscious through it all. His face was contorted in pain.

Couldn't they give him something to relieve the pain? Looking at his pale skin, she remembered how much blood he'd lost. They were probably afraid to give him anything for fear of killing him. But he was in so much pain. Looking over at Victoria, who'd been joined by Rafal, she suddenly saw a vision of Asa. He was running up the side of a building as if gravity didn't exist, pausing to look in each window he came to. When the vision was over, she let out a long breath.

"He will live," she said as confidently as possible.

"Is it a prophecy?" Victoria asked between sobs.

"It is."

"Thank you," the blonde-haired girl said as she threw her arms around Neviah from the side, careful not to get blood on her. "I can't lose him, Neviah. I can't."

"You won't," she assured her, though she had to push away the images of another, darker prophecy she'd seen months before.

"I should have been there!" Rafal said, furious with himself. "I shouldn't have left him."

"You had no way of knowing this would happen, my prince," Enya said. "There hasn't been a Shedim attack on Alya in our lifetime. How were you supposed to know?" This quieted the Chayya, but anger still dominated his features.

They remained near the operating room for close to an hour before the intensity of the doctors lessened, and their trips in and out of the room slowed. Neviah poked her head in and could see Asa lying back, staring at the ceiling until he saw her. He gave her a smile, weak but real.

A few minutes later, before shooing them out, a doctor confirmed that he was stable, but infection was always a fear. They would keep him for several days, and his friends could visit with him the next day.

The doctor walked away. Asa's friends decided that Rafal, Victoria, and Enya would stay the night. Corban had to see to matters at the school. Being a companion to a recruit had freed him of some of his duties, but it was time for him to take charge and secure the School of Flight.

Chapter 9

Miraculously, it was only a week before Asa was released, but not before he'd healed nearly every person and Chayyoth in the hospital. She'd known the waters of Alya tasted better than any she'd ever tasted before and even knew they had regenerative properties. What she hadn't known was how strong their healing effects were. As part of his recovery, Asa had to drink ten glasses of the water each day and bathe in it twice a day.

Though he was free from the hospital, it was another week before he was able to do more than just attend classes. He was eased back into the training regimen. They had become legends among the recruits now that one of their exploits could be confirmed by the twenty dead Shedim. Neviah made sure everyone knew about Asa fighting with an arrow jutting from his chest. He no longer received odd looks over his limp or injured shoulder. They knew he was a fighter, and he'd earned their respect.

Neviah was grateful to get out of many of the classes, having to accompany Corban to defense meetings. The patrols were increased and extended. The woods were flown over every morning to ensure Shedim hadn't come in the night. Even the recruits had a turn each night at guarding the barracks. The girls' barrack had it worst, with only the four of them to take turns guarding.

It was on one of her shifts in the middle of the night that Neviah pulled out the key the Neri had given her. She'd forgotten about it in the aftermath of the battle. Watching the lamplight reflect off the silver as she spun it around in her hands, her thoughts revolved around the mysterious door it opened. Supposedly, many had desired to obtain the key and here it was, held by a girl who was terrified of flying. According to Corban, the House of the Forest was somewhere at the top of Alya, a place only flight could access. How was she ever going to get the Forest Shield if she couldn't fly?

She put the key away and pulled out her book of prophecies. Afraid that she already knew what Re'u was going to tell her, she opened it to where she'd been reading. Two sentences in, she slammed the book closed, causing Victoria to start before settling back to sleep.

Neviah already knew the lines, though it wasn't until that moment she understood what they meant. It read, "There is no one who can stop the wind, neither is there one with power in the day of their death." She knew she didn't have power over the day she died. She knew that worrying wouldn't add a single second to her life. It was stupid to fear her death, especially when she'd already died once or almost died; she still wasn't sure. Still, she could not stop the dread that fell on her every time she considered flying.

Faith. It was her only defense against fear, but she was afraid her faith wasn't strong enough. What if tomorrow was the day she fell to her death? How could she not think about it?

A shadow moved across the lantern. She looked up just as Corban knelt beside her. "Why do you cry, my companion?" he asked softly, which for him amounted to a low rumble.

"I can't do it. I can't fly. No matter how hard I try, I can't make myself do it."

"You flew when Asa was taken and again to visit him in the hospital."

"Those were special circumstances," she said.

"Why?"

"I couldn't let him die because of my cowardice."

"But what if that had been the time you fell to your death?"

"My friends are worth risking my life for."

"Do you realize Tanas will bring dragons when he comes? Only the Sword of Re'u will pierce their scales. We need you in the air." She nodded her head, but he kept speaking. "Do you really want to leave Asa and Victoria to face them alone?"

She was quiet but eventually shook her head.

"Then, train with me. Learn to be a master flier as Micah was. We need you, Neviah. You need to be willing to lay down your life for your friends, even when the threat isn't immediate."

She didn't say anything for a while but looked at the nearest lantern, watching the fire dance. She eventually nodded her head. She didn't know how she would do it, but she couldn't leave her friends to face this threat alone.

"But I am afraid," he said, looking deep into her eyes, "that joining your friends in the air will not be enough." Then he, too, looked at the fire in the lantern. "The strongest steel made by man will melt like wax before the heat of a dragon's fire." He looked back at her and said, "Only a shield forged of light can withstand a dragon's breath. I will not lie to you. The House of the Forest lies at the roof of the world, the very utmost part of Alya, so high, not even the air can reach."

"I remember you telling me about it," she whispered.

"Then you know the trip can easily claim our lives."

Slowly, she reached into her pocket and pulled out the silver key again. She imagined her friends engulfed in flames. The Neri had given her the key. The shield was meant for her to claim. If she didn't, she was sentencing her friends to death, everyone to death by dragons' fire.

She stood to her feet, tired of being afraid. Anger welled up inside her. Anger at fear itself. Too long had it paralyzed her. It had nearly gotten her and her friends killed already. No more!

"We go now," she said, swinging onto Corban's back.

She had to duck for them to fit under the doorway. Once outside, Corban told one of the camp guards to look over the barracks, then took off at a fast run before lifting them into the air. Her stomach rose into her throat, but she held onto her anger and determination. Even while flying, it took half an hour before they came around the curve of Alya to where they were aimed at Colossus. As they traveled further, fewer and fewer Chayyoth homes could be seen.

"It's freezing," she said, wishing she'd grabbed a coat.

"It stays cold here year-round," Corban called back over his shoulder. She watched their progress as best she could, but it was difficult looking forward into the wind. The force of the cold air made her eyes water so badly that she could barely see anything in front of them.

The Armor of Light

Gradually, the green grasslands and forest of Alya disappeared, replaced by ugly gray rock. Above them, they could see Colossus. She had only been able to see bits and pieces of it because Alya usually obstructed the view. It was a brighter blue than she'd ever seen it, its rings extending from horizon to horizon. Corban landed, more out of breath than she'd ever seen him.

"The air is thinner here," he said.

She could feel it, her lungs pulling harder and her heart beating faster to find the little air there was. She hadn't even been doing anything. Corban had been exerting all the effort.

"Let's walk for a moment," he said.

She jumped to the ground and walked beside him as he caught his breath. It took several minutes for his breathing to normalize. His eyes glowed and his wings reflected beautifully as they were bathed in the bright light of Colossus. The light brought out artful designs in his wings she'd never noticed before.

"It gets worse from here," he said, stopping so she could remount. "We are near the top. From here, there will be no air."

"How long until we get to the House of the Forest?"

He shrugged, lifting her slightly. "I don't even know exactly where it is. No one does."

"Faith to finish," Neviah said with a smile.

"Faith indeed," he said. "There are hundreds of square miles to cover once we're up there." Neviah pulled out the key and looked at it.

"I've held my breath for two minutes before, but I wasn't trying too hard," she said.

"Without training, most humans max out around three minutes before passing out, I believe. I can hold mine for more than seven. Remember, it feels good to let a little breath out at a time, but don't do it. Fill your lungs until it is painful, and don't let it out until you are sure there is another breath to take."

Taking deep breaths, they began the final leg of their journey. Canyons opened up under them, only to be replaced by jagged peaks and wasteland. Corban flew faster than she thought possible, flying high so he could rest while gliding back down. A minute went by, and there was still no sign of anything.

Her lungs screamed for her to release the air she was holding, but she remembered Corban's advice. He looked back at her, worried when her body began to spasm with the effort of not breathing. Corban started to circle back, but she grabbed his head and faced him north again. Only through faith could they find the shield. They were soon past the point of no return. Three minutes must have gone by because her vision was dimming. Black spots seemed to float around in the air in front of her.

She let some air out of her lungs when she couldn't stand it anymore. It felt good, but when the instinct to breathe tried to take over, there was nothing to breathe! It was like she had duct tape over her nose and mouth! Her head was sinking forward of its own volition when she saw it loom up in front of them.

It was a giant wooden structure surrounded by jagged rocks reaching into the void above them, resembling ancient and gnarled cedar trees. The ancient structure was enormous, covering several acres of land. Hundreds of pillars surrounded a center building, which rose up in front of them with Colossus as the backdrop.

With a new burst of speed, Corban raced among the pillars. On the side of the building, low to the ground, was a small door. They landed roughly, Neviah thrown to the ground where the rest of the wind was knocked from her lungs. Then she was floating in the air. No, Corban was carrying her with one arm. She could barely see through the tunnels of her eyes. The world was getting further away with each hammering beat of her heart. Somehow, she had the motor skills to pull out the key, and with Corban's guidance, she put it in a lock and turned it.

The door sprung open, and she stumbled through and into fresh air! Her lungs pulled desperately at the cold, clean air. The darkness still threatened to take her until the oxygen had worked its way into her blood. With her balance restored, she turned and saw Corban still standing outside. She walked toward him, but suddenly she couldn't breathe.

Stepping back into the air, she motioned for Corban to come in. He shook his head and pointed at the doorway. It was extremely narrow, too narrow for him to enter.

To prevent using up some of the reserves in his lungs, he signed,

"I'll return."

Then, he was gone. She watched him fly away before turning to the darkness beyond the edge of the door. Every moment she tarried put Corban in more danger. The more trips he made, the more tired he'd become and the more likely he would suffocate. Pulling out the Sword of Re'u, she let its soft blue light guide her.

It wasn't long before she saw light ahead. After Asa's account of the trials he'd faced, she approached warily. The corridor narrowed even further until she was standing before two open doors.

Centered above the doors was a placard that read, "Choose." The door to the right was suddenly awash in light. She stepped closer as a little girl ran by laughing, followed by a toddler and then a man with light brown skin and black hair.

The man scooped up the toddler, who squealed as he was held in the air and spun around. Neviah gasped when the man turned enough for her to see his face. It was Adhira but older, his boyish good looks replaced by the strong, handsome face of someone close to their thirties.

Placing the little boy down, Adhira crouched and looked around. The girl peeked out from behind an ottoman and screamed as Adhira saw her. He chased her around the ottoman until she made a break for it, running around a chair.

Then Neviah saw herself, older with only the slightest hint of wrinkles forming at her eyes, sneak up and grab the little girl from behind, picking her up and smothering her with kisses. The girl squirmed free, roaring like a monster and chasing her brother around the room.

While older Neviah was distracted, watching the kids, Adhira grabbed her around the waist and spun her around, lifting her easily from the ground with strong, pleasantly muscular arms.

He drew his face close to hers as he set her down, and just when their lips were unbearably close together, he said, "So what's for dinner?" Then the scene froze, with older Neviah scowling up at older Adhira.

Present day Neviah laughed and shook her head. "You always have to go for the joke." Despite her laughter, she found tears in the corner of her eyes. Before she could fully process the different emotions she was feeling, images began playing in the other doorway.

A family she didn't recognize was sitting around the dinner table. The scene changed and another family was walking through a field. Change: a family was playing on a beach. Over and over, the scenes transformed, showing family after family. The scene changes sped up, showing her hundreds of different families. It went on for a while until the images froze with dozens of people dancing at some sort of festival.

Neviah stepped back. Choose. With the certainty that only came when Re'u was revealing something to her, she knew each door to be a possible future. Her future was now in her own hands.

"I don't have to die," she realized, looking at the door on the right. She could grow old with Adhira and have a family. Her eyes strayed to the door on the left. For her to have that life, that wonderful dream of a life, she would have to sacrifice all those other futures. Hundreds, maybe thousands of lives would be impacted. No, not impacted but lost.

But she wanted to live! Fresh tears welled up in her eyes as she reached for the door on the right. The children, her children, could be seen in their frozen chase in the background. It was a future that could never be. The cost was too high. Slowly, as the tears streamed from her eyes, she closed the door, sparing one last look for the family she would never have.

She walked through the door on the left and came to a sliding halt when a gigantic chasm appeared before her. She found herself standing on a narrow balcony overlooking a gorge that continued forever into darkness. On a pedestal, a few feet away from her, was the Forest Shield. It shone with its own blue light, revealing the symbol of a bird in flight made out of inlaid gold across its silvered front. Asa had gone through so many trials to get to the Sword of Re'u, having to solve the maze, the room of mirrors, the dream monster, and not to mention the rock monsters and the desert itself. She had expected more.

Neviah guessed gaining the nerve to fly, obtaining the key, finding the House of the Forest, and choosing the door were trials of their own but she expected something more difficult. There was a narrow path leading to the shield with sheer drops into nothingness on each side. She took a small step forward, and the floor rumbled. The rocky path in front of her collapsed, and the stones fell into the darkness below. She waited for a while but never heard the stones strike the bottom.

Looking up, she realized her easy walk to the shield was now a long jump across the chasm. Sitting down, she stared at the shield. It was hopeless. The jump was impossible. She'd made a similar leap before when she was back on Earth and managed to make it across an alley from rooftop to rooftop, but that was a time when she had no fear of heights. She didn't have it in her anymore. That jump was before she knew how she'd die.

She ran her hands over her ponytail pulling it over her shoulder and stroking it. Looking up, she made a startling discovery. The pedestal was inching away from her. She stood to her feet and confirmed her fear. There was an ever-growing gap between her and the shield. She backed up. But what if this was how she died? There was no time. If she was going to jump, it had to be now.

Pushing off the wall, she ran forward with all the strength she could muster. Three steps, four, then she was flying through the air, not daring to look down while she hung in the air above the gaping mouth of darkness below her.

The platform raced toward her, but her momentum gave out as she reached out for the rocky path. Her fingers brushed the stone but found no purchase. A cry escaped her lips as she fell backward into the darkness. The wind rushed past her. This was it: her death.

Neviah closed her eyes and immediately felt arms slide around her. They were strong but human. She looked up to see the dark silhouette of a man holding her and she knew in her heart it was Re'u.

"Am I dead?" she asked.

A laugh. "No, Neviah. You will never truly taste death."

"I won't?" she asked.

"Not the final death. I will always be there to catch you," he said and then he was gone, and she was standing on the pedestal in front of the Forest Shield. She reached out her hand and took the shield. There was a strap inside the shield that fit around her forearm and a handle to grab with her hand. It weighed nothing at all. She drew the

Sword of Re'u and banged it against the shield. The ringing echoed through the chamber, resounding like two crystal glasses struck together.

She stroked the intricate gold and silver intertwined around the edge of the shield and marveled at how deftly it was woven into the bird that adorned it. When she let go of the handle, the shield shrunk to only a fraction of its original size, looking like nothing more than a wristwatch. She heard the sound of skidding rocks outside. Corban! The crumbling pathway was whole again. She ran to the entrance as fast as she could.

"I'm coming!" she yelled, having just enough foresight to take a deep breath before running out onto the barren surface of Alya. Corban dipped his shoulder, and she leaped upon his back. Knowing how close their first trip had been to disaster, they sped from the vault like a bullet into the morning light.

The air in the vault must have been of better quality because her vision was just beginning to spot when they hit a pocket of denser air. It was like walking through a forcefield. Neviah could feel her companion's lungs expanding and contracting as he pulled in the air.

The Chayya didn't stop to rest but pushed further to the south side of Alya. The recruits were just coming back from a run when Neviah and Corban showed up. Her friends and the other recruits came up to them as they landed. Asa looked good after his first run since surgery.

"Where have you guys been?" Asa asked.

"Look at your wrist," Neviah said in reply. He and Victoria looked down, shocked to see what looked like a silver bracelet on each of their wrists resembling intricate tattoos.

"What is this?" he asked, looking at the design.

Neviah let her shield grow to the size of a buckler, small and round. "This is how we defeat the dragons."

Chapter 10

Having indestructible shields, the teens no longer used wooden swords and shields when they practiced with each other but instead fought with their amazing silver swords. They'd gotten much better under Adhira's tutelage. There were a few times he even talked Mordeth into showing them a few things.

"At last, someone understands," the sword master said to Neviah as he had them practicing their sword art. "I should have chosen you for a pupil instead." Neviah smiled at the praise.

She looked over at Adhira, who appeared unaffected by the comment. He was used to it. Mordeth was always pointing out how the others did everything better than the Indian. She knew the compliment was meant to make Adhira try harder, but it still felt good to be told she was doing good.

"Faster, boy," Mordeth said to Adhira. "You are still too slow."

They were standing in small circles carved by their swords into the ground. They were spinning in circles, focusing on one "enemy," which was nothing more than a stick in the ground, before spinning to focus on another. From her days of self-taught dancing, Neviah was good at it.

"Your neck is faster than your feet," he reminded the group. "Find the target with your eyes as fast as possible so you will know what's coming before your body has caught up. I must get back to the city. Keep practicing." He picked up his sword and scabbard before heading back.

Victoria fell to the ground, dizzy. "Like this," Neviah said and demonstrated a perfect ballerina spin, pausing to look at one enemy, then the other.

Behind them, there was a loud thump that brought their attention that way. A sack of grain lay fifty feet to the south. Rafal landed and picked it up, looking at them sheepishly before springing back into the air.

Neviah watched the Chayyoth for a moment. Corban had them practicing their catching skills. They would give the sack to him, and he'd fly up high and toss it. Their goal was to grab it before it hit the ground. Neviah looked at Asa and swallowed big to show her consternation.

"Don't worry," he said. "We'll be fifty times higher than they are now." Was that supposed to be comforting? "They'll have longer to catch us," he explained to her raised eyebrow. "As long as we're not going too fast," he finished more to himself.

"What do you mean by going too fast?" Neviah asked.

"Oh, that's right. You missed the class on falling."

She had missed a bunch of classes with Corban having to attend meeting after meeting. He had been put in charge of the task force focused on how to use the teens and their weapons most effectively should war come.

"The longer you fall, the faster you go. If you fall too long and reach terminal velocity, even if your Chayya catches you, he won't be able to pull up in time."

"Couldn't they just flap their wings?" she asked, trying not to picture her death.

"Not at those speeds. The best they can hope for is to hold their wings perpendicular to the ground and slowly bank out of it. The faster they're moving, the longer they need to pull up."

They looked up again as Corban tossed the sack. It was Enya's turn. She quickly dove after the bag and grabbed it between her paws. She then smoothed out of her nosedive and glided until the force of the fall was spent, and she could flap her wings again. From the air, Rafal pointed to something in the east. Neviah followed his direction and saw a single gray-winged Shedim walking down the main highway toward Uru.

"Victoria," Neviah said. "Can you make the shot from here?" It was several hundred yards, but she knew her friend could easily make the shot. The question was more to see if she was up to it.

"Yes," she said, letting her sword turn into a bow and her shield retract to watch size. She pulled back the string with a silver arrow notched.

"Stay your weapon!" Corban called as he landed in front of them. Victoria lowered her bow. "It is the emissary from Chaldea. It has been a month, and he is here to talk to the Patriarchate."

That evening found Neviah and Corban standing beside the king of the Chayyoth. Adhira and Mordeth were there too. They were on a balcony that overlooked the elders below. There was no talking as one of the Patriarchate rose and moved to stand in front of the Shedim.

The Shedim spoke first. "High King Tanas requires your answer. Will you join him in ushering in a new world order, or will you oppose him?"

"We have spoken with our people and will vote now to settle this matter." Turning to the Patriarchate, the man said, "Vote yay if you wish to submit to the rule of King Tanas or nay if you wish to remain a sovereign nation."

Starting with the first person, the Patriarchate began their vote. The first five were nays, but the next person voted yay. Hushed conversations sprang up all over the chamber. Neviah wondered why someone would vote to ally with Tanas. Then again, she'd once been fooled by him, too. Or perhaps they voted out of fear.

In the end, there were thirty-one for the allegiance but thirty-nine against it. Neviah relaxed from the death grip she had on the railing. The majority of the elders weren't fooled by Tanas' lies.

"We do not wish war," the orchestrating Patriarchate stated seriously. "But we will not support this Tanas as king of the world."

The Shedim nodded, showing no outward sign that the decision mattered to him. "Tanas also wishes there to be no war but the survival of man; yes, even the survival of all intelligent beings depends on a united world. Ba'altose killed many thousands until Tanas united the kingdoms and defeated him. The rest must join us or stand against us."

He stepped closer to the railing separating him from the elders. While he spoke, he looked at them each in turn while walking down the railing. "Many of you see the wisdom in the words I speak. This is evident from the way you vote. I know you see strength in this form of government, how your once warring tribes were united by the notion of equal representation. Do you not now see the flaw? Half of you would embrace us as allies, while the other half would have us be enemies. Yet the difference of a few votes decides everyone's fate. It is nothing but the tyranny of the majority.

"Therefore, Tanas, King of Princes, has one last offer. A dragon will be sent to each of your cities at the head of his armies. If you do not agree with the decision your countrymen have made for you here today, you will have one last opportunity to join us." He spun away from the silent elders, making his cloak flap around behind him. He quickly exited the hall.

"He sure knows how to make an exit," Adhira said as they made their way out of the building, surrounded by arguments.

Outside, the city was in turmoil. Knowledge of the decision had already spread through the packed streets. Some people were openly praising the vote, while others were dangerously close to rioting. Neviah mounted Corban, and they took off into the air just as a fistfight broke out between two men near them.

Corban didn't take them to the School of Flight but stopped at the Spring of Life to get a drink. It was a magnificent pond as large as an Olympic-sized swimming pool. The water was over a hundred feet deep but was so clear that Neviah could see all the way to the sandy bottom.

She knelt beside Corban and brought some to her mouth with a cupped hand. It was the best-tasting water she'd ever had. When she'd had her fill, she leaned against a large rock.

"How can so many people be willing to follow Tanas?"

"Because Tanas is the great deceiver, Iblis."

"Iblis?" she asked. Asa had said Tanas was a dragon in disguise named Iblis, but that was all she knew.

"Iblis is how he is known in dragon form," Corban said. "He's one of the Ancients and has been weaving this web for centuries."

"I just don't understand how people don't see it. He's allied with dragons and Shedim. Even if they don't think Tanas is a dragon, they should still know he's up to no good. Do you think any of the Patriarchate will break away from the others?"

Corban motioned with his head for them to start walking. "I don't know. Some voted to join Tanas because they believe he is genuinely the savior of the world. Others want to join him because they believe no one can stand against such an army as he's assembled."

They walked in silence for a while. She liked that they still did a lot of walking. It made everything feel less rushed, which she needed since it felt like the world was hurtling toward chaos.

"When Tanas has been killed, then they'll know he's not their savior," she said with as much confidence as she could manage. Corban remained silent. "You do think he can be killed, don't you?"

He was slow to answer like he was tasting each word before he spoke it. "Yes. With the Sword of Re'u, anything is possible."

"What is it?" she prodded. He was holding something back, she was sure.

"There is nothing in vision or prophecy that says he dies."

She thought about all the prophecies she'd seen and read. There was nothing that told her Tanas' fate.

It was evening before they arrived at the school. Word had already gotten to the students that they were at war. Their excitement ebbed when they caught sight of Corban.

"Form up," he said.

Within a minute, everyone was rounded up and standing in formation at attention.

"At ease," he began, and everyone relaxed, continuing to look at him, Neviah by his side. "We have accelerated your training as much as possible, but there was only so much we could teach you in one month. With the exceptions of Asa, Rafal, Victoria, Enya, Neviah, and myself, you will not be participating in the early days of this war."

Complaints sprung from humans and Chayyoth alike.

"Not fair?" Corban said, picking one of the complaints. "Am I to put you with units that have trained together for years? You wouldn't know a single one of their standard operating procedures. They can respond to each other's movements with such precision that it is as if they are separate parts of the same body. You would slow them down, cause confusion, and get companions killed."

"Sir, could we form our own unit?" one of the humans asked.

Corban shook his head. "You don't know anything yet. You are missing eleven months of training and have absolutely no experience in aerial combat."

"Why do they get to go?" one of the Chayyoth whined.

Neviah was shocked at how undisciplined they'd all suddenly become, even more so at Corban allowing it. If the other instructors heard them, they'd be doing pushups until their arms fell off. Still, Corban was humoring them, trying to convince them they weren't ready.

"Asa, show them why you have been chosen."

Asa looked around for a second before pulling out the Sword of Re'u and walking over to a large stone that lay next to a tree. He effortlessly cut through the stone, which fell apart into halves.

"Neviah, show them why you have been chosen."

She wondered for a moment if she should do the same thing as Asa but decided to use the bow. She shot an arrow that passed through Asa's stone, then continued until it had passed through a tree and a fence post and disappeared into the woods.

"And Victoria, show them why you have been chosen."

She looked around for a moment, her shyness threatening to win out. Then she took a deep breath and pointed to a tree. A small fire appeared on one of the branches, spreading quickly until much of the tree was alight. Then, a small cloud appeared above the tree, and rain fell on it until the fire was gone, leaving the branches smoking in the failing light of the sun. It was the largest display of her gift Neviah had ever seen.

"Any more questions?" Silence. "Get your rest. There is much training still ahead."

Without further complaint, the recruits went their way.

Corban called together those who would see combat. "You will continue with your regular training, but you will receive additional flight lessons with me."

"Will we be assigned to a unit, sir?" Rafal asked.

"No, we are our own unit. King Hayrik has given me full discretion in training you and on how to utilize your unique abilities and weapons. And besides, what I said to the other recruits is also true about you. Your inexperience in aerial combat can get companions killed if they are expecting something of you that you're not ready to give."

The next day, it was obvious any progress Neviah and her friends had made socially with the other recruits was gone. No one approached their now ostracized group.

"They're just disappointed they don't get to go fight," Asa said between classes. "They will come around eventually."

Neviah wasn't so sure, but the whole situation with them seemed almost childish.

Their flight class was as scary as usual. Neviah knew she had to fly and didn't run from it anymore, but it was still terrifying. It was a walk in the park compared to Corban's private lesson.

"You want us to do what?" Neviah exclaimed at her companion.

"You need to learn how to fall," Corban insisted. "I want you to jump from your companions' back." They were already a couple of miles above the ground, the Chayyoth flapping their wings to keep them in a circle. "Face the ground and open your arms to make yourself as wind-resistant as possible."

"Like this?" Asa said and rolled off of Rafal. Neviah and Victoria screamed as he tumbled away from them. Rafal darted after him, closing the distance quickly. As he neared Asa, the Chayya slowed, dipped his head, and scooped up his companion so Asa was where he needed to be. It took them a minute to return to the group.

"Not bad," Corban said. "Now, Victoria, it's your turn."

With a nervous look at her friends, she jumped from Enya's back. Her Chayya caught her in seconds, grabbing her arms and letting Victoria climb onto her back.

"Now you, Neviah," he said.

"You must be crazy if you think I'm going to..." her words were cut off by Corban's sudden barrel roll. She'd had her arms crossed and flew from his back without a chance of grabbing on.

She didn't scream. She couldn't. Her eyes were fixed on the world below as it rushed to meet her. Was this it? Her death? She felt something nudge her legs, and as quickly as she was dumped off, she was back on her companion, soaring through the air. She grabbed around Corban's neck as tight as she could. So relieved to be alive that she forgot to be mad at him.

"Not bad for your first fall," he said over his shoulder. "Open your arms to slow your fall more next time. You'll get better."

"Next time? I'm not doing that again!" Anything else she was going to say disappeared from her mind when he dumped her off a second time.

Chapter 11

Lessons continued for several months, giving some of the recruits hope the war would hold off long enough for them to finish training. Those hopes were destroyed by the first reports from the border scouts. There was an army of three thousand horsemen approaching Sarepta on the Moriahn border to the east. No one seemed worried because the city was heavily fortified with enormous walls defended by two thousand of the city's own soldiers, each equipped with a bow. Horsemen had no way of taking such a city. They didn't even have siege equipment.

The next day, another scout arrived with news from the north. Two armies of ten thousand men each, both with siege equipment, were marching on two of the border cities. The Moriahns readied a large force of their own, which headed that way. The Chayyoth waited.

Two days later, several scouts arrived. There were five other cities surrounded, though there were still no Shedim sightings. No dragons. The Moriahns didn't have any more soldiers to spare from their main force in the capital in case Uru was attacked, too. On the fifth day came the first dragon sighting. Uru was in a panic, supporters of Tanas taking to the streets while the opposition readied their belongings in preparation for a journey to the safety of the mountains to the south.

"There is a force to the south made up of men and Shedim," Corban said to their group of six. "And yes, they do have a dragon. Two groups of one hundred companions each are being sent that way, and we're going with them."

"To the south?" Neviah asked, confused. "I thought the dragon was spotted in the north."

"I heard it was the east," Enya said.

Corban nodded. "You are all correct. So far, there have been ten confirmed dragon sightings in Moriah."

There was a collective intake of air.

"Why south, then?" Asa asked. "Aren't there more cities being attacked in the other directions?"

"Yes, there are," Corban said. "But we cannot let the stronghold at Daggers Pass be overrun. In the event Uru is taken, the people must be able to escape to Esdraelon, which is through the mountains."

"Esdraelon?" Asa asked. "I haven't seen it on any maps."

"It is an ancient fortress built into an enormous plateau with tunnels vast enough to hold a million people. The Moriahns could hold those tunnels for years if they needed to."

"Does the enemy know about it?" Asa asked.

"I doubt it. Daggers Pass is manned by a couple of hundred soldiers, and Tanas only sent a small force to subdue it. If he knew of its strategic value, he would have made securing it a top priority."

"But if we send Chayyoth there but nowhere else, won't he suspect it's more important than he thought?" Asa asked.

"No doubt you are wise beyond your years, Asa," Corban said with a nod toward the boy. "But our tacticians have already worked out several diversions, sending other troops to several of the smaller battles. Rest assured, they are brainstorming brilliant strategies."

"Of course," Asa said. "I tend to ask too many questions."

"No such thing," Corban said.

An hour later, they were among the largest group of Chayyoth Neviah had ever seen in one place. Armor was strapped onto humans and Chayyoth. The mounts received steel helmets, which covered their brow and snout, as well as thick leather breastplates, while the riders wore hardened leather armor and helmets.

"This will slow me down too much," Enya complained over the bulky armor.

"But it will stop a spear from killing you," one of the men from the armory said.

"If I wasn't wearing this," she countered, "no spear would be able to catch me."

With Corban's permission, Enya was fitted with a set of scout armor instead, which was hardened leather but thinner. The humans were given food, water, bows, arrows, and spears to carry along with their shields and swords. Each Chayya ended up with an extra hundred pounds of gear at least.

"Why don't we have spears?" Neviah asked.

"Three reasons," Corban said, adjusting his armor as she pulled on the straps. "One is that Enya and Rafal have not had a chance to become accustomed to the weight it adds. Two, you have swords that can cut through anything. Three, and most importantly, you do not know how to fight with a spear."

She nodded. They hadn't made it to spear training yet.

"Take these," Corban said when the gear distributor walked up with three sets of goggles. "You were supposed to receive these during the mid-training races, but you need them now."

It took three hours to get the groups ready for flight. Leaving Alya and orienting themselves to the land below, they hugged the ground in multiple tight V formations, not unlike a flock of birds. Neviah and her friends flew just behind the rear formation. They moved through valleys, rising no higher than the tallest trees. The goggles made seeing far easier.

Neviah didn't allow herself to think about the coming fight. She preferred to remain as calm as possible and that meant thinking about other stuff. Asa, flying on Rafal to her right, was doing enough worrying for the both of them. She smiled. Asa always fretted so much while approaching danger, but once he was in the thick of it, he was the bravest person she knew. She was the opposite. As long as it didn't deal with heights, she remained calm and confident until things went wrong. Then, she worried.

Victoria was unreadable. She was always quiet, no matter if they were going to war or to pick flowers. Enya and Rafal looked eager. Rafal had been to a battle before but had never done any fighting. Enya had only known how to be a servant most of her life.

Their excitement would fade the moment their ignorance of fighting did. Neviah smiled again at the way her thoughts were going. She was looking at it all as if she were some hardened veteran. She shook her head and leaned closer to Corban to reduce wind resistance.

Two hours passed before they landed on the side of an extremely large hill. A single scout pair was sent. They were near Daggers Pass, they were told. On the threshold of battle, the wait for the scouts was excruciatingly long.

One of the men crouching beside Asa tried to intimidate him with talk of fighting. "I once saw a Shedim spear three men off their horses with one throw. They're twice as strong as a man, you know."

Asa pulled down his collar to show the arrow wound in his chest before saying, "I believe it. I've met them before."

The man blinked for a moment, his grin fading. The Chayya on his right leaned toward him and said in a whisper loud enough for several people to hear. "Those are the children who killed Ba'altose." Quiet laughter followed until they were hushed by their squadron leaders. Moments later, the scout returned.

Corban relayed the report. "There are five hundred men and four hundred Shedim camped at the mouth of the pass. The dragon is spewing fire at the walls."

"What's the plan, then?" Asa asked.

"We are the plan," Corban said. "Unless we take out that dragon, he'll turn our entire unit to ash."

Asa donned his determined look.

Corban continued, "We are going to try to take the dragon by surprise. I want to lead with arrows, but if they don't do the trick, we'll have to get close for sword work. Most importantly, follow my commands. We don't know what will happen. The Sword of Re'u has not been tested against dragon scale."

"The sword will hurt the dragon," Neviah said, though she remembered Ba'altose wielding a sword that could block the Sword of Re'u. That had confused her at the time. She'd thought the Sword of Re'u was stronger than anything else. Maybe the weakness was on their part. Either way, the sword was their only chance.

"Let's go," Corban said.

Neviah and her friends mounted up. The wind was soon washing over them as they flew toward the stronghold.

When the monstrous, green-scaled dragon came into view, her heart nearly stopped. Time had lessened Nebo's size in her memory. A wall formed a half circle around a small stone barracks. To the rear of the fortress was solid rock. Anyone passing through the narrow valley would have to move right past the defenses. It was perfectly protected from siege weapons, which couldn't be brought against the walls due to its narrow passageway. Nothing could breach those walls. Nothing but a dragon.

The behemoth beast towered above the walls, its green scales dully reflecting the noonday sun. It spewed an endless stream of fire against the massive stone buttresses. Before their eyes, rock was turned to liquid as it melted and flowed down the valley like a river of lava. Within moments of their arrival, the wall was reduced to nothing but a melted waste, and the barracks had begun to succumb to the heat of the dragon's breath. The fire never ceased or diminished. Neviah wondered if anyone inside was still alive or if the smoke had gotten to them.

Corban motioned for the others to flank the dragon while he and Neviah came from the rear. He made the bow sign with his paws, and Neviah let the Sword of Re'u turn into the silver bow. Wordlessly, she drew back an arrow and let it fly. Two more arrows flew at the large target from the sides.

Neviah had misjudged the distance. Her shot went wide and clipped a wing, spraying oily liquid all over the rocks as the dragon's ancient blood was spilled. The dragon jerked back from its task, causing Victoria's perfectly aimed headshot to miss. Asa's arrow penetrated the mass of muscle in the creature's back.

The dragon turned to face the first real threat it'd ever had. It roared in rage, a sound that sent a shudder through Neviah. Looking at Victoria, it let a jet of flame shoot from its mouth toward her. Even with Enya's speed, they couldn't dodge it in time. The Chayya tucked her head as Victoria's shield grew larger than it had ever been before, covering both human and Chayya in a half-sphere. The fire engulfed them, passing around the sides of the shield until they looked like a falling meteorite. The fire suddenly stopped as another arrow pierced the dragon's hide. Neviah remembered herself and joined Asa in raining arrows down at the dragon, giving their friends time to regain altitude and fall back. Every time she loosed an arrow, another would appear on her string, and she would let that fly, too. Free of the fire, Victoria shot again.

While the dragon was writhing from Asa's and Neviah's arrows, Victoria's struck the monster square between the eyes. Its last roar was cut short as it collapsed to the ground. The molten stone flowed around the dragon's body, half entombing its giant frame. They had defeated their second dragon.

Corban made the sign to regroup. They came together just as a company of Shedim crested the hill behind the dragon. The enemy formation broke apart as some continued toward the companions, and some stopped in shock at seeing the dead dragon.

"Fire!" Corban yelled at her over his shoulder.

Neviah rapidly fired as many arrows as she could. Combined with her friend's arrows, Shedim began to fall from the sky. The Shedim were almost upon them when the other companions broke from cover and formed a counter-assault. A wall of spears crashed into the Shedim, slaying many. Then, the fighting began in earnest.

Neviah laid low to Corban as he came up under a Shedim. She twisted and shot the creature in the stomach with an arrow while her companion grabbed another. Corban raked his claws, cutting through leather armor, wing, and flesh, sending it screaming to a certain death below. Three came at them at once.

"Tuck left!" Neviah called out.

The wing moved out of the way just as her shield became a barrier one of the Shedim crashed into, nearly unseating her. The command saved Corban from a sliced wing as the Shedim tumbled away unconscious.

"Fly!" she yelled a split second later, letting him know his wings were safe while she simultaneously let her bow turn into a sword. She sliced through a second opponent's blade, armor, and flesh. Corban killed the third.

Coming up behind two Shedim who were struggling with a single Chayya, Corban reached out and ripped a wing off of each, sending them spiraling to the ground far below. Neviah clipped a Shedim's wing with her sword as Corban came upon the enemy flank.

"Hold!" she yelled as she had an idea. She let the sword turn back into a bow and shot an arrow down the enemy's flank. It traveled through many Shedim before she lost sight of it. "Done!" she called to give control of their movement back to Corban.

An arrow suddenly thudded into Corban's shoulder armor, causing him to backpedal a moment. "Mind the archers!" he yelled back to her.

Shedim archers had risen above the battle and were shooting into the fray, perhaps indiscriminately, since their own troops were struck too. She pulled back an arrow, intending to take out a few archers, but it wasn't needed. Enya rushed in from above the clouds to pass down their line from behind. Victoria's sword traveled down the Shedim like a terrible scythe clearing blades of grass.

That was when the enemy broke. Some of the companions attempted a pursuit, but the two group commanders called for a regroup. The human enemies were attempting to shoot arrows up at them from the ground, but they were too far away. The companions had gravity on their side, however, and loosed every arrow they carried into the men, who had nowhere to hide. At that moment, Neviah completely understood the phrase "like shooting fish in a barrel."

It made her sick to shoot down at them. They seemed so helpless. She reminded herself that every enemy killed couldn't then kill a friend later. The enemy had instigated the war, after all. She paused in her shooting to gasp as a wave of energy passed through her. Asa had healed her and was flying through the friendly lines on Rafal, healing everyone. Corban's arrow had popped out of his shoulder, and Neviah didn't feel any pain in her arm anymore. She hadn't even realized she'd been wounded until Asa healed her.

When the enemy was eliminated, all except the few dozen or so Shedim who'd escaped, the Chayyoth landed to collect their dead. Fifteen companions lay dead, seven Chayyoth and eight humans. One Chayya lost a rider, and he stood protectively over his human's broken body. An arrow protruded from the man's neck. Tears flowed from the Chayya's eyes.

Corban had to pause from helping move a fallen Chayya when Neviah put her arms around him and squeezed him tight. She knew he would be standing over her body like that one day. She hoped he would have the strength to go on. Corban patted her shoulder before continuing with their task.

There was cheering as men emerged from the melted ruins of

the barracks. They had survived the dragon's attack by hiding in a cellar deep in the rock, which had protected them from the heat. Soot covering their bodies showed the smoke had nearly gotten them. Using old cots and blankets, the human soldiers helped to make gurneys to carry the dead.

Thanks to Asa, there were no wounded. The dead Chayyoth were each carried by four others. Their companions were carried in the arms of a single Chayya. Corban carried one. So did Rafal and Enya since they didn't have the extra weight in armor and weapons most of the wind warriors carried. The Chayya who'd lost his companion scooped him up ever so gently, tenderly pulling him to his chest and carrying him into the air.

The flight back to Alya was just as silent as the one that took them to battle, only this time it was out of respect for the fallen. They stopped often to switch bearers. Their homecoming was a mix of cheers and tears. The majority of the companions had returned, so the cheers won out over the cries. Neviah saw a female Chayya trying unsuccessfully to comfort her husband, the Chayya who'd lost his rider. Corban walked over to talk with them.

Adhira was there to greet them. "How'd things go?" he asked with arms crossed and eyebrows raised. How could someone look so cocky when they were just asking a question?

"Victoria got the big kill this time," Neviah said. The other girl blushed.

"Arrow in the face for the win," Adhira guessed, holding his hand up for a high five. Victoria gave him a weak one.

Neviah wondered how many questions he'd already asked without their knowing it.

"And I don't see any wounded, so Asa gets one, too," he said, and Asa gave him a high five. "Then there's Neviah. What do we keep you around for again?"

She was just about to punch Adhira square in the face when Corban strode up in a hurry. "Come, Neviah. Other scouts have returned, and we need to be present at the briefing."

Shaking her fist at Adhira, she followed her companion. When they got to the meeting, the scouts were already reporting. The blood drained from her face. Their victory in the south was nothing compared to the losses elsewhere.

Chapter 12

All of the cities on the eastern border had conceded to Tanas without a fight. A dragon had come to each gate, and whether from fear or actual support, the leaders gave in to the demands. Now, the enemy had free access to a number of inner cities, all less fortified than those on the border. There was little anyone could do since the largest part of Moriah's forces had been sent north.

Groups of companions were dispatched to various areas, but each skirmish ended in defeat. The enemy was too numerous, and furthermore, twenty dragons had been confirmed in Moriah. One of the northern cities had been melted to the ground by no less than three of the behemoths. Refugees were pouring into Uru from the countryside until every street was packed with the homeless. Chayyoth helped evacuate as many people as possible. They brought stories of such horror that even the strongest supporters of Tanas dared not say so openly anymore. The day's briefing the companions received was laced with desperation.

"The Moriahns sent their main force here," a venerable rider said, pointing at the large map spread across a table. "The only thing that separates them from an enemy force twice their size is the Deepwood Forest. The Moriahns could hold the enemy in this pass here." He traced a line from the Moriahns' position to a road that divided a mountain range. "The only thing keeping them from moving to the pass is the enemy force here." The place he pointed to was on the opposite side of the forest from the Moriahns. "There are a couple thousand Shedim, which would be challenging enough if it weren't for the three dragons that accompany them. They're the ones who destroyed Jarmuth."

The battle-hardened Chayyoth and their riders showed no

outward signs of fear or concern.

"How many companions will we be sending?" Corban asked.

"King Hayrik has approved sending half the Chayyoth army," the man responded. "There will be three thousand of us."

"Are there special orders for my team?"

The man looked at Corban. "None. Can your companions handle three dragons at once?"

"If yours can keep the Shedim off our backs, we'll take care of the dragons," Corban answered without a hint of boasting. To him, killing the dragons was as possible as eating bread for lunch.

Adhira was there to see them off the next afternoon. "You guys, be careful. I'm sure these dragons have heard of their buddy's death and will be watching out for you."

"We'll be fine," Neviah assured him.

"I'm itching to help, but I have to wait for the fight to come here," he complained. "Maybe I should have been a rider."

"You wouldn't have liked it," Neviah said.

"Why not?"

"We never get to sleep in."

He laughed, but when the order came to leave, Adhira's face became serious. "Come back, Neviah. All six of you."

She nodded before Corban ran forward and launched them into the sky. Everyone's confidence swelled at seeing so many of their brothers in arms moving with them. They covered ground quickly but made camp when the light of the day faded. The weather was pleasantly warm, which was good since no one was allowed to make a fire. Talking was kept to a minimum in case enemy scouts were around.

Neviah and her friends found a soft, grassy spot to relax in that evening. They were bathed in the soft blue light of Colossus as they lay silently looking at the sky. She tried not to think about the people who were likely dying in battle at that exact moment. The next day would bring more death, but at that moment, at least she had something beautiful to look at.

She wasn't sure if it was the man screaming or the guttural howls that woke her from sleep. The warriors were up and ready to fight in seconds. Everyone slept with their weapons and there were no tents to obstruct the ranks quickly forming. All around them, in the dim light of Colossus, it looked as if the shadows were coming to life and attacking.

The creatures that sprang from the woods, Se'irim, were the stuff of nightmares. They were awkward, hairy creatures, no taller than a man, though they stood hunched with long arms that looked as if they belonged to creatures twice their height. Their hands ended in jagged claws, each longer than a dagger. Howls escaped from cruel, fang-filled mouths, grotesquely oversized as they loped across the open ground. Their nocturnal eyes glowed gold in the pale blue light. No sooner had the Chayyoth and their riders formed lines than the assault crashed into them.

The companions held firm under the initial charge, where the Chayyoth's superior size and armor made a nearly impenetrable wall. The back rank of riders sprung into the air, raining down arrows on their enemy. The press of the creatures was so great that it looked like the ground was a large, oily black wave undulating toward the companions, threatening to overpower them.

The Se'irims' monstrous claws were impossibly sharp. Neviah saw one of the creatures slash through a Chayya's hardened leather armor right in front of her, leaving deep furrows in his chest before the Chayya bit the monster's head off.

Neviah and her friends made use of their bows, bringing down creature after creature.

"Skyward!" the order echoed down the lines, and everyone able to spring into the air did so. The companions who were already airborne pumped arrows into the enemy front line to free up their allies who were desperately trying to break free of the melee.

Many Chayyoth and humans lay dead or dying on the field. The monstrous Se'irim were formidable foes on the ground. Fortunately, they couldn't fly, and they weren't too smart. Instead of retreating to the cover of the woods, they fought over the remains of the dead companions while the living riddled them with arrows. The morning light had just begun to spread over the battlefield when the last of the creatures fell.

"And those are Se'irim," Corban said grimly as they landed. "We can add them to the list of monsters that serve Tanas."

It took several hours to sort out the allies from the enemy. The dead companions, nearly a hundred, were buried, being too many to bear back to Uru. The Se'irim, hundreds of the vile beasts, were left where they died. There wasn't time to burn them and they had another battle to get to.

Though no one spoke of it, Neviah could tell the losses angered everyone. They took up the flight path from the day before and were ready for a fight when the enemy came into view. Tents and fires spread far across the hillside as the enemy remained camped. They were holding positions for some reason. The Chayyoth ignored this camp. Humans were of little concern. They'd be easy enough to deal with once air superiority had been gained. If it could be gained.

The Shedim enemy was already airborne, flying in formation, and on their way to meet the companions in battle. The Shedim force was larger than they'd been briefed, and at their rear flew three enormous dragons. Neviah tensed as the lines neared one another. The humans readied spears on the front rank while the ones behind them shot arrows. The Shedim led with arrows of their own, and many on both sides fell to the projectiles. With bone-shattering crashes in front of her, the two lines met.

The companions drove deep into the enemy ranks, but the Shedim threatened to spill over and under with their superior numbers. The rear ranks of companions met them, and it was a game of plugging holes the Shedim continued to make. Neviah shot several arrows that brought down many of the enemies at a time.

"Stop wasting your shots!" Corban ordered. "Your arrows aren't needed on lesser targets!" She immediately understood. The dragons were the biggest threat and hung back from the fight, no doubt waiting for the teens to appear. So, they did.

Corban motioned for them to climb higher into the sky. They traveled so high that the air was extremely thin before they leveled out, Enya and Rafal flanking them. Corban pointed to each pair and then a dragon below. Asa and Rafal had the red. Victoria and Enya had the green. Neviah had the brown, which, of course, was the biggest.

As they began their dives, their arrows traveled ahead of them. The wind whipped Neviah's ponytail around so forcefully it became a stinging whip against her neck. She ignored the stings and continued to fire at her target. She led some shots and fired some to the left and right of the dragon, trying to get a good spread. The result was a wall of arrows streaking down at the brown dragon. They were five hundred feet away, then four hundred. Three hundred.

A reserve unit of Shedim, which had been holding formation behind the dragon, shot forward and used their own bodies as shields against the projectiles. The arrows pierced them and kept moving, but the impacts, coupled with their angle of movement, sent the arrows flying in different directions, some killing more Shedim but most flying off to do no further harm. Neviah fired as fast as she could manage but there were too many Shedim willing to sacrifice themselves. Suddenly, she and Corban were the projectile.

Corban lowered his armored head to use as a ram. Neviah hung low to his neck as they plowed through the wall of enemies. The Shedim attempted to come in behind them, but they were moving too fast. As soon as she was free of the bodies, she rapid-fired several more arrows. The Shedim shield having failed, the dragon was already moving away. Most of the arrows missed. She was a decent shot, but firing from the back of a constantly moving mount at an evading enemy was difficult. Two arrows did manage to pierce its lower back and one hit the tail. The dragon banked low, but they pursued.

Too late, Corban realized what the dragon was doing. Arrows filled the air all around them as they pulled up and away from the human archers below. Her companion took several arrows in his wings, but his armor protected his vital organs. Once out of the archers' range, they had a bigger problem.

The dragon had wheeled around and was coming straight for them. The Shedim they'd outrun were nearly caught up, preparing to assault them from the rear. The dragon opened its mouth, lined with razor-sharp teeth. More terrifying was the stream of fire that bellowed from its gaping maw. It was bright white as it enveloped them.

The Forest Shield sprung up to protect them, growing until it was large enough to bend the fire around them. The Shedim behind them were incinerated as the fire was redirected toward them. Corban strained to move them forward as the fire stalled their flight. Neither of them could see anything. It was all Neviah could do not to be pushed off her companion. Though the fire didn't touch them, heat threatened to overwhelm them from the sides, above, and below. Sweat poured off her face, and her lungs labored for the oxygen the fire was burning away.

Then, it was like they hit a brick wall, more like Corban did, anyway. He stopped dead and she stumbled forward off of her companion, sure to keep her shield out in front of her since the fire never ceased. She gained her feet, and her shoes found a solid grip on a surface that felt like rough concrete. Risking a glance behind her to see where her companion was, trying to figure out what had happened, she saw teeth all around her and the red tongue she was standing on. She was in the dragon's mouth!

With the fire still pushing strong, the dragon closed its mouth. At least it attempted to. The Forest Shield created a barrier the dragon's powerful jaws couldn't break. Leaning forward with all her weight, she was able to put one foot in front of the other, forcing her way deeper into the dragon's throat. The dragon bit down again, and she had her chance. She took the Sword of Re'u and drove it up as hard as she could. The fire stopped instantly, and a roar of pain replaced it, pushing her back a few steps. She let the shield shrink as she jumped up and drove her sword higher into the dragon's head. She followed this with two arrows for good measure.

Neviah plunged into darkness as the mouth closed. She tried to run to the giant teeth to carve a way out but instantly became weightless. The dragon was falling! She tumbled around, striking something hard at each impact. Her silver sword shined its bluish light, giving her a terrifying view of the inside of the dragon's mouth.

She was quickly covered in the dragon's blood and slid across the tongue, skinning her knees and elbows. She couldn't stop her tumbling but started to swing the sword of Re'u wildly. Finally, she was able to puncture a hole large enough to let some light through.

She caught a glimpse of the ground as it appeared through the tumble. It was growing rapidly closer.

Light suddenly flooded her tomb, and a familiar roar met her ears. Corban stood on the dragon's lower lip and strained to raise its mouth enough for Neviah to see him. She tumbled away, landing at the back of the dragon's throat. She could tell which way the beast was tumbling finally and readied herself. When gravity shifted, she sprang off the fire pouches, pushing herself toward her companion. She impacted him, knocking them both free of the dragon. The teeth snapped closed so quickly that Neviah was almost crushed.

She was free-falling, and despite her panic, her training kicked in and she held her body parallel to the ground, arms out to create as much resistance as possible. Corban quickly banked out of his fall, scooped her up, and slowed their plummet with a long swooping dive on wounded wings. They had just paused to look back when the dragon struck the ground with such force it caused the ground to shake, felling several trees.

She snapped her eyes back to the sky, seeing if her friends needed help, but Victoria's dragon was already dead, lying across the valley from the one Neviah killed. Asa and Victoria were riddling Asa's dragon with arrows, and Neviah knew the creature was done for. The army of Shedim was in full retreat, once again leaving the humans below to the mercy, or lack thereof, of the companions.

The Moriahns reached the battle below and partially surrounded the larger human force. With the help of the Chayyoth and their riders, they ran the enemy into the forest, clearing the field of victory. The cost had been high, though. The bodies of numerous companions littered the hills and forest below. This time, when they returned, the wails of grief would outweigh the cheers.

Chapter 13

Fewer than fifteen hundred, little more than half the companions, returned from the battles. Though they defeated a flying force more than twice their size, there was no boasting, no cheers. How could anyone celebrate when they'd paid such a high price to bring down just one of Tanas' armies? There were many such forces marching through Moriah. The superiority of the companions in battle mattered little if they lost the war to attrition. The only redeeming outcome from the battle was that the Moriahn foot soldiers had suffered few casualties. They were moving back to the capital to regroup.

The day after the companions' return, a scout arrived with some good news at last. The enemy force, which had landed near the port cities in the southeast, had moved further east, away from the main population centers in that region.

When a second scout reported the next day, they realized the news wasn't as good as they'd thought. Tanas' armies in the north had also moved east, while the eastern armies stopped their marches altogether. The enemy wasn't fleeing but gathering. Few of the eastern scouts showed up to report more on the matter.

"They are gathering the five fastest companions to scout the cities to the north and northeast," Corban said the morning three days after the Battle of Three Dragons.

Neviah and her friends nodded, thinking he was just passing along information.

"I want Victoria and Enya to go," he said.

Shocked, Victoria pointed at herself to make sure he wasn't talking about another Victoria.

"You are the fastest fliers I've ever seen. I need you to report to command at once. I've already secured your position."

Enya and Victoria gave a quick "Yes, sir" before saying a quick goodbye and flying into the night. Asa stared after them.

"They'll be fine," Rafal said to him. "They aren't going to fight, and nothing can catch them." Asa nodded but continued to gaze into the darkness.

"You and I have other business to attend to," Corban said to his companion before walking across the clearing into the woods. Neviah followed.

"What is it?" she asked.

"You and I have been tasked with a scouting mission of our own."

"Where are we going?"

"Very far, into the mountains east of Moriah."

"There are plenty of actual scouts," Neviah said. "Why don't they send them?"

"They have," he said, stopping and looking her in the eye. "None have returned."

She stared back at him, digesting this new development. Companion scouts were unequaled in stealth or speed. If Neviah and Corban were being sent, then something else was needed.

"What is it?" she pressed, searching his face for any feelings that would tell her what to expect.

"We think the enemy may have found something," he said.

"Found what exactly?"

"There are artifacts from the Dark Days that could unleash unspeakable evils on the world. We sent the first scouts in when we received word that the enemy was digging."

A sense of urgency immediately washed over her.

"You feel it too," Corban said, studying her face. She nodded.

"We have to hurry," she said as the need to get moving increased. "Every minute matters now." Without waiting for a reply or for him to lower his shoulder, she grabbed a handful of mane and pulled herself up. In four quick strides, they were airborne. They paused only to grab provisions from camp before taking to the skies again.

As they switched from Alya's gravity to that of the world below, she looked out over the surrounding countryside. Uru was surrounded by makeshift tents and communities. The refugees were overwhelming the city's resources. What were they going to do when

Tanas' armies arrived?

Corban flew them south, quickly passing over Moriah's rocky beaches and out over the ocean. Once they were out of sight of land, Corban turned east. The waves were lazily pushing in toward land, and Neviah could see their winged shadow reflected off the water several feet below.

Fear was a funny thing. Though she'd been flying often lately, her fear of heights threatened her, drawing her thoughts continually to her inevitable death. Trying not to think of the fear was actually making her think of it more. There were plenty of distractions while flying in formation, but flying with just the two of them was sending her brain into overdrive. To calm herself, she reached around to the side pouch on her pack and pulled out a hairbrush.

Even though the wind beat at Corban's mane, it was matted with days of grime. He had been so busy that he hadn't bathed in a week. She ran the brush through his long silver hair, starting at the top of the mane and pulling it through the knots. She smiled a few strokes later when she had a straight patch showing among the tangles.

Corban turned his head to look at her and said, "You're not doing what I think you're doing, are you?"

She hid the brush behind her back and shrugged. He turned his eyes back to the horizon in front of him, shaking his head and mumbling something about it being a long flight to go.

The sound of thunder brought her attention to the darkening sky. They were flying into a storm. Could lightning strike them in the air? Corban beat his wings, gaining altitude as the thunderclouds approached. They lost visibility as they entered the clouds, the moisture dampening their clothes and fur.

She had to squint against the sudden brightness as they broke free of the clouds to glide just above the storm. Every now and then, the grey clouds would brighten as they flared with lightning, accompanied by a nearly deafening boom. Just before each flash, she felt a slight vibration in her ears, and the hair on her arms stood up. It was terrifyingly beautiful.

Later in the evening, after the storm had passed, they found a mountaintop cave to sleep in. Another day of flying brought them to an island. Both checkpoints were stocked with a few dry foods and contained natural springs, which allowed Neviah to refill one of her empty water skins with fresh water. There was a barrel on the first stop filled with water from Alya, which Corban nearly drained.

On the third day of their journey, she took a long draw from a creek trickling down the island's single large mountain. Corban drank from the large water skin he carried.

"Today, we reach the edge of our scouting grid," Corban announced. "We need to remain vigilant. And," he said, reaching back and running a large paw over his beautifully braided hair, "I need to maintain a certain degree of...formidability."

"Braids can be scary," Neviah teased.

He stared at her hard, which she thought looked so adorable with the braids.

"Okay, okay, I'll fix it while we fly," she laughed.

By the time she had his mane smoothed out, they were flying over land again. Huge mountains sprang up all around as they glided low between them. The valleys below were covered in dark green conifers. It was beautiful, but the scenic tour was eventually replaced by reality when she spotted a large encampment in the distance.

She pointed it out to Corban, who lowered their flight path until they were skimming the treetops. They banked away from the encampment toward a large, bare mountain. It looked out of place among all the other peaks covered in vegetation.

Corban suddenly wheeled them around and descended into a sparsely wooded area. When they were on the ground, he made the sign for silence and inched forward to the edge of the trees. Beyond the forest was a clearing and mountainside clear-cut of trees. Though the field was devoid of the larger foliage, it was far from empty. Large boulders and debris littered the entire area. It looked as if a giant tiller had run up the side of the mountain.

"Explain," Neviah signed.

Corban grabbed a strange-looking pinecone off the ground. It was blue and greasy-looking. The Chayya pointed at the mountain, then the pinecone. He broke off the top of the pinecone and pointed between it and the mountain again. Someone was leveling the top of the mountain.

They froze as a tremendous crack thundered through the valley.

Neviah looked up to see a car-sized boulder tumbling down the cliff face. It followed the curve of the hills sloping away from the mountain and rolled straight toward them at a tremendous speed. Corban launched them into the air as the boulder's path became clear to him. It crashed through the trees below them like a giant bowling ball toppling pins.

Corban flew north and began a methodical scan of the surrounding area. Each side of the mountain revealed similar desolation. They had to swing wide when they came upon its eastern face. Hundreds of weather-stained tents of varying sizes were strewn all over the forested area. Tanas' colors, red and white, adorned several standards. The camp occupied the only ground free of debris. Sure to stay out of visual range of the enemy, Corban flew back and forth several times to take in the layout of the encampment. His eyes were able to see great distances without aid, but Neviah had to pull out her newly issued telescope.

Between the camp and the mountain was a smaller camp that had even shabbier tents. A crude log wall had been constructed all around it. Was it meant to keep people out or in? Maybe the missing scouts were there.

She spotted a steep path zigzagging up the cliff face. There was a pulley system to the side of it. Indiscernible material was being lifted to the top of the mountain, counter-weighted with another lift carrying large rocks.

Corban looked back at her, pointed at his eyes, then at the top of the mountain. She nodded. They needed to know what the excavation was all about. Had the enemy found an artifact? If so, what did that mean?

Corban circled around to the opposite side of the mountain from the encampment. He flew away, deeper into the valley, before turning back to face the behemoth. Rising steeply into the air for several hundred feet and flapping hard enough to make Neviah wonder if she had just suffered whiplash, Corban carried them high into the air. Then, he swooped down toward the earth below.

Their speed increased until they leveled out, the terrain flying by in a blur. By the time they reached the wasteland before the mountain, they were speeding like a bullet, only exposed for the few seconds it took to cross the open ground. Corban hurtled toward the mountainside, showing no signs of slowing.

"Umm!" Neviah let out when she was sure they would smash into the unyielding rock in front of them. At the last possible second, Corban tilted his wings, and they were skimming up the side of the mountain. The ground flew away from them as they climbed ever higher up the side of the cliff.

To calm her racing heart, Neviah pretended like the side of the mountain was actually the ground. Instead of calming her, the thought made her dizzy. Why couldn't the enemy be looking for artifacts in a tunnel somewhere? Or in a nice quarry?

So perfect was Corban's speed and timing that by the time their momentum was spent, he had only to step onto a jutting rock without so much as flapping his wings. There was a cacophony of sounds echoing from the area above them. Stepping from Corban's back and making it a point not to look behind her, Neviah slowly climbed the angled rock in front of them.

Close on her heels was Corban, the only thing between her and the open air behind them. Metal could be heard chipping away at rock, which only grew louder as they neared the excavation. A rock the size of Neviah's head suddenly appeared over the edge in front of them. She held up her arm to deflect the blow, which would have been useless if it had not been for the Forest Shield. The shield appeared just in time to deflect the rock with a loud crack, knocking her backward. Corban's strong arms scooped her up and side-stepped the rock as it tumbled out over the cliff.

They froze for a moment, looking like wax figures on exhibit. The crack of the rock against the shield had been deafening. Pebbles tumbled from above the steep stone they occupied as a head peeked over the top. Neviah didn't know what to do as she met the eyes of a large black man holding a pickax. Then came the biggest surprise of all. The man winked at her and disappeared from view.

Neviah felt Corban's muscles relax before he set her down. She looked at him, confused. He looked at her as if she were an idiot.

"He is Moriahn," he whispered.

Neviah remembered the fenced camp they had seen down in the valley. Maybe every black person in that world was Moriahn.

"They are prisoners," she said.

"Tanas' men are using them for slave labor."

"Even in this world," she mumbled while shaking her head.

"What?" Corban whispered.

"Are we going to rescue them?" she asked, switching to sign language.

"No," was the return sign. Corban did not elaborate but instead motioned for her to continue up the rock.

As she peeked over the edge of the rock, she saw the man who had winked at her a few yards away. His back was to them, and he was chipping at a large boulder dangerously close to the edge. Torn clothes covered in gray dust hung in rags over his muscular frame. She turned her eyes from the man to the rest of the dig site.

The entire peak had been flattened. Several holes speckled the terrain as some workers dug deeper into the softer areas of the ground. Nearly a hundred Moriahns were scattered around the cleared mountaintop, most swinging a pick or shovel while others hauled debris to the cliff edges. Intermingled with the Moriahns were a handful of guards with the emblem of the red horseman on their breastplates and swords in hand. Men with cocked crossbows stood sentry at the far side of the clearing, the greatest deterrent for a revolt.

Neviah ducked down out of view while Corban had a quick look. Yells erupted, causing Corban to drop his head below the crest of the rock.

"Did they see you?" she signed. He shook his head.

"They found something," he whispered. His face was stoic, but the trepidation was obvious in his tone. "Something large."

Chapter 14

The yelling was soon replaced by soft thuds of shovels and picks at the center of the cleared area. Corban and Neviah risked watching the scene. All eyes were focused on the men digging. With so many excavating such a small area, the dirt and rocks quickly vanished. At first, it looked like they had uncovered a large black chunk of metal.

After an hour of digging, however, it became clear the object wasn't a natural formation. As rocks were pried from the object's surface, smooth pillars as dark as night showed themselves to be part of an intricately crafted arch. At the top of the arch, pillars spiraled into hundreds of smaller supports, resembling a large spiderweb over an empty center. When the area was clear, a large crater had been created, sloping in toward the ancient doorway. A black set of stairs circled the archway, leading toward and then away from the artifact.

Neviah suddenly realized that was exactly what it was. They had uncovered an artifact from the Dark Days. But what did it do? With the find completely uncovered, no one seemed to know what to do next.

At length, a man who easily cleared seven feet tall appeared from the pathway leading to the top of the mountain. Though he wore the armor of the enemy, Neviah had to admit that he was the most handsome man she'd ever seen. His unusual height caused her to look at his neck. A ruby-encrusted gold medallion swung from a gold chain. A dragon! The dragon in man form nodded at a guard and the others moved to start stripping the Moriahns of their shovels and pickaxes.

Without saying a word, the dragon man walked into the crater, grabbed a Moriahn by the back of his neck, and dragged him toward the artifact. The Moriahn was the man who had winked at her. Being quite large himself, he pulled against the dragon's grip but not a stride was broken as they traversed the stairs. Without pause, the Moriahn was picked up and effortlessly tossed through the archway. Gasps escaped the throats of everyone gathered, even the enemy soldiers. The man didn't come out on the other side!

Neviah looked questioningly at Corban, but his eyes were locked on the doorway. She turned just in time to see the space within the archway turn black. Men on the other side began to scream and trip over each other to get out of the crater. From Neviah's position, she could not tell what was happening on the other side of the arch.

Then she saw it. Like tendrils of smoke, slender black appendages reached around and gripped the side of the archway. Then, they stretched out slowly as if testing the air. An oily mass accompanied the appendage-like fingers. Not in nightmare or the horrors she'd so far experienced had she seen something so hideous.

The creature looked as if it were covered in oil. It had a face like a wolf; only in place of fur were fur-like spikes that dripped a white substance that sizzled when it struck the ground. The poisonous spikes covered its entire body. Its two legs were double-kneed. When it moved, the way it walked had a fluid roll that was almost graceful. Its hollow sockets looked around the clearing, falling on the one who'd summoned it. The dragon approached the creature, equal in stature.

When the dragon was standing right in front of it, the monster reached out and touched the medallion hanging around his neck. It quickly let go and bowed low to the ground. The dragon man said something, and the creature stood again. He said something else Neviah couldn't hear, but she read the body language perfectly as he pointed around him. They were going to throw all the Moriahns through the archway!

Several fights broke out at once. Swords swung, men yelled, and blood flowed as the unarmed Moriahns were subdued. A small group of men were able to overwhelm a couple of guards at the cost of some of their lives. This resulted in four Moriahns remaining free, two now armed.

Neviah looked to Corban for the signal to help. He put a massive paw on her shoulder and shook his head.

"We can help!" she signed quickly in frustration, then pulled her book of prophecies from her backpack and let it turn into the silver sword.

He shook his head again and pointed at himself and her before making the sign for death. Then he made the sign for mission.

She looked back to the scene she was helpless to stop. Crossbows were leveled at the Moriahns but the dragon held up a hand to stay the bolts. The spikey creature was approaching the four escapees. They backed up until they had nowhere else to go. It was either jump off the cliff or face the creature and they were seriously considering the first option.

The two men with swords sliced the air in front of them as a warning, but the creature was undeterred. Suddenly, four spikes shot from the creature's hide and stuck in the men's chests. They fell to the ground, screaming and clutching at the barbs.

Above the screams, Neviah could hear the dragon boom, "Get them through the gate before they die." A dozen soldiers ran to carry out his orders, sure to stay as far from the nightmarish porcupine as possible.

Two enemy soldiers had been badly wounded in the skirmish. One soldier was putting pressure on a deep gash in another man's leg. The other soldier lay in a ball, holding a stab wound from a sword that'd found its way under his armor.

"What are you doing?" the dragon demanded when he saw the soldiers trying to save the two casualties. "Get them through the gate, as well. Before they die!"

The soldiers hesitated. These were their brothers in arms. When the dragon man took a step toward them, any trace of hesitancy evaporated, and they were moving with urgency toward the archway, friends in tow.

"No, wait!" one of the wounded soldiers cried out as they were tossed into the inky darkness.

Another creature, this one with hands like knives, stepped into their world. Neviah was ripped from the spectacle when Corban pulled her down.

"We have seen enough," he said, his voice concealed from those above by the screams of men being fed to the gate.

"What is that thing? What is going on?" She could not keep the hysteria out of her voice.

"The creature is a Shayatin, an abomination crafted of shadow."

"A Shayatin? But Shayatin are small and shadowy and like to reanimate corpses."

Ba'altose had worn a crown that allowed him to summon and control the creatures.

"Those were Lesser Shayatin. This is a full shadow gate, allowing Shayatin to cross over. It is a gateway between the Abyss and our world. A Shayatin cannot enter this world under its own power. Only the living can pass through. Be glad this shadow gate is not large enough for a Greater Shayatin." Corban spoke as if he were merely giving a lesson in class. Did he feel any fear at all?

"Greater Shayatin? They get bigger?"

"Yes. Now, mount up."

She grabbed his mane and swung to his back.

Corban moved to the edge, seemingly unaffected by the screams behind them. He hunched and sprang from the cliff, the valley coming dizzyingly into view. When Corban spread his wings, Neviah caught sight of movement right beside them.

"Tuck right!" she yelled instinctively. The battle-hardened Chayya immediately tucked his wing, but it was too late. The Forest Shield sprang up, but she could not turn in time to deflect the spear-sized bolt as it pierced Corban's wing and buried itself in his side.

They tumbled through the air, Neviah's training the only thing keeping her on her companion's back. She hunched down closer to Corban as he managed to open his left wing and stop their tumble. They were hurtling toward the ground and spinning dangerously close to the cliff face.

Neviah leaned out over the good wing to help redistribute her weight, tucking her book of prophecies under her stomach so she could make use of both hands. She could feel his muscles straining against the wind as it tried to force his wing open more. She leaned out more until she was practically lying on his good wing. They were able to get enough control to pull away from the mountain.

Their descent slowed but Corban had no control of their direction.

They made it out over the forest before a gust of wind turned them around. They were thrown into a tailspin, and without the ability to flap his wings, Corban was powerless to stop it.

The trees rushed up to meet them. They struck the first limb, knocking Neviah from the Chayya's back. Her book of prophecies flew from where she had it tucked under her body. She let the Forest Shield spring around her like a round sled and could hear limbs crunch as her impenetrable shield plummeted through the forest. When she came into contact with the ground, all the breath was stolen from her lungs as she smashed up against the inside of her shield.

The shield became a bracelet again, and she lay on the leaf-strewn ground, straining for air until a breath finally came. Rising quickly, she stood and leaned against a nearby tree. Her shield arm felt like it had been run over, but aside from scrapes and bruises and an intense wave of nausea, she was okay. Swallowing the bile that came into her throat, she looked around for Corban. She spotted him on his side not too far away and stumbled toward him. He slowly righted himself but remained kneeling.

"How bad is it?" Neviah asked in a rushed voice. His breathing was erratic and raspy. He did not reply.

She looked him over. Nothing appeared broken. When she came around to the large bolt pinning his wing to his side, she impulsively sucked air between her teeth. The bolt was barbed down its length until it disappeared beneath Corban's flesh. Tears sprang into her eyes.

"Did it get your lung?"

He nodded while she was trying to decide the best way to deal with the large spear. Removing the bolt wasn't an option; it was preventing him from bleeding out. If she tried to pull out the piece embedded in his wing, it could puncture the artery running through it. She would have to use the Sword of Re'u to cut it away above and beneath the wing.

She looked around for her book of prophecies but didn't see it anywhere. After searching around the nearby trees and still finding nothing, she closed her eyes for a moment and took a deep breath to calm herself. They didn't have much time, and she needed her sword.

When she opened her eyes, she was standing at the base of a tree with low-hanging limbs.

"Climb." The word rang in her head. It was rare for Re'u to speak so directly, but without a moment's hesitation, she began to climb, focusing on the limbs above her and not looking back until she was a good way up. She could see Corban kneeling below her tree. Why was he moving? She made the sign for halt so he wouldn't move again. Was he trying to make the wound worse? Males were the same in all species. Tough at the expense of intelligence.

She was about to resume her climb when she saw a squad of twenty or so enemy soldiers approaching through the woods. They couldn't have been the men from on top of the mountain, but they were enemies, nonetheless. Neviah looked up. She could see the book of prophecies nestled in the tree several limbs above her.

The soldiers hadn't spotted Corban yet but were heading straight for him. The companions made eye contact. She had to get the sword and get back to him. He suddenly shook his head, his ragged breathing causing chest spasms. Then, he made the sign for mission again. She hesitated. If they both died, their allies wouldn't know about the shadow gate. But she couldn't let them kill Corban.

She resumed her climb, only to be halted by shouts below. Corban was limping into the cleared area between the woods and the mountain, and the soldiers spotted him! They rushed forward and quickly surrounded him, spears ready to strike. Neviah rushed up the last couple of limbs and grabbed her book of prophecies. She let it turn into a silver bow and drew down on the first soldier her eye came to.

How many could she kill before they slew Corban? When one of the soldiers motioned with his spear for Corban to come with them, Neviah lowered her bow. They weren't going to kill Corban, not immediately anyway, but were taking him prisoner. That was good, she told herself.

She could go for help. It had taken them several days to fly. It would take a month to walk it. Corban would be dead by then for sure. He had told her to put the mission first. Neviah shook her head as she climbed back down the tree. She couldn't do that, not without her companion.

She would just have to rescue him.

Chapter 15

She followed at a distance. The enemy escorted a slow-moving Corban through the barren zone while Neviah traveled in the shadows of the trees. No more boulders fell from above. They'd found what they were looking for. Neviah considered the shadow gate. Could it be destroyed? If not, she wondered if the creatures, the Shayatin, could be killed or sent back.

She was forced to stop when Corban and the troops came near the soldiers' encampment. It became difficult to see her companion as he was taken through the maze of tents. When he was lost from view, she followed where his path would take him to a large black tent at the center of the camp. There were guards positioned around the perimeter.

Looking to the sun where it hung a little above the horizon, she sat under a tree and waited, thinking. The cover of darkness would work in her favor. All she had to do was make it to Corban, cut the bolt from his side, and they could fly far enough away to where the enemy couldn't find them. It was a simple plan, and she was sure Asa would have come up with a better one, but it would work. It had to.

When the shadows grew long, she assessed her clothing. The sky-blue armor was not the best camouflage for a night mission. Remembering some of her training, she used her sword to cut into a tree. Using a few leaves, she took the sap from the tree and rubbed it all over her. She then dug up some earth with her hands and began applying it over the sap. By the time darkness engulfed the valley, she was impossible to spot.

The night air was warm with a slight breeze coming from the south when she stepped out into the open. She had watched the soldiers for the last couple of hours while she waited and was comforted by their lax patrols. They did not expect an attack in the middle of nowhere. She was halfway through the open field on her way to the camp before she realized something was amiss. The soldiers, with their red and white tunics over shining armor, were no longer chatting as they had been and were huddled away from the spot where they'd been standing.

Neviah strained to see what had them so cowed when a shadow moved in front of an oil lamp. The shadow continued to move until, finally, it came into view between two lamps. Neviah dared not so much as blink for fear of attracting any attention when she saw the beast.

It was a horse that looked as if it were made of the night itself. Blood-red eyes peered out from under a thick black brow. It was enormous, nearly twice the size of a normal horse. It had a shadowy aurora emanating from it, almost as if oily black smoke was perpetually rising from its body. Thick plate armor covered the beast's chest and snout. The Shayatin horse was plenty of reason to give her pause, but the rider was a whole new level of terrifying.

The rider was humanoid, only large enough to make the horse look a normal size. Black armor adorned his body from head to toe. A normal man would not have been able to move under its weight. The helmet was complete with a guard that covered his face in a fanged grimace. Every piece of the armor had a honed edge that rivaled a sword in sharpness.

Neviah took a steadying breath, lowering herself to the ground when the Shayatin pair moved away. If they got in her way, she would deal with them. There was no other choice. She began an excruciatingly slow crawl toward the tents. Every now and then, the armored horror made his rounds, forcing her to pause. Being a creature of shadow, it might be able to see in the dark, so she was sure to use the strewn rocks and brush to her advantage.

As she grew closer to the monsters' patrol, there was nothing left to hide behind, so she made a quick dash for the nearest tent and ran inside with sword ready. She was greeted by darkness and soft snoring. She used the sword tip to cut a slit in the back of the tent and peeked out. No one was stirring in the center of camp. Cutting the hole larger, she slipped out and over to another tent. Even under the cover of darkness, Colossus above left few shadows deep enough for her to hide in. What she wouldn't give for some cloud cover.

She ducked behind a tent as the Shayatin horse and rider came into view. She was glad they were looking the other way because there was little cover where she was. As soon as they disappeared from view, she hurried between several tents, careful not to trip over ropes and pegs.

When she made it to the large black tent, she found a stack of crates to hide behind. Voices could be heard on the other side of the fabric.

"I don't care if it does die before we can throw it through the gate," a man was saying. "The Chayya may have information we can use. Scouts are always privy to what is going on at command."

"But, sir," came a less commanding voice, "the dragon has ordered every prisoner to be put through the shadow gate."

"I know, I know," the first voice said in frustration. Neviah could hear the soft crunch of dirt as the man paced. "But he could not possibly have foreseen us capturing a Chayya alive."

"Do you want to take the chance, sir?"

There was a pause.

"No."

"And remember, sir, we may yet find the rider. Humans are far easier to...persuade than Chayyoth."

"Fine. Ready the prisoners, then come and get me. I want to see this shadow gate myself."

"Yes, sir."

As footsteps shuffled away, Neviah waited. She strained for any sounds that would indicate her companion was in the tent. Nothing. She wondered if she should have followed the other man, but if Corban was inside, she didn't want to leave him.

She used her sword to cut the tiniest of holes in the bottom of the tent and looked in. The room was lit by lanterns. A man was seated at a desk, looking over yellowed parchment as he took notes with a pen he periodically dipped in ink. Corban's helmet was lying by his feet!

Neviah could see everything on the right side of the hole she made, but a partition obstructed her view of the rest of the tent. She considered moving but in order to see what was on the other side, she would have to be standing in one of the two main paths that crisscrossed in front of the tent.

She considered taking the man by surprise but if her companion was not in the tent, she would be alerting the entire camp for no reason. She waited. The minutes seemed to stretch. How long did it take to "ready the prisoners"? Her weariness was just causing her eyes to droop when she heard scuffling feet inside the tent again. The other man returned. He moved to the side of the tent she couldn't see. She decided to wait until they led Corban out of the tent. She would ambush them, free Corban, and they would be airborne before anyone could respond.

"We are ready, sir."

"Good. Grab the Chayya and take him to the lift. I doubt he could make it up the path in his condition."

This was it. She let her sword become a bow and drew down on the edge of the tent when she heard the men exit. The first one came into view, a short man with a stocky build. She waited a beat, and the second stepped into her line of sight. She was just about to loose the arrow when she realized there was no Corban. She quickly shrank back behind the crates and cut a hole in the tent large enough for her to pass through. She ran around the partition to reveal an empty tent.

They must have moved Corban without her seeing. Maybe he was never in the tent to begin with. She fought the urge to curse as she strode for the hole she'd made. Before she could leave, a vision flashed in her mind. She saw a man in a full set of black armor. Around him were the bodies of thousands of people. The moment the vision ended, her eyes strayed to the parchments on the table. If she was going to follow the two men, she had to leave immediately.

But they said they would put Corban on the lift. She remembered where that was. She'd spotted it while she and Corban scouted the mountain. What was Re'u showing her?

Moving to the table, she picked up the first piece of yellowed parchment. It looked like a topographical map. She couldn't make out anything useful from it, so she quickly rifled through the other papers. There were many more maps. She froze when her fingers uncovered a drawing. She moved the other papers to the side to reveal a drawing of a helmet. It was black and twisted, looking like someone had melted a normal helmet until it was pockmarked with bubbles and abnormal crevices. It was the helmet from her vision. She traced the words that were drawn at the bottom of the paper: Nightmare Helm. There was a checkmark next to the name. Under it were drawings of other pieces of armor, just as twisted, the rest of the armor set from her vision. Attached were maps with Xs drawn on them.

She hoped the enemy never found such things, whatever they were. Maybe if she destroyed the maps, they wouldn't be able to find any more artifacts or shadow gates. She searched through the desk until she found a candle, cut it very short, and lit it on the desk's oil lamp. She set it among the papers so the flame would be about the right height in a couple of minutes. Then, she squeezed back through the hole in the tent.

Rushing between tents, she tripped on a rope, stumbled, then continued her rush to the edge of camp. Reaching the last tent, she knelt behind a cart and waited. The armored Shayatin on horseback rode past. The pair never stopped looking out over the cleared fields and never changed pace.

Neviah was rocking with anticipation. She kept looking over her shoulder. Had she not set the papers close enough to the flame?

"Come on already," she muttered. The horseman came into view again, passing near her cart. Suddenly, horse and rider spun around, facing her direction. Had they spotted her?

"Fire!" she heard a soldier yell from somewhere in the camp.

The cry was taken up by others as men ran from their tents toward the fire Neviah had started. The Shayatin hesitated, looking around warily. Neviah allowed herself to breathe again when the creatures rode off toward the center of camp.

The mountain loomed before her, a titanic shadow silhouetted by the blue planet above as she sprinted away from camp. It was dark enough to make the run hazardous for her footing. She banged her shin on a felled tree, giving her a considerable limp until she fell into what could only be a crater made by one of the fallen boulders.

"I don't have time for this," she grumbled as she climbed out. She slowed her pace to avoid a few other obstacles. The silence of the night surprised her. The camp ruckus behind her quickly deadened as she moved nearer to the mountain. The only sound was her breath and the soft crunch of dirt beneath her shoes.

After rounding a large boulder, Neviah was able to see the light of lanterns ahead of her. She slowed when she heard voices.

"If a human becomes one of those monsters as they pass through the gate," a man said, "I wonder what a Chayya would become."

"I don't think that is what happens," came a second voice, much younger than the first.

"They say it is like trading one on our side of the gate for one of the Shayatin on the other side but how do we know that is what is really happening?"

"Are the Shayatin stealing people's souls?" the younger guard asked.

"No. I think the Shayatin just take their lives. All we know for sure is that it takes a person crossing into the gate for a Shayatin to come out of the gate. Who knows what happens on the other side."

"So, every person that goes through allows a Shayatin to come out."

"I believe so."

"How many Shayatin are there?" the younger one asked.

"Millions. More. The gate leads to a whole new world, I think. There may be enough Shayatin to exhaust every life form that ever existed. We'll see what comes down after the Chayya goes through. Though, I can't imagine anything worse than what's come down already."

If they were talking about Corban, he could already be on his way to the gate. She low crawled up to a felled tree and looked around it. The two men were seated on a stump with their backs to the mountain.

Pulling out her sword, she raised herself into a crouched position, ready to pounce. Killing two distracted guards wouldn't be too difficult. Suddenly, a vision appeared before her eyes. Adhira was in a cage with his arms bound behind his back and something covering his eyes. Then, she saw the face of the young guard who was sitting only a few yards from her.

As quickly as the vision had come, it was gone. With the vision came the overwhelming certainty that without the young guard, Adhira would die. But the guard was one of the bad guys. Kneeling back down, she waited. Somehow, the young guard's future was intertwined with Adhira's. She would have to find a way past the guards without killing them.

Beside them was a complex pulley system which was in use. Looking up, she saw a lift slowly making its way down. The lift creaked, drawing the attention of the guards.

"Get ready," the older soldier said. "I think we have another one." They moved beneath the lift, throwing long shadows against the cliff face from the single pole lantern. A rope came into view from above, and the soldiers grabbed it. Digging in their heels, they pulled the lift to the side, away from the pulleys. With a dull thud, the lift landed heavily on the ground.

Wood creaked as a monstrous form stepped from it. The Shayatin, black as the night around it, covered in scales and with a scorpion-like tail, glared at the soldiers. The men looked at their feet. The creature made a guttural noise, which sounded like a tormented laugh. Neviah ducked behind the log when the monster turned. After a moment, it finally strode off into the night.

She looked again when she heard the pulleys creaking back to life. When the lift was a couple of feet off the ground, the soldiers resumed their seats on the stump. The rope hanging from the lift was slowly rising into the darkness above. It was her only chance.

Neviah stood and let her bow appear, drawing down on the men as she sidestepped toward the rope. Their backs were still toward her.

"That one wasn't as bad as the one with all the eyes," the young one said. "But I'd still hate to run into any of them in a dark alley just the same. Or even a well-lit alley."

They would have been easy kills, but she reminded herself the younger one, at least, had some future role to play. The rope was a foot above her head. She quickly tucked her book of prophecies into her armor and jumped. Her hands tightened around the rope, sliding until her grip stopped at a knot tied at the end of it.

The ground beneath her was swallowed by the night as she rose further into the air. Fighting off a small panic attack, she held on for dear life. With the mountain blocking out the light from Colossus, she could barely see the rocks right beside her and she figured not being able to see was probably for the best. She had no clue who or what was at the top, but they would have a hard time seeing her. Just as she was beginning to wonder how long she could hold on, torchlight became visible above.

"Where are the rest of your kind?" a man asked flatly as the lift came to a stop.

"The idiots wait to see if the Chayya will allow one of the great beasts to come through," came the guttural reply. "It is not the size of the sacrifice that matters, only the size of the gate." The wooden lift groaned in protest as the creature stepped on.

"You are too heavy," the man said, surprise in his voice. "Let me attach another weight, or you'll fall to your death." Boots crunched on gravel as the man walked away.

"Hurry up, human!" the Shayatin growled back.

Neviah didn't know what her next move should be. Her arms were burning from holding her weight, and when the man returned, she would be sent back to the guards waiting below. Reaching out, she put her feet against the rock face, which took some of the weight off her arms. Slowly, she climbed the rope a little so she could get a better view. When she was right beneath the wooden planks, she peered through the space between them to see one of the monsters standing on it.

It had the head of a snake, its large fangs hanging over the bottom lip. They dripped a white fluid. It looked like the Shayatin was salivating, waiting for the chance to bite someone. Suddenly, its head snapped around. The monster spun in circles as if it knew it was being watched from somewhere. A forked tongue tasted the air just before the creature turned its black-eyed stare downward, looking directly at Neviah.

She let go of the rope with one hand and reached into her armor for her sword. The lift jerked wildly as the creature reached around the planks and grabbed Neviah by her wrist. She froze with fear and did not struggle as she was pulled topside, lest she be dropped to her death. Her hand closed on her book of prophecies, but that arm was pinned beneath the creature's considerable grip as he grabbed her with the other hand.

The House of the Forest

"Another one for the gate," the Shayatin said as it spun toward the mountain. It still had a vice grip on her wrist, but when her back was no longer toward the hundred-foot drop, her mind cleared, and she took action.

The Forest Shield sprang open, severing all the fingers on the snake's hand holding her. It hissed in pain as Neviah fell to the wooden boards. She jumped back a step so her feet were on solid ground while simultaneously drawing the Sword of Re'u.

She paused for a split second, trying to think of something clever to say. Where was Adhira when she needed him? With a quick horizontal slash, she cut the ropes holding the lift, sending the Shayatin hissing and falling into the darkness.

She didn't know if the impact would kill the beast, but at least she knew they could be wounded. Spinning around, she tried to look past the torchlight but couldn't see the man who'd been guarding the lift. Maybe the work he went to do had distracted him from what had just happened. She let her sword become a bow and sprinted up the path to her left. It quickly curved away from the edge to a small rise, giving her a view of the entire mountaintop.

The excavation had become more of an arena. Hundreds of soldiers and Shayatin had gathered around the shadow gate. There was something strange about the men she could not quite put her finger on. Torches were strewn all over the place, leaving some areas well-lit while others remained in shadow.

There were an alarming number of Shayatin and no telling how many had already left the mountain. As she looked on, more of the black monsters were emerging from the shadow gate. She breathed a sigh of relief when she caught sight of her companion. He was in the middle of a line of Moriahns who were being fed forcibly to the gate. She estimated a couple of minutes before it was his turn. There was no doubt in her mind Corban was the night's main event.

As she was about to move to her right to get closer to him, she caught sight of a strange scene just below her. Soldiers in a line were standing nervously in front of one of the smallest Shayatin. It had appendages coming off its head that oddly looked like dreadlocks, though they appeared sharp as knives.

"Do you swear eternal allegiance to Iblis, the King of Princes?" it asked in a rumbling voice.

"I...I do," the soldier directly in front of the monster said. He was looking around him like a cat who'd been cornered.

The Shayatin held up a gnarled staff with a jet-black jewel set atop it. The jewel flashed red, and the man gasped, and immediately, his posture straightened.

It was more than that, Neviah realized. The man was actually taller, with broader shoulders as well. There was a black dragon burned into his forehead with dark veins spreading from it down his neck, disappearing under his armor only to reappear on his arms. Whatever walked away was no longer the same man he was a moment before. She knew then what was odd about the soldiers. Many had already been transformed by the Shayatin.

Turning from the scene, Neviah hugged the ground as she moved around the shallow vale closer to Corban's position. She hoped the dried mud covering her body protected her from the keen eyes of the monsters around her. Their attention was elsewhere anyway. She made it to within twenty feet of her companion, but a Shayatin moved next to Corban and grabbed ahold of his mane.

"What say I speed things up a bit!" the creature yelled. Cheers and roaring guffaws responded as the Shayatin shoved its way to the front of the line, pulling her companion along. Corban was dragged to the steps of the shadow gate.

With a roar, Corban swatted at the monster, and the Shayatin stumbled backward through the gate. This was met with much laughter from the gathered enemy. Another much larger Shayatin approached the injured Chayya.

Neviah was out of time. She had no plan and no reason to think she wouldn't die there that night, but she stood and pulled her bowstring to her cheek. She loosed the arrow, which took the Shayatin in the shoulder. It stumbled back into the mass of soldiers behind it.

Before the shock of her appearance was over, she sprinted down the hill toward Corban. A soldier stepped in her way, attempting to grab her. His grim determination turned to confusion when her bow miraculously turned into the silver sword. She cut him down without breaking stride. Movement to her left alerted her to raise her shield. It sprang up just in time to deflect poison quills from one of the Shayatin, some of which struck nearby enemy soldiers.

Crossbow bolts sailed through the air. One whizzed past her head, and she raised her shield just in time to block several more. Another soldier stepped in her way but made the fatal mistake of putting his back to Corban. The Chayya's claws raked across his back, dropping him to the ground.

Neviah leaped over the man and used her sword to cut the bolt under her companion's wing. She grabbed his mane and was leaping onto his back when something barreled into Corban's other side.

Halfway between the ground and Corban's back, Neviah had no way of bracing herself. As she was slung backward, she saw Corban grappling with a Shayatin, frenzied laughter permeating the air from those gathered. She reached out to brace her fall, but she found no purchase as she tumbled through the shadow gate.

Chapter 16

Hair whipped around her, and flakes of dirt fell from her skin due to the wind assaulting her as it poured through the shadow gate. All around was a mixture of dark hues. The sky, if it was a sky, was purple and black with red lightning rending the barren land around her.

Neviah hovered there, a couple dozen feet above the ground, and could see for miles. The land was desolate, with charred patches as far as the eye could see. There was no vegetation, water, or anything else that would bespeak life in that world. Yet, directly below her were thousands of black Shayatin, weapons ready and fighting each other to be directly beneath her. If she fell, she would be dead before hitting the ground. She looked up.

Though the door had been upright in the world of the living, it was now above her in the cursed land she'd fallen into. Just as she was falling through the shadow gate, she remembered her shield. She gritted her teeth against the pain in her wrist, but the Forest Shield was the only thing keeping her from falling to the creatures below. It completely covered the gate, leaving her to hang awkwardly by her wrist. She was helpless. Lifting her feet, she tried to hook them on the edges of the gate, but the shield was in the way.

She considered making the shield smaller but didn't want to risk it becoming too small. Something caught her attention to her left. She studied a mountain that was as black as the Shayatin below. There was movement, she was sure. With horror, she realized there wasn't anything moving on the mountain. The mountain itself was moving!

Even the Shayatin were keeping a watchful eye on the Greater Shayatin as it approached. The creature moved so slowly that Neviah wondered how many hours it would take for her doom to come upon her. Her shield moved, sending blinding pain through her arm.

Looking up, she saw two massive paws curled around the edges of her shield; then, she was pulled upwards. It quickly became sideways as she reentered a world less desolate and fell heavily to the ground, landing on top of a dead Shayatin, missing its head.

"On my back now!" Corban commanded. All around them was fighting. The Moriahns had formed a circle around Neviah and Corban. Without weapons, they were being slaughtered. She looked back at the shadow gate, then to the sword in her hand. She had to try.

She swung at the side of the archway nearest her. The sword bounced off with a shower of sparks, numbing her hand with the impact. That was why the shadow gates had been buried, she realized. Even the Sword of Re'u couldn't destroy them.

She turned back toward the fight, which was all but over, and wasted no more time before jumping from the gate steps onto the Chayya's back. He took off straight into the air, jerking her backward so hard she could feel the pressure in her teeth.

Bolts flew through the air, but they were ineffective as the pair quickly fled into the safety of the night and out of sight. Looking over her shoulder, Neviah saw the last resistance fall under the enemy swarm. She wanted to go back and help but knew what Corban would say. The mission always came first. She silently thanked the men who had just died to help them escape, though they didn't even know them.

Neviah turned her attention back to her companion. She let the Sword of Re'u glow so she could inspect Corban's wing. There was crusted blood where the wound had scabbed over but fresh lifeblood was pouring out with each pump of the Chayya's wings. A piece of the bolt was still buried in his wing, the barbing making the wound reopen.

"We need to land," she said over his shoulder. "You are losing too much blood."

"We have to get as far away as possible," he said weakly. "They will be looking for us to head straight back to Uru, and that is what we must do."

"We are far enough away for me to patch you up really quick. Now, land!"

Corban looked over his shoulder for a moment. He didn't say anything, but Neviah realized they were dropping altitude.

Colossus showed brightly, allowing them a safe landing near some heavy foliage. Neviah jumped from his back as soon as his paws touched the ground. She gingerly lifted the wing to inspect his side. The spear puncturing his lung was gone, leaving a hole. Air bubbles were mixed with blood as it dripped to the ground. She couldn't believe he was still able to breathe.

"You need something smooth to cover the wound," he rasped. She looked around until she found a large leaf, but it was too dry. It cracked and flaked away when she applied pressure.

She remembered her backpack and pulled it from her back, opening one of the smaller pockets. The inside lining was made of plastic. She deftly cut the flap off with her sword and pressed it against the wound. Corban's ribs expanded as he took a deep breath.

"That is much better," he said with a cough, his voice mostly back to normal, if a little weak still.

"Can you hold it in place while you fly?"

He nodded, reaching across his body to hold it in place. She turned her attention to the spear jutting from his wing.

"It's bleeding a lot."

"I think it may have cut the artery during the fighting."

"I have to remove it if I'm going to patch the wound."

"I know."

She was wondering what to do when the Sword of Re'u turned into a rapier all on its own. She stood with the blade poised above the wing.

"This is going to hurt," she warned as she pushed the blade into the wound. The wing jerked involuntarily, pulling a grunt from Corban. "Keep still!" she said as she slowly moved the sword in a circle around the edge of the wound. She was thankful that the sword couldn't cut Corban.

When the last piece of the bolt had fallen from the wound, blood started to pump out faster.

"Pull your wing in tight to your side," she said. He did so, using the wing to hold the plastic against his lung wound as well. She pressed her backpack against the outside of the wing, but the blood continued to flow. "I can't stop the bleeding," she said, her voice cracking as she fought to hold back a sob.

She suddenly became aware of hoofbeats coming from the east. Corban's head was hanging low, and he looked around, disoriented. He'd lost too much blood. She quickly guided him to a dense patch of brush and was able to gently help him lay on his side. She hoped that with all his weight on the wing, circulation to the wound would be completely restricted.

She knelt down beside her companion and watched the direction the noise was coming from. The ground rumbled as the Shayatin pair galloped into view. It was the black armored knight from earlier, hunched over his gigantic horse. The horse was moving faster than anything Neviah had seen, which was an amazing feat with such a large Shayatin on its back.

The pair flew past, stirring the vegetation with a gust of wind as they passed. She breathed a sigh of relief and turned her attention back to Corban. His breathing looked stronger than before they stopped, but he was struggling to keep his eyes open. Though his eyes glowed in the darkness, they were duller than she'd ever seen them at night.

"It's going to be okay," she said, though she didn't know how that could be true. They were hundreds of miles from Uru in the middle of nowhere, and if Corban moved, he would bleed to death.

She pulled out one of her water skins, one that still held water from Alya.

"Drink," she commanded, holding the skin for him. She made him drink it all.

She became aware of the rumbling ground just before the horse burst through the brush to her left. She raised her shield and dug the edge into the ground, but the beast slammed into it before she could brace herself fully. The force of the charge knocked her back several feet, where she rolled to a stop facedown and dazed.

Her vision swam as pain throbbed in her left eye. She could already feel it swelling. She had enough awareness to look up. The horse wobbled sideways before bending its legs to lay on the ground.

The impact with the Forest Shield had left the beast dazed as well.

The monstrous knight on its back was completely unharmed, however. The Shayatin stepped from the horse's back, rising to its full height. Neviah stood and staggered a step but managed to keep her footing, rising to stand barely at the height of the black knight's chest. When it took a step toward her, Neviah pulled her silvered bow to her cheek and fired an arrow at the Shayatin.

It held up a wrist as thick as her leg, and suddenly, a shield sprang from what looked like an identical bracelet to the one she wore. Through the shield, she could see roiling black and purple clouds and red lightning flashes. Her arrow went into the shield and disappeared. Was the shield some sort of shadow gate?

He drew a sword from his scabbard that looked as if it were made from smoke. It wafted and danced with the wind as the knight continued its advance. Neviah stilled herself and readied her sword. The Shayatin stabbed at her faster than she thought possible for such a large creature. Her shield sprang up in time to deflect the blow, knocking her back a step.

The knight paused, reassessing the girl's armament. The Shayatin stabbed at her again, and she saw her chance. Neviah twisted, holding her sword perpendicular to the ground to deflect the blow. The enemy sword shifted like a shadow, the Sword of Re'u passing right through smoke before the cursed blade solidified again.

The only thing Neviah could do to escape the enemy's counter-slash was to step in close. The Shayatin's shield sprang up before her, and she found herself being sucked half into the shield. She managed to catch herself with her knees and quickly reached back with her shield arm. The Forest Shield widened to deflect a swat from the shadow blade and gave her enough leverage to pull herself back.

She managed to break combat and jump away from the monster. They circled each other for a moment after, reassessing. The Shayatin was definitely stronger and faster. The Sword of Re'u wouldn't be able to get through its shield without her getting sucked into whatever dimension lay on the other side.

She wondered what the monster thought of her. Small though she was, she had a shield that could stop its shifting blade and a sword that could do some real damage if she were to make it past its shield.

Her eye was throbbing and so swollen she could barely see out of it. Out of the corner of her good eye, she noticed the horse rising to its feet again. Great. Why face one unstoppable foe when she could face two?

She turned and fired an arrow at the horse. The animal moved, lightning fast, to the side, and she lost sight of it as the knight swung at her head with its blade, trailing wisps of shadow behind it. She brought up her shield but stepped back as the blade turned to smoke and rematerialized as he tried to get through her defense. She ducked the blade, then turned and stabbed at the Shayatin's armored chest. He brought up the gate shield, forcing her to pull back from her strike.

The pounding of hooves behind Neviah caused her to instinctively dive to the side. The horse corrected its course at the last moment to prevent it from smashing into the knight. She shot arrows rapidly at the pair, forcing the knight to raise its shield and the horse to dance until it was behind its master.

The enemy's shield was the only thing keeping her from victory. She paused for a second in her shooting, waiting for either of the Shayatin to poke their heads out. The knight looked above his shield, but the arrow wasn't fast enough and was lost to the void. She shot several more arrows, trying to buy time.

She suddenly realized the horse was no longer behind its rider. The rustling to her right was Neviah's only warning, but she did not have time to react. The horse ran into her, head bent low. The saffron armor on the horse's head dealt a glancing blow to her right shoulder. She screamed in pain as she felt the sharp edges of the saffron digging into her flesh. Her book of prophecies fell to the ground, and her blood ran hot down her arm to soak the sleeve of her tunic.

The horse reared above where she lay on the ground, its hooves raking the air. Neviah held up her shield, and the hooves crashed against it. The edges of the Forest Shield buried themselves in the ground all around her, creating a protective dome. The night air rang with the banging as hoof strikes continued to rain down.

The assault soon stopped, and she could hear the horse take a few steps back. She risked a glance out from her cocoon and saw the Shayatin knight warily approaching, even though the horse was now guarding her weapon.

Neviah ran a finger along the razor edge of her shield and immediately remembered her training. Everything was a weapon.

The knight raised his sword as he simultaneously pulled his shield in close to protect himself. When the shadow blade slashed down at her, with all her strength, she knocked it aside with her shield from her position on the ground. The Forest Shield shrunk to watch size as she rolled closer to her enemy. When she felt the monster's metal studded boots dig into her back, she winced but took advantage of their proximity.

Her left hand darted up behind his shield to grab the leather strap that was holding it to the Shayatin's wrist. Fire, like acid, shot through her leg as the enemy blade sliced across her calf. She gritted her teeth and let the Forest Shield grow to the size of a buckler, completely severing the enemy's arm. The Shayatin shield fell to the ground, nearly enveloping Neviah in the gate as she pushed it aside and scampered behind the knight.

The Shayatin howled as it dropped the smokey blade and grabbed its stub of a wrist, which was pouring black smoke. Neviah kept an eye on the horse, which stood unmoving. Sparing a glance for the enemy shield, she saw the shadow gate was open, though the shield was slowly shrinking. The Forest Shield grew to the size of a tower shield before Neviah dug the bottom into the ground for leverage. Planting both feet in the small of the Shayatin's back, she pushed as hard as she could.

Her own screams pierced the air as she felt the severed calf muscle in her left leg protesting with pain. The Shayatin stumbled forward a step and turned to face her as it stepped onto its own shield. It clawed the air as it fell into the shadow gate, a primeval roar escaping the helmet that masked its face. At the last moment, the Shayatin managed to dig its gauntleted fingers into the earth. It hung there for a moment, its hand the only thing keeping it in the world of man.

The ground finally gave way, and it dragged a clump of grass with it as the knight fell back into the Abyss from where it came. Just before the enemy shield shrunk back to the size of a watch, a small shadow the size of a cat jumped out.

It was a little imp, its skin as black as the other Shayatin she'd seen.

The House of the Forest

It had tiny horns on its head and daggers for fingers. It sneered at Neviah and ran toward her. She reached out and grabbed the shadow sword, which had become a black book. The shadow blade sprung up, but before she could swing at the imp, a giant hoof stomped down on the small creature. Smoke wafted up from beneath the hoof as the horse looked down at Neviah. She held up the blade, trying to blink away the tears filling her eyes. Her calf felt like it was on fire.

The horse took a step forward, but she moved back as best she could, bringing her shield up. The Shayatin stopped but continued to stare at her. She was losing a lot of blood from her leg and shoulder. She let the shield shrink and without taking her eyes off the horse, she ripped the sleeve not already covered in her blood from her tunic before wrapping it around her other shoulder. She used her teeth to pull the knot tight. The horse still did not move.

She tore another strip from her cloak to wrap tightly around her leg. Using the Forest Shield as an awkward crutch, she was able to stand on her one good leg.

"Go," she said, waving her new sword toward the woods behind the horse. "Get out of here." The Shayatin did not move. She hopped toward her sword and scooped it up before tucking the black book under her arm.

The horse surprised her by picking up the gate shield with its teeth and holding it out to her. She expected some trick. Her mind soon moved back to her companion, and she slowly moved that way, putting most of her weight on the shield. The horse followed at a distance.

Corban was exactly as she'd left him. The blood on his fur was drying but she breathed a sigh of relief only when she saw there was no blood on the ground around him. His position lying on his wing was staunching the blood flow and allowing him to breathe. She knew there was no way to move the mighty Chayya without killing him.

What was she going to do? She didn't know how long he could last the way he was. She shook him lightly. He groggily lifted his head an inch off the ground.

"Tell me what to do, Corban."

He slowly lowered his head again without responding.

"I don't know what to do," she whispered, looking around until she found the horse. The Shayatin was standing a few feet away with the strap of the shield between its teeth. What was it up to? A thought occurred to her. As best as she could, she hobbled over to a large bush and cut it free. Then, after arranging it and some other brush around her friend, Corban was hidden.

"I'm crazy," she told herself, looking from her companion to the enormous horse. After a moment, she turned and slowly limped her way over to the horse. "Why aren't you trying to kill me?" she asked frankly. "What do you want?"

The horse did not answer but took a step toward her. It lowered its muzzle until it was within arm's reach. She slowly reached out despite the pain the movement caused her shoulder, still not sure what the beast was up to. When her hand touched the black nose, she felt a wave rush through her, like goosebumps all over her body.

"*We would be unstoppable!*" Neviah jerked her hand back. The words had rung out loudly in her head, like an intrusive thought jumbled with her own thoughts. It was as if she thought the words but more forceful. The horse didn't say anything else.

"You can talk," she said. The horse nodded. "You can talk in my head." The horse nodded again. "But I have to be touching you?" Another nod.

She looked between the horse and Corban. The waterskin with Alya's water was gone. If his wounds did not kill him, he would die in a few days without that water. She had to get back to Moriah, and soon. She reached out and touched the horse again.

"I need to travel west," she said. "Will you take me?"

"*We will weave a path of destruction wherever we go. Together, we can conquer kingdoms!*"

Neviah was taken aback by the fervency of the statement. "I don't want to conquer anyone," she said. "I just need to get help for my friend."

The horse didn't look away from her. "*Your friend will die. Join me, and we will be as powerful as the Ancients!*"

"No," she said forcefully. "I just need a ride."

The Shayatin didn't say anything for a while. When it spoke, it was business-like. "*I will take you where you need to go in return for*

The House of the Forest

the Vapor Blade and the Abyss Shield."

"Done," she said without hesitation. She took the shield from the horse's mouth. "But I will hold onto them until we get to Uru."

The horse nodded as she put the book of prophecies and Abyss Shield into the remnants of her backpack. She had torn it up to save Corban but it still had the main pocket intact. The Vapor Blade remained in her hand.

Neviah moved around to the side of the horse but realized she would not be able to put the necessary weight on her right leg to climb. It would have been difficult anyway, with the stirrup the same level as her shoulder.

"I am injured," Neviah said.

The horse knelt, which made it the height of a normal small horse.

Neviah leaned her weight back onto the Forest Shield so she could put her good foot into the stirrup. She pushed herself away from the shield and was able to grab onto the saddle horn and gingerly pull herself up. She put the foot of her injured leg into the stirrup after adjusting the leather strap for length but made a mental note not to use it. It was going to be a bouncy ride without use of one of her legs.

"There is a waist strap. I suggest you put it on if you do not wish to fall from the saddle."

"Okay," she said, wrapping the thick strap around her waist. "Head southwest until we see the ocean. Moving west from there will lead us to the city I seek. I need you to be fast."

Laughter echoed through Neviah's head as the horse took off at a breakneck speed through the woods. She hoped the Shayatin didn't have any surprises in store for her.

"What is your name!" she yelled against the tumultuous wind in her ears.

"*Euroclydon,*" it responded.

Re'u chose that moment to show her a piece of the Shayatin's future. It would kill hundreds. If she didn't need the creature so desperately, she would have slain it without a moment's hesitation. Instead, she rode off into the night with it.

Chapter 17

Neviah's thoughts troubled her as horse and rider sped through the mountainous terrain, the beauty of the rising sun feeling like a mockery of the travesty from the previous night. Her thoughts of Corban were often interrupted by other, less constructive thoughts she struggled to suppress. She thought back to their fight with Ba'altose and his blade of power. The Sword of Re'u had been able to cut through everything else but that blade.

That was until she attempted to destroy the shadow gate. The silvered sword had bounced off of it as if it were just another metal blade. She shook her head. It didn't make any sense to her at all.

"The Sword of Re'u should've been able to cut through anything," she mumbled.

"If you take up the Vapor Blade," said a voice inside her head, *"then you would not have to cut through an enemy blade. You could simply pass through it. You could slaughter…"*

"Enough!" Neviah yelled, pushing the horse's words from her mind. She felt the blood rushing through her veins as she tightly gripped the hilt of the Vapor Blade. She became aware of the hate boiling inside of her, and it shocked her. Anger at the monster's intrusions was understandable but she never thought herself capable of the loathing she felt for the beast.

She remembered Corban and focused on him again. He had become such a large part of her life. She couldn't imagine life without him. Why did the world have to be such a horrible place? The leather reins creaked in her grasp as her thoughts turned to Tanas' betrayal. She seethed as the Shayatin glided impossibly fast over the gently rolling hills, which were rapidly replacing the rocky peaks. Never in her life had she moved at such speeds, even in a car.

Her thoughts soon slipped back to the war. If Tanas had been what they all thought he was, none of the evil occurring in Moriah would have happened. She hoped she would be the one to kill the traitor. The many ways she could slay him played over and over again in her mind.

A sharp pain in her left leg brought her attention back from her brooding. The gash throbbed against the makeshift bandage. Euroclydon's gallop had been surprisingly smooth until he turned a sharp right, forcing her to put weight on the injured leg.

"What is it?" she asked out loud when the horse came to a stop between a copse of trees.

"*Look.*"

She did as the Shayatin suggested and peered through the foliage. There was a large force sprawled between two hills just shy of being full-fledged mountains. The human soldiers wore Tanas' red and white colors.

"Just go around them to the south. We need to find the shore anyway."

"*It will cost us time.*"

"Not as much time as this pointless conversation!" she snapped.

The horse rocketed to the south. It was nearly an hour before they came to another passable valley. They were forced to stop again, the valley filled with tents and soldiers.

"*Further south?*" the Shayatin asked, and though Neviah wasn't familiar with mental communication, she thought she detected a hint of smugness.

"That must be Moriah's border," Neviah said, exasperated.

"*We will likely find the same at the next pass,*" Euroclydon said, reflecting her fears. "*If we can't go around, that leaves one option.*"

"We go through," she said.

"*What is the plan of attack?*" the horse asked.

"I have no plan or the time to come up with one. Let's go."

Neviah felt the horse in her head again, but instead of hearing words, she felt what the horse was feeling. As the Shayatin galloped toward the human line, there was a strong sense of joy emanating from it.

Shouts echoed through the camp when the perimeter guards saw them. Men formed up in tight ranks directly in their path. Three hundred feet away, Neviah had the Vapor Blade turn into a bow and loosed an arrow toward the enemy line. The arrow looked like an inky shadow as it zoomed through the air. It struck a man in the front rank and passed through two others before it lodged itself in a pole. The tenor of the shouts changed.

"*Ah! Fear!*" the beast said.

Neviah was only able to shoot one more arrow. Euroclydon covered the ground too fast for anything more. Her shield sprang up to protect her and the left flank of the horse, the bow turning into a sword as they bore down upon the men. Some ran while others held their spears at awkward angles to keep out of the steed's path.

It must have been like a nightmare come to life for the enemy as the Shayatin smashed into the soldiers. Spears snapped, and shields splintered at the impact, echoing through the surrounding hills like a gunshot. The horse's black armor was a battering ram, carving a bloody path through the disjointed ranks.

Neviah lashed out with her sword, slicing through weapon, armor, and man with each sweep of the blade. She felt the thump of weapons against the shield, but no one dared face her sword arm.

After passing through the rows of men, Euroclydon turned to face them again. Those not dead or fleeing reformed amid the calls of a man on a white horse. The animal looked like a pony compared to Euroclydon. In one swift motion, Neviah let the sword turn into a bow, loosed an arrow, and let it turn back into a sword again. The man was lifted from his saddle with the impact of the black missile. The sight was exhilarating.

"*We should kill them all,*" Euroclydon said.

Neviah sneered at the cowing men. She could feel a thirst inside her, one that had been buried deep. She wanted to do just as the horse suggested and kill them all.

"No!" she commanded, as much an order to herself as to the horse. An image of her wounded companion flashed in her mind. For a moment, the monster resisted the tension she put on the reins. She doubted she had the strength to turn the Shayatin if he disobeyed.

She could feel the horse's disappointment filter through as it finally turned. The pair blew through the rest of the encampment like a tornado, trampling and slicing any soldier unfortunate enough to find himself in their path. The way Euroclydon zigzagged through the tents, the unfortunate were many.

Tidal waves of hate emanating from the creature threatened to overwhelm her. Several times, she caught herself enjoying the chaos and destruction they were causing. She did manage to, for the most part, keep them heading in the right direction. By the time they reached the other side of the camp, the soldiers no longer dared hinder their path.

"*We should finish them off,*" the horse insisted. "*One soldier should be allowed to escape to tell others of our power. We could be the nightmares...*"

"Enough!" Neviah said as forcefully as she could manage. "Quit trying to poison my thoughts! Let's go. You made a deal."

The horse continued.

She came to the realization the Shayatin was affecting her thoughts and actions somehow. It was as if the worst parts of her were brought to the forefront of her mind, and every negative emotion became a driving force.

She raised a hand in front of her face. Crisscrossed across her dark brown skin were tiny spider-webbed coils of black veins. They were so black they almost looked purple as they pulsed. A shadow-like black smoke, very faint, formed around her hand, untouched somehow by the wind.

The black veins reached to her elbow and stopped. Neviah immediately filled her thoughts with her friends, prophecies, and their mission. The veins quickly receded and shrunk until they were barely visible on the back of her hand.

Her thoughts were interrupted when she felt an itch between her shoulder blades. Looking up, she saw several hundred Shedim filling the midmorning sky. She shot an arrow straight up, surprising the lead flyers but missing her target.

To Euroclydon, she said, "I thought you were fast. Why are the Shedim gaining? I am starting to think you are all boast."

Anger filtered through their telepathic connection, but their speed increased. The wind buffeted her as if she were in a steep dive atop Corban. She ducked her head to decrease the resistance and looked to the side, relieved to see the Shedim rapidly falling behind.

Hours went by before she realized how far they'd come. They were deep within Moriah's borders. Far to the south, she saw the blue line of the ocean stretching as far as she could see from east to west. They covered in one day what had taken her and Corban three. By the light of the setting sun, Uru's magnificent white walls glowed on the horizon, Alya dominating the sky above.

Neviah breathed a sigh of relief when she saw a squadron of twelve Chayyoth with their human companions descending toward them from Alya. Their approach had not gone without notice. She used the reins to stop the Shayatin as friendly troops landed all around and encircled them.

Before the squadron leader could speak, she slid from the back of the monstrous horse to land heavily on her good leg. She was barking orders before she hit the ground.

"Send your fastest flyer to the School of Flight to find Asa and Rafal. Bring them to me now."

"What authority do you…"

"This is my authority!" she growled, letting the Forest Shield spring up under the lead Chayya's snout. He shot a quick glance to the Chayya to his right, who took two quick steps before launching into the air.

Neviah felt the horse brush against her shoulder.

"*What of our agreement?*" Euroclydon asked, his eyes moved between the companions and her. She again considered killing the monster. She cared nothing about being made a liar for breaking their deal. Despite her disdain for the beast, she slowly withdrew the Abyss Shield from her backpack and placed it along with the Vapor Blade into the saddlebags laid across the animal's rump. Before it could move, she grabbed the horse's faceplate and pulled its massive head down next to hers.

"When the time comes, and your paths cross, know this." She looked unblinkingly into its eye. "The choice you make will decide your fate as well. I will find you. I will always find you. And no deals struck in the dark will save you next time. The next time I see you, I will kill you."

"*Whose path?*"

She didn't respond but held the Shayatin there for a moment longer, staring him in the eye, before letting go. The creature stared at her sideways, studying her face for a moment. The Chayyoth stepped out of the giant horse's way as it dashed off. In seconds, the heavy sounds of its hoof beats were gone as the Shayatin disappeared from view over a low hill.

"If you should see that horse again," she said coolly to the gathered companions, "kill it on sight." With the animal gone, she began to feel a considerable weight lift from her spirit. The anger finally ebbed, and her mind felt like it was clearing.

The human atop the lead Chayya opened his mouth to say something but stopped and pointed behind her. She managed to hop in a circle to see the flyer returning with Asa and Rafal in tow. They landed beside her.

Before either could speak, Neviah said, "Asa, heal me." He reached out and brought a gasp from her as his gift healed her gashed leg and shoulder. Pulling herself up behind Asa, she pointed east. "Fly that way as fast as you can!" she ordered.

Neviah had just enough sense to wave at the squadron leader to follow as Rafal ran forward and took flight. The leader kept pace with them as Neviah relayed everything she could remember about the last few days. Uru was out of sight before the squadron leader sent a messenger back with the dire news. Four pairs of companions accompanied the threesome as they rushed east.

"It is going to be okay," Asa said over his shoulder. "Corban is the toughest Chayya I've ever met."

She nodded but didn't trust her voice at the moment. Her guard had been up the entire time she was with Euroclydon but with her anger finally melted away, her concern for Corban filled her thoughts again. The forests and mountains of Moriah sped away below. After the sun had fallen below the horizon, her eyelids began to droop.

She shook her head and slapped her own cheek, unable to remember the last time she'd slept. Flying felt immensely slow after riding aback the Shayatin, though they were likely covering ground just as quickly. She let her forehead rest on Asa's shoulder.

Tears streaked down her cheeks to drip onto his shirt. If he noticed her crying, he didn't say anything. After traveling many more miles, she was able to collect herself and was wiping away the tears on her face when she noticed they were losing altitude. Asa tapped Rafal on the shoulder, and the Chayya visibly shook himself before flapping his wings to regain height. The squadron leader flew over to them.

"We need to make camp," the Chayya said.

"Then make camp," she replied. "We will continue to fly."

"Your Chayya is exhausted," his rider insisted.

Asa held up a hand and said, "We will continue. We need the rest of you well-rested for the search party. Follow in the morning."

The man and Chayya looked between them for a moment before nodding and flying off into the night. The rest of the squad followed them to the ground as the teens continued.

"Could you get Rafal to tell me what you have been up to?" Neviah asked when she noticed they were descending again. Asa nodded and leaned forward to talk into Rafal's ear. Rafal turned his head to look at them out of his right eye before speaking.

The Chayya spent much of the night relaying his and Asa's training over the past few days. The conversation gravitated away from training to Chayyoth history, food, and sports. It was enough to keep Neviah somewhere between the land of dreams and being groggily aware of what Rafal was saying. Her main purpose in engaging the Chayya was to help keep him awake.

"Why don't you get some sleep?" Asa said after she slapped her face for the hundredth time.

She shook her head. "I can't. It just wouldn't be right, you know." Asa nodded, though she wondered if he really understood.

When the sun rose, it was right in their eyes. "That'll make it easier to stay awake," Asa said with a smile.

Neviah didn't bother to respond or smile back. She appreciated his attempts to distract her, but the sunrise served as a reminder of how long her wounded friend had lain with his injuries. As the sun moved across the sky, it counted down the precious hours they had left to save him, if he was even still alive. Twice, they had to stop so Rafal could rest.

When the sun dipped toward the horizon again, she began to recognize familiar terrain. Panic gripped her as she studied the treetops. Everywhere she looked seemed the same. Corban and she had fled in the middle of the night before dropping into the woods. From the sky, it would be impossible to tell where they'd landed.

"We need to land," she said.

Asa relayed the order, and they were soon on the ground. She hopped off and took a moment to let the feeling reenter her stiff legs.

"Which way?" Rafal asked as Asa sprang from his back beside Neviah.

She quickly spun in a circle, arm raised and ready to point. Only she didn't know which way to point.

"It's okay," Asa said, obviously reading the panic in her eyes. Turning to Rafal, he said, "Start a spiral above us and slowly work your way out. I will head northeast, and Neviah will go southeast. Stay low and don't go anywhere near the mountain and camp."

"It will be impossible to find you again in the dark," Rafal said.

Asa pulled out his book of prophecies and let it turn into the Sword of Re'u. It gave off a beautiful blue glow. Rafal nodded and took flight.

Neviah was about to turn, but Asa grabbed her hand and said, "We will find him." He gave her hand a squeeze and ran off into the forest as twilight settled across the valley.

With sword in hand, Neviah raced into the woods. Her legs felt wooden, barely responsive as she trudged through brush and briars.

"Corban!" she called above the nighttime insects as they took up their endless cadence. Her brain was a fog, and she knew that she should be worried about enemies hearing her, but she no longer cared. Every moment mattered. She had stopped the major bleeding in Corban's wing, but there was no way to know if it was enough.

The night drew on, and Rafal stopped by twice to check on her progress. She began to doubt whether they had stopped in the right area. She could be off by miles in any direction. The sun rose, and Rafal did not come back for a while. Whenever he came back again, she'd decided to go to the mountain where the enemy had uncovered the shadow gate. It was a risk, but from there, she might be able to recreate their flight path.

Rafal tarried still. Neviah's breaths were coming in great gulps, but she refused to stop to rest. She tripped on a tree root and fell to the leaf-strewn ground, where she paused a moment on hands and knees. Behind her, the flap of wings and heavy footfalls told her Rafal was behind her. Wiping the back of her hand across her eyes, she stood and turned around.

Her breath caught in her throat as she looked with wide-eyed disbelief, seeing Corban standing before her. Rafal landed with Asa upon his back, but Neviah barely heeded them as she buried her face in Corban's mane. Her strength gave out then, but her companion's strong arm held her up. She felt hands grab her around her waist, and Asa managed to help her onto Corban's back.

"Thank you," she whispered as they took flight.

Chapter 18

Days passed with no report from Victoria or the other scouts. The news about the shadow gate only increased the fear and rumors already plaguing the city. Their enemies were not only growing in number, but thanks to the shadow gate, they were growing in power as well. The companions maintained a defensive posture while the leaders endlessly debated what to do. Many civilians were evacuating to Esdraelon, the hideaway to the south.

They spent the downtime training with the recruits again. It felt strange going back to lessons after their recent exploits, but Neviah reminded herself there was still so much to learn and threw herself into the routine. After more days passed with no news, she was grateful to have something to take her mind off her own worries. Though Corban was now safe at her side, Victoria and Enya were still in harm's way.

After training on the third day back, while Corban was showering, her mind drifted to her own death, as it often did now that she was flying every day. It was inevitable. Everyone died, but she felt like hers was drawing close. She feared her next battle could be her last. Holding her book of prophecies in her hands, she ran her fingers over the soft cover. When she did fall, Re'u would be there to catch her. That's what he said in the House of the Forest. After reading countless prophecies and having several visions of her own, she'd learned that Re'u's words were not always what she expected they meant. But she did know they were true. It didn't mean she wouldn't die.

There were worse deaths, she told herself, and she had to suppress images of numerous examples from her experiences in that world. Yes, dying from a fall wouldn't be so bad.

"I heard you killed dragons," Ebbe said as he came up beside the bench she was sitting on. The large Chayya, Biyn, was with him, as well as some of the other companions who'd made them their unofficial leaders.

"I couldn't have done it without my friends, and we wouldn't have had a chance without our companions," she said.

"What was it like? Being in combat?"

She thought a moment before replying, "Terrifying. Horrible. Exciting. It was hard to sort through the different emotions at the time. It still is, I guess."

"Could you tell us how you found the sword?" one of the human recruits asked as he walked up.

Neviah was taken aback by their sudden interest in her. She thought they'd decided to hate her. Maybe hearing about the battles and realizing how many kinsmen hadn't returned sobered them to why the instructors wouldn't let them fight.

Thinking for a moment, Neviah started with their first encounter with Tanas and told them everything that'd happened to her to present. They were already familiar with the part about Nebo since Asa had told them about it, but she put her own perspective on it. She admitted to being so afraid of heights that she couldn't climb out a window with Adhira, even though she knew it messed up Asa's escape plan.

"But you've been flying with Corban. How did you master your fear of heights?" a Chayya asked.

"I haven't," she admitted. "I'm terrified every time I'm more than a foot off the ground. At some point, I realized that the only way to put aside my fear is to have something more important than myself to fly for, to fight for."

From there, she continued the story, spending extra time on the recent battles. This fed their hunger for information on the fighting while simultaneously giving them a real idea of what to expect.

"I wish we could have been there," Biyn said.

"I'm glad you didn't have to be," she responded. "I have no doubt all of you would have done well and proven yourselves to be great warriors. It is always best to be as prepared as possible, though. Take me, for instance. There is nothing special about me at all. I'm just a girl from an orphanage in a random city. Yet I was chosen, given this sword," she let her book of prophecies turn into the blade. "Now, I do what is best for our people. If the instructors want you here to train more, then this is where you should be. Period."

Ebbe was nodding. "You are right," he said. "I just wish there was more we could do, you know, to help."

She stood and approached a freshly shampooed Corban. Over her shoulder, she said, "I think the next battle may come to us, and if it is anything like I think it will be, we'll need all the help we can get."

✶✶✶

Over the next two days, twelve extremely exhausted scouts returned, Victoria and Enya showing up last. Though the scouts had reported briefly as they came in, on the evening of the second day, King Hayrik had them all gathered to report in detail.

"Surrendering is the only option," one of the riders said to start off the briefing on the second day.

"Even if we could triple our forces, we wouldn't stand a chance," his companion added.

This put the entire room into a buzz. They were gathered in the great hall with the Patriarchate, King Hayrik, and many military leaders. Someone pounded a gavel until the conversations died.

"We require numbers," King Hayrik called down from his balcony seat, "not advice."

"The enemy was impossible to number, my king," one of the Chayyoth said. "They were as innumerable as the grains of sand upon the ocean shore."

"You exaggerate," one of the Patriarchate insisted.

"I'm afraid he does not," another Chayya said. "If I were to venture a guess, I would say his forces exceed three hundred thousand."

This sent the room into a complete uproar.

"Impossible!" someone called out.

"We must concede!" someone else said.

It was many minutes later before order could be restored.

The companions continued with similar reports. The picture they painted grew bleaker with each scout. There were tens of thousands of Shedim. No fewer than forty dragons were present, well over a hundred thousand foot soldiers, tens of thousands of armored horsemen, and an equal number of archers. Several packs of Se'irim had been spotted, which undoubtedly meant there were many more around somewhere. Corban shared their report. Shayatin were pouring from the shadow gate. Tanas had also managed to recruit a giant rock monster, which Neviah didn't look forward to seeing again.

Every scout's advice was the same. They should concede to Tanas' demands. Even if they attempted to flee, the enemy air units would crush them all. Throughout the reports, two scouts remained silent: Enya and Victoria. The Patriarchate were about to call a vote concerning their options when Corban spoke up.

"Not all the scouts have reported," he said, drawing everyone's attention. "Enya, Victoria, what have you to say?"

All eyes turned to the last of the companions. The two exchanged a few words, and Enya was the first to speak. "The numbers are as have been stated." The Patriarchate nodded and began to turn back to their conversations. "But," Enya said louder, regaining their attention. "I do not believe the situation is hopeless. We must fight."

Bitter laughter. The room was half filled with it.

"And how do you suppose we conquer such a superior force?" one of the Patriarchate asked.

Enya looked at Victoria, and the girl stepped forward to speak. "It's the dragons," she said softly. She was asked to speak up. "The different groups of Shedim were camped around the dragons."

Enya added, "We think that if we can kill the dragons, the Shedim might lose the will to fight when their taskmasters are gone."

There was laughter again, but this time, Corban spoke over them. "She is right! If we can but gain the skies, the ground forces would have a difficult time breaching the mighty walls of Uru."

"They barely even have siege equipment," Enya said. "They are depending on the dragons for that, too."

"But can your team kill forty of them?"

Corban thought for a moment but shook his head. "It would be difficult to even draw near them with so many Shedim in the air."

"Then, if the last two scouts have no further news, it appears as if our options have been unchanged."

"There is one more thing," Enya said. "We flew past the enemy to the border cities, the ones who sided with Tanas." She looked around the room to make sure she had everyone's attention. "They were all burning."

Silence. It took the gathered a while to process this new information. "There have been no other reports to this effect," one of the Patriarchate said. "Who else has seen this?" He looked around at the other scouts, but they all shook their heads.

"No one has flown that far," a Chayya scout said. "The sky is thick with enemies."

"How did you two make it there and back unseen?"

Enya spoke up again. "We didn't. Go unseen, that is. The enemy chased us, but we outflew them every time."

Several people murmured about the credibility of the two females. Corban spoke up. "I vouch for them. They are both above reproach. I believe them. We would be wise to heed their words."

The debating began again in earnest. After an hour of deliberating, only two options were left. They either had to surrender to Tanas and hope he kept his word, which Neviah knew he wouldn't, or they had to flee to the south to the mountain hideaway. The Patriarchate put it to a vote and a large majority chose to flee, likely helped by Enya's and Victoria's revelation concerning the destroyed cities.

"What is the decision of the Chayyoth king?" First Chair of the Patriarchate asked.

King Hayrik moved to the railing of his balcony. "The Chayyoth will stay and fight until all of your people and ours are borne to the safety of the mountains."

"Then, we will increase the evacuations immediately," the First Chair said.

Neviah knew it would be easier said than done.

"What's up?" she asked Adhira as he strode onto the flight

training field a couple of days later.

"Me," he said, adjusting his backpack to his other shoulder. "We're going to be neighbors."

"Why?" she asked with as much disdain as she could muster. She could never let him know how much she had missed having him around, annoying jokes and all.

"Because I couldn't go another day without looking into those beautiful brown eyes of yours," he said, causing her to roll those same eyes. "How have you been?" he asked, more serious than usual.

"Fine."

"Asa told me you went on quite the adventure. I hear you got the first Shayatin kill in a few thousand years."

"Yeah," she said with a smile. "I hadn't thought about it like that. I think the honor goes to Corban, though."

"Can I get your autographs?"

"Why are you really here?" she asked with a sigh.

"It's no longer safe in the city. Mordeth and I are moving up here until everyone is evacuated. I'll be in the barracks with the flying recruits."

"What's going on in the city?"

"You mean aside from the riots?"

"Riots? Adhira, just tell me what's going on."

"The Patriarchate issued orders for everyone to prepare for a city-wide evacuation. Well, not everyone wants to go. The authorities tried evicting people, but that led to full-scale protests, which turned ugly. Troops have been sent throughout the city, but with the streets already crowded with refugees, the evacuation is slow."

"What is wrong with people?" Neviah exclaimed. "Don't they know Tanas isn't a savior? He's coming here to kill us! All of us."

"Apparently, they see things differently."

"You and Mordeth came here to get away from the protests?"

"Sort of." He sat down on the grass beside her as Corban returned from putting their training gear away. "There is a rumor going around that Tanas isn't attacking Moriah to conquer it. People believe he is after the four of us. Some even think that by handing us over to him, he'll leave."

It took a while to fully process the news. After all they'd done for that country, defeating dragons and Asa healing hundreds if not thousands, the people were turning their backs on them. She thought they'd found a home among the Moriahns.

"Not everyone feels that way, not even a lot, really," Adhira said as if he could read her thoughts. "Just enough to make the city unsafe for us."

"What makes them think Tanas is after us?"

"I don't know," he said with a shrug. "I think people still believe he killed Ba'altose. And we say Asa killed Ba'altose. Maybe, in a way, we set them on opposing sides."

"And people are choosing Tanas," she finished in frustration.

"Some," Corban said, finally joining the conversation. "His web of lies is very cleverly woven."

"I can understand some being fooled at first, but now it should be obvious who the good guys and bad guys are," Neviah said.

"People believe in Tanas because they are afraid for the alternative to be true," Corban said. "If Tanas will not accept concessions, it means the Moriahns will have to give up their homeland and flee from a force no one can stop. They have abandoned reason for blind hope."

"How can we make them understand?" Neviah asked. "If they stay, they'll die."

"I'm sure many will find wisdom before the end," her companion assured her.

"I just hope it's not too late when they do."

"Look at that," Asa said, walking up with Victoria, Enya, and Rafal in tow.

"I haven't seen a storm like that in a while," Adhira said. The eastern horizon had turned completely black. No light could penetrate the dense clouds, covering the land in darkness.

"Well, a storm like that might slow the evacuations," Asa said, though he was unusually preoccupied by the black mass. The few clouds dotting the sky above were moving east. That meant the black mass was moving against the wind.

"That is no storm!" Neviah realized, jumping to her feet. "It's an army!"

Chapter 19

There was a tumult of yelling and orders barked all around them as people and Chayyoth realized a battle was upon them. The teens and their companions were frozen to the flight field. After coming to the realization the approaching darkness was the enemy, Neviah began to make out the different blocks making up the formations. She imagined she could even make out the tiny specs of the individual Shedim. They were miles away, but that could mean mere minutes by flying speed.

"What do we do now?" Asa asked Corban.

"You wait for orders," he said, lowering his shoulder to indicate he wanted Neviah to mount. She did, and they were soon flying over treetops. Corban stayed low, which she knew was his way of helping her cope with flying. Trees gave way to an open field that was once richly adorned with grass and flowers. Thousands of booted and furry feet had transformed it into a large brown blemish on Alya's surface.

The companion army spread as far as she could see, from forest edge to forest edge. There were close to seven thousand pairs. Hundreds had voluntarily come out of retirement. It was a formidable force, but she couldn't keep her eyes from straying east. Tens of thousands of Shedim made the number of allies seem small and insignificant.

Corban landed near a large gray tent the Chayyoth hierarchy used as a command post. Neviah jumped to the heavily trodden ground, and they entered. King Hayrik was already there as well as most of the other leaders. A short wait brought the remainders.

"As you can tell," Hayrik began, "our position is direr than we thought. Ever has Alya been a refuge for our people. A million men could not take her from us." He paused to look at the faces of the gathered. "Unfortunately, there are more than just men coming against us. The Shedim outnumber us ten to one. We cannot hope to win out against them."

"What are you saying, my king?" one of the Chayyoth asked.

"We must abandon Alya." That statement broke down the resolve of everyone in the room as many began speaking at once.

"Impossible!" one Chayya said.

"We've already moved the majority of the young and infirm," another said.

Corban raised his paw. The conversations continued for a while, but one by one, the others gave him their attention. He lowered his arm and turned his attention to Hayrik. "I am with you, King Hayrik, whatever your decision. I have only one concern."

"Speak, my friend," the king said.

"We cannot survive without water from the Life Spring."

Hayrik nodded. He'd expected the question. "I have two answers. The first is that the evacuation is a precaution. It is possible that, by some miracle, we may return to her if the battle goes well. The second is for us to retrace the flight of our ancestors across the sea." Silence. Neviah didn't know what to think. She knew little about Chayyoth lore or ancient history aside from what Rafal had shared with her, and even that was foggy at best.

Corban was the first to speak again. "How much time do you need?"

"It will take hours to finish evacuating everyone to a safe location, and Uru is still full of people."

"People who do not want to leave," a rider said.

"Yes, there are many who would welcome Tanas with open arms, but there are still those who linger in the hopes that they can weather the storm of battle. If the city walls are breached, there will be thousands of Moriahns attempting to flee."

"What is the battle strategy, my king?" Corban asked, always getting to the point.

Everyone leaned toward the large map laid on a table. Above the map was wire mesh, creating a three-dimensional representation of the sky above the Uru countryside.

"I want the First and Second Wings to hold these positions here and here," the king said, pointing to an area of the aerial map to the east. "The Third Wing will hold back. I don't have to remind you that we are severely outnumbered. When the enemy attempts to surround the first two wings, the Third will stem the tide where possible."

"What of the ground tactics?" a Chayya asked.

"The Moriahns will be on their own until the air battle is decided. They've pulled their men behind the walls where they can hold out for days against Tanas' land-bound troops. I do not want your men wasting a single arrow on a ground soldier. The only hope of victory lies in air superiority. Save your arrows for the Shedim."

"Any word on the dragons?"

The king shook his head. "There has not been a single dragon reported."

"Maybe they're sitting this one out," a man suggested. "Now that we have a way to kill them, they show their true nature."

Corban shook his head. "They will show. Likely, they'll wait for the fighting to begin."

The news seemed to rattle Neviah more than the others. What trick did Tanas have up his sleeve?

"What should we do?" Neviah asked, referring to her friends. She rarely spoke at the war meetings, but with no dragons to fight, they could be used elsewhere.

"Help where you can," the king said. "But I do not want you to engage in any close combat. You are too valuable to lose to a lucky spear. In fact, I'm attaching you to the Third Wing. If a dragon shows, your standing orders take precedence."

Their standing orders were to take out the dragons by any means necessary.

"If there are no further questions, you are released to meet with your captains. Use any strategies you see fit to carry out my orders. Be swift. Be brilliant. That is all."

When they walked out of the tent, Neviah noticed the enemy had gained much ground. They no longer resembled a storm on the horizon. They looked like a tidal wave looming above them.

"How long until they reach Alya?" Neviah asked as she climbed onto Corban's back.

He looked up at the sky. "They could be here in minutes if they flew at full speed, but they are moving at a gliding pace."

"Why don't they rush in?"

"They are resting on the currents from their long flight. If they rushed in now, they'd be too tired to be effective."

"Then, why don't we rush out to meet them while they're tired?"

"Because we want to delay the fighting as long as possible while the civilians are evacuated," Corban answered.

"That makes sense," she said as Corban flew them back to camp.

Neviah quickly relayed their orders to the others. They went to their respective barracks to gather their few belongings. She put her change of clothes into her backpack but hesitated before reaching into the bottom of her drawer and pulling out her iPod. Victoria was watching her.

"I might as well leave it," Neviah said, trying to sound flippant. "The battery died months ago when we thought we were going to die in the desert."

"Can I see it?" Victoria asked, reaching out her hand. Neviah handed it over.

The blonde girl took a deep breath and let it out before touching her fingers to the charger connection. The screen immediately lit up. With a smile, she handed it back to Neviah. The battery was full.

"I wasn't sure if it would work," she said.

Neviah put her free arm around the girl and hugged her tight. "I can't even begin to explain how much this means to me."

"What's that?" Enya asked, walking over.

Neviah picked one of her favorite songs and put one of the earbuds in the Chayya's ear. Enya's eyes opened wide. "How is this possible?"

"Where we come from, a musician's song can be recorded on one of these, and we can listen to it whenever we want to."

"It is wonderful," Enya said. Neviah let her finish the song, listening with the other earpiece. Corban stood patiently at the door to the barracks, looking toward the sky.

When they were done, he said, "The wings are gathering. We must leave soon."

They filed outside, where Neviah paused to look back. Alya was being evacuated. Would they ever come back? She'd come to think of the place as home. Reluctantly, she turned, mounted up, and let Corban carry her away.

They landed in a large field outside the Third Wing armory. It was a buzz of activity as Chayyoth were issued heavy armor before moving into the field. Several companions were riding down the ranks, putting them into formation.

When Neviah approached the large opening in the side of the armory, the man looked over his glasses at Corban and then at Neviah. "Do you need help with his armor?" he asked slowly.

"I've got it," Neviah said. "I've helped him with his armor before."

"This isn't standard issue, dear. This is heavy armor. And your companion is as large as they come."

"I'll be fine," she said. They wore hardened leather amor when fighting took them far from Alya but how heavy could this armor be?"

The man looked between them a couple more times before yelling over his shoulder, "One size five!"

They moved forward and waited as the pair in front of them were issued their armor. The Moriahn was given a breastplate, which he hefted onto his back like a backpack. Then, he took two duffle bags and followed his companion out of the armory.

"One size five," a heavily muscled man said with a smile, hefting an enormous breastplate onto the table in front of her with a loud thump. She looked back at Corban, but his face was unreadable.

She put her back toward the table and tried to slide it onto her back like the other rider had done. It barely slid a couple of inches. With a grunt, she pulled again, using her lower back to pull it mostly off the table. It took a couple more tries, but she was finally able to get it onto her back. She took a couple of steps away on shaky legs.

"Don't forget your bags," the man said, holding them out to her. She snatched the bags from him, almost losing the breastplate in the process. She vowed to come back and slap that grin off the man's face.

Putting one foot in front of the other, she emerged from the armory, following Corban, who had the decency to set a slow pace. Her legs were burning already.

"Here is good," he said when they had just entered the field.

Neviah let everything she was holding fall to the ground, rubbing her back as she scowled back at the armory.

"How can you fly with all this weight?"

"It is not easy," Corban said, helping her lift the breastplate and holding it to his chest while she fastened the leather straps around his neck and arms. "But the Shedim will be lightly armored. We need every advantage we can get."

She looked around at all the other companions, over a thousand pairs going through the same motions she was. Anticipation mixed with fear cast a shadow over the preparations, hanging in the air like an ever-deepening fog. With every strap she tightened and every buckle she fastened, the coming battle felt more real. They were about to fight a far superior force. Many of the companions around her wouldn't live through the day.

Neviah's fingers fumbled as she secured the last few fasteners, trying to fasten the armor plates to his haunches. Then, Victoria was by her side, helping her tighten the straps. They shared a smile. Asa, Rafal, and Enya stood ready, Enya the only Chayya on the field wearing the hardened leather armor. Just the sight of them gave her strength.

They mounted up as the order was echoed down the lines. This was it. It was really happening. The flights began to launch themselves into the air one at a time.

"Follow me," Corban said. They were soon airborne, following after the Third Wing.

When they transitioned out of Alya's gravity, she became aware of the Chayyoth force spread out in front of her. Seeing all three wings, thousands of companions, flying in formation filled her with awe. They were a flying wall that seemed impossible to penetrate, filling her with confidence, which only lasted until they neared the enemy.

The sheer number of Shedim dwarfed the Chayyoth army. They were like a mass of insects that only grew larger the closer they came. The Third Wing stopped where they'd been ordered to wait, but the other two wings continued on.

Suddenly, the Shedim noticeably picked up speed. So did the Chayyoth, their companions shooting arrows as the masses neared.

Hundreds of Shedim fell from the sky, only to be replaced by more. The two forces were soon hurtling toward one another, spears extended on both sides. Neviah gripped Corban's mane and leaned forward as she watched, daring not to breathe as the two forces came together.

There was a bone-shattering impact of armor as the forces' convergence echoed back to her position. Hundreds of bodies fell from the sky, mostly Shedim but many companions as well.

The companions plowed into the Shedim, their superior size and armor wreaking havoc through the enemy lines as their spears reached through to the following ranks. Blood drained from Neviah's face when the rear rank of Shedim rose up above the front line. They were a tidal wave of soldiers, cresting over the battle to come crashing down on the ever-decreasing number of companions.

Hand signals were passed around the Third Wing, and then they rushed forward. Just as the wave of Shedim started their descent onto the First and Second Wings, the Third crashed into them. Corban, Enya, and Rafal held back, following their orders not to take part in close-quarters combat. They were close enough, however, to pour their silver arrows into the ranks of Shedim. Their arrows felled Shedim by the handful, but there were always more. It was like scooping away a handful of dry sand on the beach just to have more sand fill in the hole.

Not too far from them, Neviah saw a Chayya get his wing severed. His companion fell off as he spiraled out of control. Without hesitating, Rafal shot forward, and Asa jumped from his back, eliciting screams from both Victoria and Neviah. With his arms flat at his side, Asa sped like a bullet toward the falling Chayya. Rafal folded his wings and dove for the other rider.

Asa reached the Chayya and grabbed at his mane but missed. He tumbled away but was able to right himself and reached out again. Neviah saw his fist tighten on the mane while simultaneously healing him. The Chayya spread his wings, and Asa put a foot on each wing to add strength to them as the Chayya tried to pull out of his hurtling descent. Neviah held her breath.

They managed to level out and then climbed skyward. Rafal had successfully caught the rider, and Neviah cheered as rider and mount were reunited. Asa transferred to his companion, and the ones they'd saved flew back into the fight; Asa and Rafal took up their positions near their friends.

After the initial impact with the Third Wing, the companions engaged the Shedim in a three-dimensional fight to climb higher than their opponent. The Chayyoth thinned and stretched as far as they could, but the Shedim were too many. They flowed around the companions from above, below, and both flanks. Neviah and her friends were in a frenzy of firing, but what could they do against tens of thousands of Shedim?

Neviah had an idea and ceased firing, waving to get Victoria's attention. When the other girl was looking her way, Neviah pointed at the Shedim, back at Victoria, and then made the sign for lightning. The blonde took a deep breath and let her bow turn into a sword as she laid it across her lap. Neviah took up her bow again and resumed firing. She wasn't as good as her friend, but there were so many enemies that it was impossible to miss. Intermittently, she looked back to the other girl.

Victoria was in deep concentration, which was in itself a miracle with everything that was going on. For a while, it seemed as if nothing was happening. The enemy continued to swell, and the Chayyoth were forced into a controlled retreat to keep from being surrounded. The fighting was coming closer to Neviah and her friends, but they dared not move for fear of interrupting Victoria. Enya held them in place with rapid wing flaps that she wouldn't be able to maintain for long.

A few Shedim broke free of the mass and dove for them. Neviah dropped one with her bow, with Asa dropping two before they were on them. Corban shot forward and raked several aside while Neviah stabbed and slashed where she could. The companions made quick work of the enemy squadron, but it wouldn't be long before the thickest part of the battle was upon them as the enemy pressed forward, forcing back the companion army.

Neviah rubbed a static shock she received from Corban's armor. It was then that she became aware of the hair standing on her arms. Her companion's mane was rising with the sudden charge in the air. They turned their eyes to Victoria, where her hands were covered in tiny bolts of lightning. Enya's fur was puffed out, making her look like a giant stuffed animal. The lightning grew in size, enveloping Victoria and her companion but not harming them. They could hear it crackling as the bubble of energy expanded further and further before she held up her hands, and the lightning disappeared altogether.

Suddenly, with a thunderous crack, as if a cannon had been fired right next to them, lightning shot from her outstretched hands. It spread in a dense spider web covering the entire perimeter of aerial combat. Each of the thousand different bolts found a target among the Shedim. The bodies rained to the ground below, gouging a hole in the enemy ranks that couldn't easily be filled. Neviah felt sick to her stomach at seeing so much death happen all at once. Victoria retched over the side of her companion.

As devastating as her attack was, however, it barely made a dent in the Shedim numbers. Fortunately, their confidence was shattered. The Shedim momentum stalled, and the companions took full advantage of their fear. The Wings cut deep into the enemy, pushing them back the way they'd come. The Shedim lines broke and they were soon in full retreat. The companions pursued, cutting down many enemies before the order was given to fall back and regroup.

Neviah knew they'd be back. There were still so many Shedim in the sky that the ground below them was shaded from the sun as if from a passing cloud. Looking down brought her attention to the ground battle, which she hadn't known was happening. Tanas' forces were assaulting the walls of Uru below where the Chayyoth held air positions. There were giant, scaly creatures with horns covering their bodies, pulling stones from the walls under a hail of arrows, which neither seemed to harm nor deter the creatures.

Neviah got her friends' attention and made the sign for archery and then the sign for big enemy. They nodded, and silver arrows showered down on the giant creatures. The enemy's siege was halted when their last sieger fell to the projectiles. The humans cheered, but Corban brought them back to reality.

"We haven't won yet."

Neviah looked to the east, where the fleeing Shedim were slowly reforming. Behind them was another mass that could only be described as a floating mountain. She could only see the behemoth through momentary gaps left by the reforming enemy. Then, the Shedim separated into two groups, one on each side of the mountain, and Neviah saw it for what it really was: an enraged seven-headed dragon with blood-red scales. Iblis had joined the battle.

Chapter 20

If Corban hadn't been holding Neviah up, her legs would have failed her. Iblis was a monster beyond anything they could have imagined. Red scales covered a body so large that it didn't seem possible for his wings to keep him in the air despite having a wingspan several hundred feet wide. Each of his seven heads sported a horn just above the eyes. The two end heads, as well as the center head, also had a horn on top of the snout.

The messenger that came to give them their new orders wasn't needed. If they didn't stop Iblis, no one would. They came together, hovering as tightly as they could so Corban could tell them his plan, but before opening his mouth, a roar sounded from behind and below them, followed by another, then another. Scattered across the battlefield below, men began turning into dragons. The dragons hadn't skipped the fight; they'd hidden in plain sight! Neviah couldn't keep count but there had to be more than twenty dragons launching themselves into the air all around them as more transformed still.

Not all were headed for the companion army, as Neviah would expect, but most made a straight line for Alya and Uru. The refugees! They were going to kill the civilians. There were caravans of people leaving the western gate of Uru. Civilian Chayyoth were still transporting the remaining young, old, and infirm from Alya to the mountain pass. They needed more time.

Corban looked between the large group of dragons and the colossal Iblis. There were only the three swords in the air. What were they supposed to do? From somewhere on the wall below, a silver arrow streaked skyward and hit one of the dragons in the head, sending it crashing down onto the city streets, collapsing several buildings under its bulk. They had Adhira, too.

The House of the Forest

The sight shook Corban from his moment of indecision. "You four must delay the dragons," Corban said loudly to the other two sets of companions. "Neviah and I will have to handle Iblis." With those broad orders, Corban turned and flew toward the approaching seven-headed dragon. The Chayyoth Wings charged in around them, splitting into two groups to take on the Shedim.

Though still far away from their target, Neviah shot arrows as fast as she could at the beast. Iblis was too fast. Many arrows meant for his heads were easily dodged. Others were blasted away with his fiery breath. Arrows wouldn't do the job. They needed to get in close so she could use her sword. There were too many heads. It would be difficult to come close enough to the dragon without being blasted with fire.

Hundred-foot streams of fire spewed forth from each of Iblis' mouths as they neared, consuming companions and Shedim indiscriminately. Many companions were turned to ash in the first few seconds. The remaining companions were forced to flee the fiery attacks.

Altering their course, Corban began climbing higher and higher into the sky. Neviah turned and kept shooting at the seven-headed monster. Even if her arrows didn't hit the intended target, at least they distracted a couple of the heads from killing companions. The temperature grew colder and the air thinner, but still, Corban climbed. All sound was lost except the wind in her ears. The air battle below looked surreal. There was fire and falling bodies everywhere, but it was absurdly quiet, all sound lost on the winds below.

Neviah soon realized what her companion was doing. They were positioning themselves behind Iblis, flying higher than the Shedim could. Corban paused in the air, right where they'd start their descent. Looking over his shoulder, his voice thick, he said, "What if today is the day, Neviah? What if today is the day you die?"

She smiled and pulled out her iPod. Putting the earbuds in, she found the song she wanted and secured the music player beneath her leather armor. The opening cords began to play.

Looking her friend in the eye and raising her sword, she said, "Then let it be today."

With a roar, Corban folded his wings, and they rocketed down, zooming through the sky like a missile. Their speed increased to the point where her vision began to spot with blackness, but she gritted her teeth and refused to lose consciousness. Her ponytail became a whip, slashing at her back and neck, but she refused to feel the pain.

A wall of Shedim formed in front of them with spears ready, but Corban didn't slow. Neviah let her shield form around her and her companion, and they blasted through the enemy. The impact jarred her arm and pulled her from Corban's back. She tumbled for a moment before putting her arms to her side and aiming her face at the seven-headed dragon.

By moving her arms slightly, she was able to alter her path just enough to where she was no longer aiming at the dragon's back but at his right wing. Somehow, the timing was right because when she struck the wing, it was on a downward push, which absorbed nearly all of her momentum. If she'd landed on Iblis' back, she would have died. As the wing rose again, she tumbled down upon the scaly back. It was like moving across polished steel.

She wanted to look around for her companion, but her arrival hadn't gone unnoticed by the Shedim. Rising to her feet, she had just enough time to block an arrow with her shield. Scores of Shedim were landing all around her. She blocked a sword swing and managed to sever two arms before she had to take another defensive stance. She blocked blow after blow, but the enemy was so dense she couldn't make a counterstrike. Iblis appeared to be unaware of the battle happening upon his back.

Neviah's shield became a partial cocoon, protecting her from the enemy strikes. She needed to move! Every second she wasted meant more lives lost. It was time Iblis knew of her presence. Stabbing straight down with the Sword of Re'u, she tore a deep gash in his scales.

She doubted it was more than a scratch to the seven-headed mountain, but it had drawn blood and his attention. The air inside the shield grew unbearably hot as one of the dragon heads blew fire at her position.

As soon as the fire let up, Neviah sprang into action, sprinting as fast as she could toward the center neck. Every Shedim around her blew away as ash on the wind.

She made it several yards before the head that'd breathed the fire recovered from its surprise. Suddenly, all seven heads were turned and looking directly at her. As seven streams of fire made their way toward her flesh, Neviah hunkered down with one of the dragon's protruding spikes at her back. The Forest Shield made an airtight wall in front of her, but the fire went on so long that she thought she'd run out of air.

She needed to inflict a greater wound than last time. Holding the shield in place, she let the sword turn into a bow. She reached down with her shield hand, barely managing to get the tips of her fingers around the string. Pulling it back as best as she could, she sent the arrow burrowing through the dragon's bulk. The fire stopped as the seven heads howled in pain. She quickly covered the space between her and the center neck, but one of the heads quickly recovered from the shock of the wound. She brought up the shield just in time to deflect the fire.

The force of the blast was so great, though, that it pushed her far to the right and dangerously close to the edge of Iblis' back. The head on the right saw her coming and attempted to duck away from the reach of her sword. The next jet of fire pushed her back and off the dragon's back between the sixth and seventh heads. With her footing lost, Neviah took the Sword of Re'u in both hands and dug it to the pommel into the seventh neck. As the head bent lower to get out of reach, it inadvertently created a direct path for her sword to slide down. She willed the blade to be as long as possible as it passed between the dragon's eyes and straight down the center of the snout, leaving a devastating gash that nearly split the head in two. There was a split second where she looked Iblis directly in his horror-stricken face, but then she was falling.

Her music stopped and the only sound was the dragon's roars mixed with the wind. The wind whipped her hair into her face as she watched the dragon writhing in the sky. Iblis wasn't dead, but he was gravely wounded. The head she'd sliced through hung limply, bleeding as the dragon retreated. The Shedim fought on but their greatest champion had been bested. Her heart went out to the companions, the refugees, and her friends. There was nothing else she could do for them. Then, she turned to face the rapidly approaching ground.

The Armor of Light

She never thought it would take so long. In her prophetic visions, she would fall, and then she would die. Terror threatened to overwhelm her, but she fought it down. As the land neared, she couldn't stop the tears that flowed from her eyes. There was so much she wanted to do with her life. She should have done more for her friends. Closing her eyes, she waited for the impact. Would she feel it?

Suddenly, two strong arms wrapped around her waist. Re'u said he would be there to catch her, but they didn't belong to Re'u. A roar filled her ears as Corban spread his wings despite the impossible speed they were falling at. Corded muscle strained against the force, bulging through the fur. What was he doing? It was too late for her. There was no way he could pull up in time!

Their fall was no longer straight down but angled slightly from Corban's efforts. The ground still rushed up to meet them. It wouldn't be enough. They were moving at an angle but their impact with the ground could not be avoided.

Just before they hit, Corban wrapped her tightly in his wings, rolled so his back was facing down, tucked his head down protectively over hers, and whispered, "Today is not your day."

The force of the impact drove the air from her lungs. They tumbled along the unyielding terrain, but Corban held firm until the end when she was flung from his grasp to crash against a tree. She lay there dazed. Her ribs were cracked, she was sure, and her left arm was broken. Fighting to regain her breath against the searing pain that came with moving, she stumbled to her feet and over to her companion's prone form.

"Corban!" she screamed as she knelt beside him. His armor was irreparably battered, and his body lay broken. She rubbed his furry cheek. "Corban?" she cried softly, though she knew there would be no answer. His mighty chest was still.

Chapter 21

"It was supposed to be me!" she wailed, holding Corban's head in her lap, rocking back and forth uncontrollably. "Why?" she cried into the fur on his face. "Why did you do it?"

It was supposed to be her lying broken on the ground. Instead, Corban died for her and left her all alone. It wasn't fair. How could he do that to her? They had a bond like nothing she'd ever experienced before, and now it was gone. Gone because dragons and evil men wanted to conquer the world.

She stopped rocking as her grief was shadowed by anger. Gritting her teeth, she balled her fist and pounded the ground. Her body shook with rage. To the east, armored knights were skirting the city's southern wall, coming straight for her. Laying her companion's head gently on the ground, Neviah stood and waited. Let them come. She would have her vengeance.

The pounding of hooves behind her caused her to turn. Adhira came to a sliding halt atop a large white horse. He looked at Corban, then at her.

"I'm sorry," he said softly.

She did not respond but instead turned toward the approaching men. The knights were far away but moving fast despite wearing full plate armor. The Sword of Re'u was no respecter of armor.

Adhira saw her intent and said, "We need to go."

She didn't respond.

"Neviah, your arm is broken, and the rest of you looks pretty banged up, too. You can't fight in this condition."

"I will kill them all," she responded, her voice a sheet of ice.

"Corban wouldn't want you to die here," he said.

She spun on him, the heat of her fury spilling over him as she yelled, "You don't get to do this!" She gestured at him with the point of her blade. "You know nothing of what I just lost!"

She ignored the hurt she saw in his eyes and turned back to the approaching enemies. Adhira didn't deserve her rage.

"Let me at least get you to Asa so he can heal you. You are no good like this."

Her arm was throbbing fiercely, shooting pain through her nerves with each heartbeat. The shock of her injuries was passing, and one by one, they were revealing themselves. It even hurt to breathe. Still, she held her position. The knights were getting closer. Their yelled orders could be heard above the grinding hooves of their mounts. Shadows trailed them, evidence they underwent the Shayatin ceremony she'd witnessed at the shadow gate. They were soulless now.

"Look at me, Neviah." When she continued to ignore him, his voice took on an edge of urgency she was unaccustomed to hearing from the always-confident Indian. "Look at me!"

She slowly turned her face up to his, tears streaming hot down her cheeks. "They killed him, Adhira," she said with a sob. "They took him from me."

"I know," he said gently.

"I can't leave him."

"You need to come with me," he insisted.

She shook her head.

"I saw what happened," he continued. The memory was too recent and painful for her to revisit, but Adhira kept talking. "He died to save your life. Are you just going to throw it away now? Come with me, or his death will have been for nothing."

He held out his hand for her. She hesitated, looking back at her slain companion, her friend. How could she leave him there?

As if reading her thoughts, Adhira said, "Corban would not want you to die defending his body."

Adhira was right. Corban gave everything for her. She needed to make his sacrifice count. Without letting go of her sword, Neviah reached her arm up, and Adhira grabbed her wrist and pulled her up behind him. As they sped away, the soulless knights overtook the hill where Corban lay.

The House of the Forest

Adhira used his sword to slice through several trees, so they fell across the path behind them. Even without obstructions, the pair would have easily outpaced the weighted-down horsemen. The two of them did not head for the western gate, where Adhira had come from, but circled around to the southern side of the city. The eastern bridge stretched over a deep canyon, which led south to the beach. It used to be a riverbed, but the water had been diverted hundreds of years past to feed the city's aqueducts. Adhira and Neviah crossed the bridge to the other side.

Everywhere on the other side of the bridge were refugees. Thousands were still fleeing the city, only to be bottlenecked on the opposite side of the bridge. The bridge itself was wide, accommodating hundreds at a time, but the caves leading into the mountain pass were a different story. Thousands of civilians were huddled on the other side of the bridge, trying to funnel into the narrow tunnels. The narrowness of the caves was supposed to be their salvation since no enemy could pursue them in force. Unfortunately, it would be the death of many if the enemy caught them outside.

A steady stream of Moriahn soldiers and civilians stretched from Uru's southeasternmost gate to the bridge as the enemy attempted to surround the city walls. Upon seeing the enemy, the stream of people turned into a panicked tide of bodies, rushing for the safety of the opposite shore.

"Form ranks on the far side of the bridge!" Mordeth yelled above the screams. He wasn't a general but was obeyed as if he were one. Hundreds of soldiers filled the friendly side of the stone bridge, holding position while the bulk of the civilians made it across. The approaching enemy soldiers were still several hundred yards from the mouth of the bridge.

Enya and Rafal landed in the middle of the bridge. They and Victoria were unharmed, but Asa's tunic was smoking, and he had a nasty-looking burn across his neck and arms. Neviah hated that he couldn't heal himself. She jumped from Adhira's horse, pushing her way through the soldiers with her good arm until she was out on the bridge with her friends. Adhira dismounted and was right behind her. Victoria and Asa jumped to the ground when they saw them approaching.

"The skies are lost," Asa said with a strained voice. His wounds must've hurt badly. Her own arm was throbbing so badly she could barely think. Asa looked into her face a moment, then reached out his hand and healed her. She looked down at her perfectly functioning arm.

"Thank you," she said, though her voice was still thick. Asa paused a moment as if he wasn't quite sure her injury was gone.

Without taking his eyes off her, he asked, "Where's Corban?" Fresh tears rolled down her cheeks, answering his question. "I'm so sorry."

Enya and Rafal bowed their heads and Victoria hugged her tight. She wanted to bury her face in her friend's shoulder, but Adhira's words pulled her back to the present.

"What are they doing?" he asked, pointing toward Alya.

Neviah had been so focused on everything happening on the ground that she'd failed to see what was going on in the sky. She looked on in horror as the dragons circled the lowest part of Alya. Asa and Victoria had killed a handful but there were still more than a dozen of the monsters. A few pockets of companions could be seen fleeing toward the east. There were so few of them left.

The Shedim held their positions to the east of the city. From that distance, they resembled a dense cloud of mosquitos. They still numbered in the tens of thousands. Neviah ran a shaky hand over her hair and down her ponytail. No matter how many they killed, there were always more.

"Get off the bridge!" a soldier yelled from the friendly side. The enemy knights were gaining momentum for a charge as they exited the tree line. Neviah and her friends were sitting ducks. Before they could take a step for cover, Adhira froze with a look of terror stamped on his face. She followed his eyes back to Alya.

The dragons had landed on the giant chain connecting Alya to the land below and were breathing a constant stream of fire, concentrated on one section of the chain. They weren't trying to capture Alya. They were trying to destroy it!

A thunderous explosion echoed through the valley and the surrounding hills as the chain was rent in two. The dragon that broke the chain was slung away as the tremendous tension snapped it around like a whip. For a few seconds, nothing else happened. Alya stood poised above Uru, where it had been for thousands of years.

Then, with a groan like the world itself was wailing in pain, Alya began to break apart. Chunks of stone the size of buildings broke off and fell to the city below. A great chasm split through the Chayyoth homeland, starting at the chain and disappearing into the clouds. Screams tore from the throats of thousands of refugees as the sundered Alya began to descend.

"There are still thousands of people in the city!" Asa yelled helplessly. The scores of people who were disillusioned by Tanas were about to meet certain death. Unable to make herself watch, Neviah turned away. That was when she saw Victoria.

Her face was flushed, both arms raised to the sky as she stared inflexibly at Alya. Neviah slowly turned back to face the broken planet. Halfway on its path to crush Uru, it hung frozen in the air. Victoria was doing it. Somehow, she was holding the weight of a small planet.

When Neviah looked back, the other girl's nose was beginning to bleed, and her arms were slowly dropping. The two chunks of Alya began to lower again.

"Asa, Adhira, grab her arms!" Neviah yelled as the boys obeyed her command. The planet stopped falling again. "Asa, don't heal her. We don't want to break her concentration."

Neviah turned around, and suddenly, they had another problem to contend with. Enemy captains were yelling orders again, bringing their knights' attention back to the Moriahns. They were soon over the shock of Alya's destruction and, within moments, were careening down the bridge toward them. The teens and their companions couldn't move without Victoria dropping the moon-sized Alya.

Why couldn't they just leave them alone? Neviah's grief-fueled rage returned in an instant. The enemy caused the death of her companion, and now they were going to kill her other friends. Letting her sword turn into a bow, she squared off with the mounted knights. The black smoke of the soulless trailed behind them.

"Take my place," Adhira pleaded from his position, holding up Victoria's arm. "I'm a better swordsman than you." He must have known she'd ignore him.

As fast as she could fire, she sent several arrows into the front rank of riders. The smart move would have been to aim for the horses instead of the riders, but she couldn't bring herself to shoot the animals.

Such was the power of the silver arrows that each one passed through several ranks of riders. The sheer number of armored bodies littering the bridge effectively broke the charge. A horseman swung down at her as he neared, thinking to make an easy kill and keep going. Instead, she let her shield grow to her full height while putting all her weight behind it.

The sword struck the shield, and the impact knocked the soldier off his mount. He was so heavily armored that he couldn't quickly stand to his feet. Rafal grabbed the man and tossed him over the side of the bridge, where his primeval screams and curses faded into the ancient riverbed. Enya and Rafal knocked aside a few more occupied horses, and then it was a foot battle. The knights climbed over their fallen comrades, making a new line with sword and shield.

Adhira was yelling something at Neviah, but it was lost with the wind in her ears. She ran to the newly formed enemy, making a gap with her bow before letting it turn back into the sword. Moriahn soldiers, led by Mordeth, caught up with her just as she came into contact with the enemy.

Her shield grew large enough to block several simultaneous stabs from enemy soldiers. The Sword of Re'u flashed out and clove a man in two, armor and all. Neviah stepped over him and stabbed another. With the Forest Shield growing and shrinking as needed, she had considerable protection from any strike coming from her left.

She roughly deflected a spear meant for her heart. Corban's words came to her then. "Graceful," he had said on many occasions. She relaxed her stance, allowing her movements to become more fluid. The blood pounding through her heart and veins provided the rhythm as she wove her dance of death among the enemy.

Anywhere she saw the emblem of the red horseman, she attacked, leaving the Moriahns behind, not caring. She was completely surrounded by the enemy, but no one could get a strike in. Many were still facing front, away from her, fighting the Moriahns, but her presence was noticed by many. And then they died. They were slow, armored for breaking ranks with horsepower.

Her path of destruction cleared an area of the bridge, bringing her near the edge. One man saw her coming, and instead of using his spear, he tried to rush her with his shield up. She simply rolled out of the way, and the shadow-shrouded man plummeted from the bridge to his death.

She felt her rage swelling with every sword stroke. It was their fault Corban was dead. They brought the war, the death. The Moriahns were a peaceful people, and they were only being killed because Tanas wanted to rule the world.

She remembered her sword biting into one of his dragon heads. She let a grim smile come to her face. Maybe she killed the monster. The smile disappeared. No, that would be too easy. Iblis had six more just like it.

The soldiers nearest her were fleeing. She tried to catch them, but the bodies of horses and men made movement nearly impossible. Suddenly, a shadow fell over the bridge. Fighting died away as every eye looked up. Hundreds of yards above them, one of the chunks of Alya was passing over. Victoria was moving it out to sea!

The size was mind-boggling. So close to the ground, the arid, rocky terrain that had been outside the world's atmosphere was now visible. A piece of the enormous chain that had held the planet in place dragged on the ground, cutting a deep trench across the Moriahn countryside. The enemy soldiers desperately tried to move out of the way as the chain moved through their ranks.

Then, she saw the chain was no longer dragging but dropping with ground-shaking impacts as each link was loosed and struck the dirt. Rocks and debris preceded the end of the chain.

A large humanoid creature, about the size of a Shedim, was chained with smaller chains to the last giant link, his arms and legs splayed out in the center of the link. Before the final link struck the ground, the chains binding him broke, and despite the three-hundred-foot fall, the creature landed on his feet. There were more chains wrapped around his body, which slowly coiled off of him, making a pile like a snake around his feet.

His face was hairy and slightly elongated, making him look canine. The heavily muscled arms and chest looked human, though larger and hairier than most. Around his neck hung a gold chain with a silver key adorning it. The key was difficult to look at, almost as if the light was bending around it and making her feel dizzy. One fist was clinched around a dark sword, which looked exactly like the sword Ba'altose used against them. It had to be another sword of power.

The creature stepped from the chains and approached the bridge. Neviah backed up to Victoria, who was still occupied with moving the two behemoth pieces of Alya. Adhira and Asa were still holding up her arms. The blonde-haired girl was sagging heavily in the boys' grasp.

There wasn't anything Neviah could do for her. She turned to face their newest foe. He must have been the Imprisoned One Corban spoke of, Siarl, she believed his name was. Was the entire war started just to free that one creature?

Neviah pulled up her bow as the creature stepped onto the bridge. He examined the bodies of the knights strewn around him and followed the trail of destruction with his eyes until they locked on Neviah. She aimed at the center of his chest and loosed the arrow. It sped for his heart, but lightning fast, he knocked the arrow aside with his sword. He hadn't even slowed his stride.

She'd only ever seen Adhira able to do that. She sent several more at him rapid fire. He nimbly dodged most while knocking away the rest. His features remained unchanged. She wasn't even worth a grimace. He stopped a few feet in front of her, in one of the few areas clear of bodies. She let her bow turn into a sword. Then, he spoke.

His voice was guttural. If a wolf could speak, its voice would sound exactly like what she heard. "Are you the greatest warrior?" he asked, almost hopeful.

"No," Adhira said from behind her, where he held their friend's arm. "I am."

"Wrong," Mordeth said, stepping from the line of Moriahns.

"He has a sword of power," Neviah said. "You wouldn't stand a chance against that."

"We will see," Mordeth said, coming to stand before the creature.

"I challenge you," the creature said.

"I accept," said the Moriahn.

The creature looked at Mordeth's sword. "You wish to fight with ordinary weapons?" he said with his first real show of emotion: disdain.

"Yes."

The creature picked up a sword off the ground. His blade of power turned into a black book, which he tucked into a satchel he laid behind him.

"Let us begin," he growled. He strode forward confidently and struck at Mordeth. The sword moved so swiftly that Neviah thought for sure the sword master was done for. At the last second, Mordeth knocked the blade aside and took a step back. Even he looked surprised at the enemy's speed.

The creature slashed several times in quick succession, putting Mordeth off balance. The key hanging from his neck bounced around as the creature fought. What did that key go to? Mordeth blocked every strike but wasn't quick enough on the last one, earning him a slice to his left arm. He broke contact, and for a brief instant, Neviah saw his eyes. He was outmatched, and he knew it.

Challenge or not, Neviah wasn't going to let him die. She shot an arrow meant for the canine's back, but as if he knew it was coming, he easily sidestepped it and continued his assault on Mordeth.

Mordeth blocked high, then low, but before he could bring up his blade again, the enemy ran him through the chest with his sword. Neviah froze in shock. She couldn't believe it was over so quickly. Mordeth was the greatest swordsman in Moriah, perhaps the world, and he fell in seconds.

She became aware of Adhira yelling.

"No!" he screamed, dropping Victoria's arm and running toward his fallen mentor. Then, several things happened at once. The first was Victoria losing her hold on both pieces of Alya.

Chapter 22

When Adhira let go of her wrist, Victoria let out a piercing cry as she made a pushing motion with both hands before collapsing into Asa's arms. As if thrown by an invisible giant, the piece of Alya hanging over the bridge was tossed so far out to sea it was lost to sight. Similarly, the chunk hanging over the city soared through the air directly toward the largest swarm of Shedim. Their deaths came so quickly that none had time to move. It happened before Adhira had taken his second step toward Mordeth.

Even though they were enemies, the sight of so many living beings dying at one time, tens of thousands, unnerved Neviah, but she didn't have time to dwell on it. The canine creature was reaching down for his blade of power as Adhira approached with the Sword of Re'u ready.

When the piece of Alya struck the ground far to the east, it caused an earthquake beyond anything she could have imagined. Though it was hurled far away, when it impacted, the world around them was thrown into upheaval. The topsoil rippled as if it were an ocean wave, knocking everyone to the ground. With a thunderous crash, the walls of Uru came tumbling down. Many of the city's buildings toppled.

An earsplitting crack ripped the bridge from its western supports, sending many enemy soldiers screaming into the widening gorge. Moriahn soldiers fled to the opposite side, though some fell through fishers created as the bridge began to crumble. After losing the northern abutment, the bridge buckled and twisted. Neviah tried to regain her feet, but the force of the falling bridge made standing impossible.

She saw Asa on the back of Rafal as they swooped in and

snatched up Adhira, who was yelling for vengeance as the Chayya's strong arms carried him off. The canine creature stood calmly on the buckling bridge, completely unconcerned about the imminent crash with the dried riverbed below. Siarl stared at Neviah as two Chayya paws wrapped around her waist. Enya lifted her in the air and deftly dodged the rubble raining from the canyon walls.

When Enya set her down near the few remaining refugees, she was able to see the full extent of the damage. The city lay in ruins, though amazingly, more than half the buildings still stood to some degree. The ground was completely distorted where mounds of earth had pushed up large trees and new valleys had been created. Far to the east, a new mountain range loomed, taller than any other. The remains of Alya.

Hundreds of thousands of enemy soldiers occupied the opposite shore from her. They had suffered heavy casualties in the quake but were still an enormous force. She thought about sending over a few arrows, but it was no use. There were just too many. There were always too many.

Nearly all the refugees had entered the tunnels, which were miraculously intact, and the soldiers were mostly inside when Victoria regained her senses and spotted something on the horizon. "What's that?"

It appeared as if the ocean was rising in the distance and was already engulfing a small island.

"Oh no," Neviah breathed when she remembered the other piece of Alya. Thrown out to sea. "Hurry!" she yelled to the soldiers still filing in. She knew it was little use. Everyone was already moving as fast as they could. The ocean rose ever higher as it rushed toward Uru.

Enemy soldiers began fleeing to the other side of the city as seawater rose over the shores, ripping apart docks and traveling up the land, washing away everything in its path. The canyon was suddenly filled to overflowing, the water lapping up the hill toward the few remaining Moriahns. The rising river did not worry her as much as the accompanying wall of water hurtling toward them.

As it approached, it loomed higher and higher, rising to nearly two hundred feet. When it reached the former shore, it began to curve out and over the land. Asa and Victoria could have flown away on their companions, but they stayed and were part of the press trying to squeeze into the tunnels. The water blocked out the sun as it brought down thousands of tons of water on the countryside.

Neviah and Adhira were the last in the tunnel. They rushed in to stand shoulder to shoulder with Asa and Victoria, who had their shields ready. Without speaking, they all held up their shields, which connected and expanded to form a wall between the Moriahns and the crashing waves. The roar of water was deafening as it beat against the mountainside, causing the entire mountain to shake. Parts of the ceiling came down near them, showering down rock and debris.

They could hear the mouth of the cave collapse under the weight of the water but the rest of the tunnels, for the most part, miraculously held. They waited for several minutes, holding their shields in place.

"Do you think the entrance sealed itself when it collapsed?" Asa asked. "It could take a long time for the water to recede."

"I'll look," Adhira said. Without moving, he nodded. "The entrance is sealed. No water is getting through."

They let their shields shrink. The tunnel had turned completely dark except for the glow coming from their swords. The soldiers in front of them continued to push forward.

It was many miles later before they walked into sunshine. Adhira sat down on the first rock he saw and put his head in his hands. Neviah slumped to the ground beside him and stared at the ground. She felt numb, emotionally and physically.

"I don't understand," Adhira said at length, echoing the thoughts in her head. "We're the good guys. We're not supposed to lose. How did this happen? Why did Re'u even bring us here?"

No one had an answer for him.

"Who was that beast that killed Mordeth?" he asked, his voice breaking to betray the emotions he was trying to hold at bay.

"He is called the Imprisoned One," Neviah said when she could trust herself to talk again. "His name is Siarl. Corban told me he was captured a long time ago and imprisoned in Alya."

"Was the war started just to free him?" Adhira asked. "Tanas killed thousands of people to free one man? Why?"

"I don't have those answers," she said, putting a hand on his. He was seething with the same rage she'd felt only hours before. Now, she was numb. "In the end, we will win," she said, though there was no weight to her words. "We just need a plan."

"I hope the plan involves a way to kill Dog Boy," Adhira said. "Mordeth was one of the greatest swordsmen in the world and the Imprisoned One killed him in moments. How can we beat something like that?"

"Maybe he died in the bridge collapse or the flood," Asa offered.

Adhira was already shaking his head. "No way. I saw him fall from Alya hundreds of feet, and he landed as if he'd jumped from the back of a horse. He's alive and he's going to play a big part in whatever Tanas is planning. You can be sure of that."

Rafal spoke next. "When I was younger, my grandfather used to tell me a story about Alya's chain, but it may have just been a story."

"Go on," Adhira urged.

"It had three purposes. The first, which Neviah just told you, was to hold the Imprisoned One until the appointed day, whatever that means. The second reason for the chain was to hold Alya in place. The third…" He hesitated, but Adhira made a circle motion with his hand for the Chayya to continue. "The third purpose was to act as one of the seals to the Abyss."

"The Abyss?" Neviah asked.

"Specifically, the place where the great beast Chemosh is kept. It is one of the most feared monsters in all creation, surpassed only by Iblis in his thirst for destruction."

"This just keeps getting better," Adhira said, throwing up his hands in defeat.

"He is not free yet," Rafal assured him. "There are three seals to the Abyss. The first was the chain on Alya. The second is a silver crown that only the Sword of Re'u can destroy."

"Oh no," Asa said, closing his eyes.

Adhira actually laughed, though it was not his usual humorous tone but one that made Neviah question his sanity.

"What?" Rafal asked, looking between them.

"Did the crown belong to Ba'altose?" Neviah asked.

"It was believed to be somewhere in the north," his words broke off when he realized what they were saying. "You destroyed the second seal?"

She nodded and said, "Please tell us about the third seal."

It took him a moment to gather his thoughts again. "The third seal, yes. It is believed to be located somewhere out at sea. It is a gate that is so massive no one can move it and no one can pick the lock. To open the gate to the Abyss requires the Eternity Key, which is said to exist only half in this world."

Neviah put her face in her hands and moaned. When she looked up, Adhira was hitting his head on the rock he'd been sitting on.

"Did you not see the key hanging from the Imprisoned One's neck?" Neviah asked.

Rafal's expression turned to shock as the memory spread across his face. "The Imprisoned One has the key!" he blurted.

"What are we going to do?" Asa asked. "We have to get that key!"

"You mean, we have to take a key from a creature that, in all appearances, is indestructible and is better with a sword than all of us combined?" Adhira said.

"What's the plan, Neviah?" Asa asked, looking across the path at her. She wanted nothing more than to crawl under the rock she was sitting against and never come out again.

"For now," she said, standing, "we keep walking."

They continued down the path for a few more miles before it led to a ravine, which then led to a wide opening revealing open grassland. The Chayyoth were gathered in a valley with many Moriahns looking on.

"What's going on?" Neviah asked.

Rafal hung his head, but Enya spoke up. "The Life Spring is destroyed," she said. "We can't stay here."

"What?" Asa and Victoria said at the same time.

"We must leave these shores in search of our old homeland. The Chayyoth and our companions must part now. Otherwise, we die."

Neviah was at King Hayrik's briefing earlier and already knew they were headed for some unreachable land over the seas.

"You can't go!" Asa said, resting a hand on his companion.

"If I don't," Rafal said slowly, "you will have to watch me slowly die of thirst."

"I can heal you," Asa said, hope clinging to his voice. "Both of you," he added, looking over to where Enya and Victoria were hugging.

"Thirst isn't something that can be healed, my friend."

"We could go with you," Asa said.

Rafal and Enya shook their heads. "Humans cannot make the trip," Enya said.

"Why not?" Asa asked.

"There is said to be a strange force there that is harmful to humans but not Chayyoth."

"A force?" Asa asked.

Rafal shrugged. "I don't know my ancient history very well. I just know that our evacuation plan, should Alya be taken by the enemy, was to go across the sea. We were told our companions would have to stay behind."

"Couldn't we still go?" Asa said. "We can find out what the force is and find a way to get rid of it or something."

"What if it's radiation?" Neviah said to Asa. "Or something similar. There's nothing we can do about that."

Tears began to stream down Asa's cheeks as he realized there was nothing he could say or do. Then everyone was crying; Adhira finally let his tears over Mordeth flow, Neviah for Corban, and the remaining companions for each other.

They were too far away to hear the order, but the king was calling all the Chayyoth close. Victoria and Asa reluctantly released their companions and watched as they gathered with their kin. The sick, elderly, and young Chayyoth were placed on hastily made gurneys so the able-bodied could carry them. The teens looked on for nearly an hour before the Chayyoth sprang into the air.

Wings carried them high into the sky until they were obscured by clouds. Enya and Rafal paused above the humans for a moment to give one last wave. Then they, too, were gone.

As the Moriahns moved on, the teens sat there, feeling completely alone even with each other's company. Neviah couldn't keep the desperation out of her thoughts. All the dead Moriahns and Chayyoth they were leaving behind. Their new home was destroyed, and the entire country was overrun. What was it all for? Why did Re'u bring them to that world if there was nothing they could do to stop all the death and destruction around them?

"Do you think they'll find their old homeland?" Neviah asked.

"Yes," Victoria said confidently, surprising them with her frankness.

"What do we do now?" Asa asked.

"I'll try to find out," Neviah said, wiping her sleeve across her cheeks and letting her sword turn back into her book of prophecies for the first time that day. The others pulled out theirs as well, and they sat for an hour reading. It was the only comfort they had left, looking for some kind of instruction from Re'u. Neviah eventually closed her book and stood. She knew what they had to do.

Chapter 23

The roar of the ocean echoed off the rocks around them as they descended a hill, which had become a new beach. From the far side of a boulder, a familiar voice met their ears.

"Put ye back into it!" a man yelled above the sound of the waves. "If that tide leaves without my ship, ye'll be carrying her back to sea on ye shoulders!"

The teenagers exchanged looks of wonder before running around the rock. Stranded on the new shore was Captain Carrick and his ship. The words *Sea Sprite* were painted gold across the side.

The crew was digging as fast as they could, trying to get the boat back into the sea before the water receded. The captain was walking up and down the new shore behind the sweat-soaked men, yelling orders to hurry up. He didn't see the teens until they were right up on him.

Turning around at their approach, Captain Carrick stared at them for a moment before saying, "Should have known ye four would show up," he said, then searched the hills behind them. "No rock monsters chasing ye this time?" he asked, completely serious.

Despite it being the worst day of her life, Neviah found herself smiling. "No, not this time."

He harrumphed before saying, "Ye wouldn't happen to know why a wave the size of Colossus just tossed my ship from one hemisphere to another, would ye?"

"Sorry," Victoria squeaked, which caused the captain to stare at her wide-eyed.

Carrick looked them over before asking, "Are ye in the mood for digging?"

Asa whispered something in Victoria's ear, and she nodded. To

Captain Carrick, he said, "If we all board the ship, Victoria can get it unstuck for us."

"I'm sure she can," he said and turned back to yell at the crew to dig faster.

"I'm serious," Asa pressed. "You trusted me once. Believe me now."

The captain looked doubtful but yelled for his men to get aboard the ship. After they all climbed up the rope ladders hanging from the starboard side, Victoria looked over the side and visibly relaxed herself. The sailors exchanged sideways glances when nothing happened. The sea was already receding, and they were losing valuable time.

Suddenly, the ship groaned, and the rear began to bob with the waves. Everyone rushed to look over the side, including Neviah. Water was rushing around the ship, making furrows in the dirt, pulling the earth away. In moments, the ship slipped free and began to move out to sea with the water. Once they were a few hundred feet from shore, everyone turned their eyes on Victoria and stared.

She shied away from the attention and picked at her hardened leather armor. Captain Carrick was the first to recover from his awe.

"Ye aren't going to have a wee girl do all the work for ye, are ye? Unfurl the mast, get the oars out the starboard side, and turn the ship about! Mind the trees sticking up out of the water!" He walked off, yelling more orders at men as he went. The ship was a madhouse of sailors running about, getting the ship ready to sail.

"So, what's the plan then?" Asa asked Neviah. This time, she had an answer.

"We are going to stop the Imprisoned One."

"How?"

She opened her book of prophecies to where she'd been reading and showed it to them.

"We still have four pieces to the Armor of Light to find."

She looked at her friends as they leafed through their own copies of the prophecies. Asa leafed through the book, reading impossibly fast. Victoria leaned back with her head on his shoulder, alternating between looking at the book and looking at Asa.

Neviah watched the pair for a moment. Looking at them, it was

The House of the Forest

hard to imagine the sweet blond-haired girl was going to kill him. Worse still was the knowledge that if she didn't, the world would end.

> **The night is far spent; the day is at hand:**
> **let us, therefore, cast off the works of**
> **darkness, and let us put on**
> **the Armor of Light.**

Other Works

The Armor of Light Series

The Sword of Re'u

The House of The Forest

The Road to War

The Tower of Leethaar

For more information, visit thearmoroflight.net.

Printed in the USA
CPSIA information can be obtained
at www.ICGtesting.com
LVHW041751071124
796013LV00006B/31